Rurik maneuver

We passed more guests too busy amusing themselves to pay us any heed. They lay in a pile of tangled bodies on a nest of cushions, feeding. I had imagined it would be different. Hands stroked through hair, lips met, and fangs pierced smooth skin. No one fought or screamed, just quiet sensual touching. *Almost erotic.*

My voice sounded hoarse. "You said Lizzy wouldn't kill the boy because she wasn't allowed. What about them?"

"Killing attracts too much public attention to our kind." He pressed himself against my back as he quietly spoke into my hair. I watched this intimate moment between predator and prey while I felt his warm breath against the nape of my neck. It gave me a flutter of confusing emotions.

His hands wandered down my hips, gathered the hem of my dress, and touched my skin. The brush of his fingernails along my thighs caught my breath. "We need to protect our obscurity, even if it is against our nature."

"You agree with this?"

"I don't have to agree with it, just abide by it. We are predators, Connie. We need the hunt." He leaned in closer from behind so his lips brushed the base of my neck, running his fangs along my skin. "We all have our weaknesses, our favorite types of prey. He won't be able to resist you." Rurik took a deep shaky breath and stepped away from me. "It's why I brought you here."

ANGLER: BOOK ONE

Bait

ANNIE NICHOLAS

Published 2010
ISBN: 1451527756; EAN: 9781451527759

Manufactured in the United States of America

Editor: Ansley Blackstock
Cover Artist: April Martinez

This is a work of fiction. The characters, incidents and dialogues in this book are of the author's imagination and are not to be construed as real. Any resemblance to actual events or persons, living or dead, is completely coincidental.

Dedication

To my family and co-workers who encouraged me
when I was down and were there every step of the way.

Acknowledgement

To the Paranormal Romantics
(www.paranormalromantics.blogspot.com)
for their support and love of things that go bump in
the night. And to Liza my grammar guru and CP.

CHAPTER ONE

Live bait made all the difference, pretty much a no-brainer. If the prey hungered, it was best to use someone like me.

I needed to attract my quarry's attention so I dressed outside the Budapest nightlife norm. The beautiful, exotic eastern European women filled the place with their form fitting, dark clothes and smoky make-up. This fashion did not complement my five foot, two inch, olive skinned, 'holy cow she's got curves' frame.

Instead, I tousled my shoulder-length, dark-blond curls and applied a little lip gloss. The high-waisted, filmy white dress, which possessed a neckline low enough I had better not sneeze, with the silver stiletto heels, made me a beacon. Time I hooked me a monster and reeled him in.

The popular nightclub jammed, and on any other night I'd be having a great time, but the crush of people made it difficult to spot anyone. Even with heels I'd have trouble seeing Rurik. I twisted and swung my hips to the pounding music as I grooved across the sunken dance floor. Tables stood around the edges so the patrons could watch.

I should have shimmied instead of turned when someone's elbow made contact with my forehead. Flailing, I tottered on my heels, tripped over someone's foot, and landed on the empty staircase.

Legs sprawled, white dress twisted too high and pulled too low, I gripped my throbbing head in surprise as the world spun. I was the picture of American class abroad.

A shadow blocked out the colored lights reflecting off the mirrored walls. It distracted me from my revealing predicament. Large, strong hands grasped my shoulders. I gazed up and my heart raced.

Rurik. The target I had hunted for in every ruin-club, open-air party, and disco in Budapest. A delicious, hunky, make-me-swoon vampire.

He lifted me to my stiletto-laden feet.

Most people don't believe in vampires, thinking them myth or legend. I know otherwise. My job comprised of luring these monsters to their executioner.

I was bait.

Rurik said something in Hungarian.

Tourists had a better grasp on the language than I

did. I shook my head. "English?" My heart hammered faster than the music's beat. I'd searched weeks for him and *he* found *me*, I couldn't have planned a better scenario.

His cold, arctic, eyes bore into mine. Even with me wearing heels he towered over me. I couldn't help but admire his dark, slicked back hair, exposing fine sculpted cheekbones, a narrow face, and a set of full lush lips—all male and very tasty.

Once assured I could stand on my own, he released m e, and brought my hand to his mouth to brush those lush lips against my knuckles. "You're an unexpected treasure, my angel," he translated over the loud music.

"Thanks." I'd lost hope of 'bumping' into him and just complied with Colby's—my employer's—routine orders. *Seduce him into following me to the hotel room close by where they waited.*

Vampire or not, he provoked a forbidden lust. *I* was still a woman, after all.

Rurik belonged on the cover of *GQ*. His black Italian suit contrasted nicely with his white dress shirt and pale skin, tailored to fit his athletic build. Everything about him was simple and elegant.

Everything except the ring on his left pinky finger. A gold antique, with a rock set in it big enough to choke on. Only the Overlord of a city could wear such a ring. It symbolized his power—like a king's crown.

His hand trailed up my arm, to touch the thin, white fabric of my dress. He said something but the music drowned him out. I didn't really need to hear him. The hunger in his eyes told me everything. He liked me.

"Do you still want to dance?" He shouted and gestured to the packed floor.

"No, I think I should quit while I'm ahead." I pointed to my forehead, where a welt throbbed with my racing heart.

He chuckled. "Then let me buy you a drink. My name is Rurik." His grasp tightened on my arm as he led me away from the dance floor. The corners of his mouth lifted into a small pleasant smile as he turned from me. It wouldn't do to flash fang and scare dinner away.

It irked me he just assumed I'd say 'yes' to his invitation. I stuffed my annoyance to the back of my mind, I didn't have the luxury for personal preferences, and I had a role to play.

We made our way through the throng of Saturday night cruisers to a table in a secluded corner. Some men sat there, then stood upon our arrival, and moved to join others who hovered within eyesight of the table. Rurik's *guards*. Things were quieter here; we could talk instead of yell.

He assisted me to a chair, then slid his closer to mine. Close enough to touch. "Are you American?"

A server walked up and set a bottle of Popov vodka in front of us with two shot glasses.

"Last time I checked." The smell of his mild, spiced cologne drifted around me.

He laughed at my wiseass remark and filled the

shot glasses, placing one in my hand.

"I don't drink," I confessed. "It goes straight to my head," I lied.

"Then bottoms up." He leaned forward, slipped his arm around mine, and tossed his vodka down.

Playing along, I faked taking a small sip, but he moved his arm up quick, and tipped my glass to a steeper angle. The contents emptied down my throat and burned as it cascaded to my stomach. I coughed and grimaced at the awful taste. Vodka never was my drink of choice.

My annoyance grew to outrage. I bit the inside of my cheeks; worried the verbal lashing on the tip of my tongue would slip out. Forced to flirt with this obnoxious creep wasn't worth my pay, but not all my job satisfaction came from the bank. I would enjoy watching Colby stake this jerk.

Rurik smiled tight-lipped. "Forgive me. I couldn't resist the temptation." He brushed a wayward curl from my face.

I leaned into his touch—even though I wanted to pour the vodka over his head—and forced a smile. Talented enough to put laughter into my eyes while thinking violent thoughts made me good at my job.

He filled the glasses again, amusement sparkling in his eyes.

I glared at the repulsive drink instead of at him, and tried to pull the reins on my mounting temper. His phenomenal packaging must only be skin deep.

Rurik gave a gentle laugh. "You're angry with me."

Perceptive. "I told you, I don't want to drink." He was a real detective, this one. I smiled at him, putting an extra quirk to my lips. "Angry is a strong word, though. Life's too short to be angry."

Waving the waiter over, he ordered something I couldn't understand, then returned his attention to me. "You haven't told me your name."

I stopped giving my shot glass the evil eye. The vodka stirred my stomach something fierce, yet called to my old vices. "I'm Connie Bence." I offered him my hand. Damn, his arrogance distracted me and I gave him my real name. *Just call me competent.*

"Nice to meet you, Connie." He took my hand and traced lazy circles in my palm. "Such a sweet morsel should have a name like..." His gaze lifted from my hand and pinned me to the chair . "Rabbit."

My already angry stomach rebelled. I took a deep breath, closed my eyes and focused by visualizing myself *not* being sick on my target. That would be two weeks of hard work down the drain, *literally.*

"That's lovely, Rurik, but I prefer Connie." I peeked and saw Rurik had moved in closer.

His eyes followed the shape of my face, down the lines of my neck, to the curves of my breasts. "I've noticed you before tonight, Rabbit, at other clubs."

I blinked. He'd noticed me before tonight? Why had he waited until now to introduce himself? A chill crept up my spine. I learned to listen to those instincts. It was time to bail out.

My employer, Colby, would be pissed. I didn't

know all the details of this case, I never did. He would cast me out to a choice location and hope I'd bring in his prize. He led a group of mercenaries I met a year ago, in Las Vegas, who taught me the ropes of my job. They scraped me from the bottom of a bottle and gave me a new life. I owed them.

Colby only dusted vampires gone bad—those who killed. If he accepted a contract, it meant he had concrete proof, and he wanted Rurik. That's all I needed to know.

A hand on my knee startled me from my worries. "I've resisted your temptations, but unfortunately you've caught someone else's notice." Rurik's fingers traced along the inside of my thigh. They caressed their way up, making contact with the hem of my very short dress.

My skin tingled but not from his touch.

An aura of power drew around my mental shields. His strength of will felt solid. It wrapped around me like a warm lover on a cold winter's day. Comfortable and secure, I wanted to give in, tired of the long, cold winter my soul experienced this past year. His power was deep and throbbing. It spoke of age and experience, more than what I'd ever dealt with.

It drew me in. Invited me to come out from behind the mental walls I'd built.

I knew better. If I did, the chances of my winning that deadly contest were nil. He'd own me. I needed to allow him to seduce me, then bring him to Colby, not get caught by mind tricks. My mental shields were built well and strong, yet he hammered at them.

Sweat trickled down my back. I'd never struggled with anyone so strong. Most humans wouldn't have noticed such an intrusion but Colby trained me well.

I met his stare and opened my legs.

Rurik raised his eyebrows and his smile widened. My distraction worked and the assault eased. "You never seemed interested in partying at any of these clubs. Just mingled, roughed up the men who got too personal. Are you going to rough me up, Rabbit?" His voice caressed me as fingers climbed my thigh to trail along my silk panties.

Bad guy or not, my libido really liked him. I had better taste than this but his naughty behavior and arrogance appealed to my darker nature—the one that wanted to be punished.

The waiter disrupted our intimate moment as he placed a drink on the table. Rurik didn't move away. He remained glued to me, one arm around the back of my chair, the other warming my loins. But mentally his attack continued to ease off. The blanket of power fell away as I focused on the waiter.

Rurik nibbled on my ear—my major weakness—which shot shivers along my sides. "I ordered you something milder to drink. It's a local delicacy, a blend of fruit juices. No alcohol." He handed me the drink.

"Thank you. I'm parched from all the dancing." It tasted like ambrosia after the vodka. It slid over my tongue and instantly relieved my thirst. "It's wonderful. I haven't tasted anything like it on my visit here."

Rurik ran his hand through my soft curls. He didn't bother with the mind tricks anymore. Instead, he looked down my dress.

I thrust the girls out. "Enjoying the view?"

He chuckled. "Immensely. You have such a natural, sweet beauty. Very old world. Lovely skin, soft hair, beautiful eyes and such feminine ... curves." His fingers started to explore more than the silk of my undergarment.

I clamped my legs together and laid a hand on his. "Maybe it's time you take me somewhere more private?" It surprised me to hear the slur in my speech. I'd only drunk the one shot and the fruit juice. The vodka must have been excellent quality to hit me that hard.

He nodded then gestured to his men to follow as we rose from the chairs.

My legs wobbled when I first stood. It concerned me. What made them so weak? Not that I'd win a race against vampires, but a stable stance gave me a better chance if things went south and I needed to run. My mental shields felt whole so I didn't think he affected my gait. Maybe the dancing did this and I should hit the gym more often.

Rurik slipped his hand into my grasp and we left together, hand in hand, weaving through the crowds. I almost lost him as a cluster of people pushed between us to get to the bar. Lost in a sea of giants, I turned a slow circle until he returned for me.

He clasped my hands around his waist and wrapped his arms around my shoulders to keep me close, pressing our bodies together as he quickened his pace.

I grinned in satisfaction.

Colby had men planted in the club, to help protect me. He ran a tight operation and had my back. They always placed a tracking device in my clothes, just in case they lost sight of me. Tonight it hid in the hem of my dress. As long as I didn't take it off the team would be close, waiting for me to bring Rurik to them so they could make a move.

I got the impression Rurik didn't plan for me to wear this dress much longer. Colby better be ready.

The guards trailed around us, slinking through the crowd.

We came out a side door where a black sedan waited. One guard got in the driver's seat while another held the back door. I stopped my forward motion. "Where are we going? I have a room just across the street." A lightheaded spell made my ankles wobble and I gripped Rurik's waist tighter.

He misunderstood my action, taking it as an invitation. He grabbed the back of my head and kissed me. His supple mouth brushed against mine, seductive and gentle. Not what I would have expected from a killer. It warmed the night.

I pulled away from his embrace. My thoughts blurred. *Not a good sign.* Alarms rang in my head. "What was in the drink?" I sounded dreamy, even to my own ears.

"No alcohol," he replied.

That's not what I asked.

His power built around me again.

This time my mental shields crumbled, gone on a fuzzy holiday. Where could Colby be? Rurik was too strong for me. His power swallowed me whole.

"We are going to a private party, Rabbit."

"Connie," I mumbled.

He sat me in the car. "It's for an important magnate in this territory. You caught his eye the other night and I want to introduce you to him." He placed my legs into the car and closed the door. That was nice of him. He wanted to set me up on a date.

He sat beside me and grinned. The fangs didn't bother either of us.

"I like parties," I announced.

"I think you'll love this one."

CHAPTER TWO

We arrived in the old part of the city close to the Danube River. Rurik's guards parked the car at the mouth of a narrow, dark alley, obscured by a fog collecting close to the ground. It was late, even by Budapest standards, and the area looked deserted. The side street we took from the Danube Promenade barely allowed the car to pass through the ancient, stone buildings that surrounded us.

Rurik stepped out of the car as one of his guards came and opened my door. The euphoric psychosis I'd experienced wore off but I still felt lightheaded. Rurik appeared beside me. "Let me help you, Rabbit." He offered his hand.

Rurik's manners surprised me but I wouldn't

accept my captor's assistance. Bad enough he got into my head. Even now my mental shield slipped through my control like sand. I pushed myself out and hoped to see signs of my rescue close by. When my heels bit onto the uneven cobblestone, I stumbled back onto the floorboard of the car. Crossing my arms under my breasts, I wished my heated stare could burn through him. Where the hell did he bring me and why?

He extended his hand again and fought with a smile that twitched his lips. His gaze left my face and traveled down to where I crossed my arms.

I followed his gaze. My breasts strained at the neckline.

"I really like that dress."

I growled and released my pose to accept his hand. "You already complimented me on it."

He chuckled as he helped me to stand and wrapped an arm around my waist to steady me. "Maybe you had too much."

"Too much what?" Was that guilt I just saw on his face? Before I could be sure, he turned us to go down the dark, little alley.

I ground my heels to a stop. "Why do we have to go down there?"

"That's where the party is being held."

"In an eerie alley? Isn't that a bit cliché?"

His smile broadened while an amused twinkle came to life in his eyes. "Yes, it is. What can I say? I'm old-fashioned." Rurik urged me to move forward. "We're late, so hurry."

I wasn't in any state to put up a fight against a quorum of vampires. "I'm not going down there with you." When was my cavalry going to swoop in and save me? The tracking device should help them find my location.

A tremor shook my chest when I took a breath and even with the cool night air, sweat trickled down my back. "No offense but I just met you. It's kind of unfair when it's three against one." The slight quiver in my voice outraged me. I turned out of his arm and gracelessly tripped again. Freaking cobblestone and stilettos don't work well together.

I leaned against the stone building and turned so it would support me. Even if I could run they'd catch me. I knew it wasn't the alcohol that made me feel this uncoordinated. My mental shields never crumbled when I drank. That's another gift from Colby's training and my past drinking habits.

Rurik's forehead creased with a frown as he collected me in his arms. "We don't have time for this, Rabbit." He pulled me close and I felt his power building up again. I was helpless as he wrapped a blanket of indifference around me, lifting away my worries and leaving me ... open.

"Ready to go to the party now?"

I smiled as I pressed my body against his and gazed into his pale blue eyes. "Ready as I'll ever be." Then I snaked my arm around his neck to snuggle against his luscious body.

His eyes widened. "Ravishing." He took my face

22

in his hands and closed the distance between our lips, but shook his head before they touched. Sighing, he stepped away and laid his arm across my shoulders. "You're not for me."

We wove our way down the alley.

"But I like you." The fog reflected the moonlight and made the stinking alley romantic. His strength and firm muscles under my hands bloomed desires I'd thought dead.

Rurik rang the bell next to a plain, steel, modern door cut into building. No lights or signs announced anything. I expected a secret knock or maybe a hidden peephole with someone asking the password. My disappointment must have shown on my face.

"What?" he asked.

"That was anticlimactic. I expected more than a doorbell at a secret party."

He peered at me from the corner of his eyes but before he could respond, a bouncer opened the door. He nodded to Rurik and allowed us in.

We entered onto the landing of a wide staircase that led down to an open basement. Rurik stopped at the top and scanned the crowd. I followed his gaze through the narrow, long space, wondering who he looked for.

The sparse décor surprised me. A bare stone foundation acted as the walls, with similar pillars spaced evenly throughout the room. Small rectangular windows were set far apart, close to the ceiling and painted over in black. I couldn't see the end of the basement since cigarette smoke veiled the room's few lights, which obscured any clear view. The stale smell made me scrunch my nose and the music pounding from the back of the hall beat with the same rhythm of my heart .

People lounged in intimate groups on couches overflowing with cushions made of vintage fabrics in rich shades of brown, red, and gold. They conversed in low tones with each other, an occasional high laugh escaped . Some smoked, some drank, and, well, some made out.

A few turned our way and watched our arrival.

I caught myself tugging at the hem of my white dress then stopped, only to find my hands fixing my hair. Rurik's control on me waned once more, his concentration focused on the crowd. The party's theme seemed of darker colors and pleasures. My plan to stand out and catch Rurik's attention backfired. I didn't want to attract *these* people's attention. I shifted over a few steps to stand behind him.

He reached back and took my hand, then gave me a gentle tug to follow him down the stairs. We drew closer to the groups. I observed several with pale skin, predatory grace, and the occasional flash of fangs. I'd never been around so many vampires before. It never occurred to me they met in social gatherings.

I knew enough about vampires to do my job. Otherwise, their way of existence was a mystery to me. Even after a year of experience, Rurik took me from that club without much effort. I'd never encountered anyone like him.

When Rurik turned his power at me it affected my mind like Valium. The more worried I got, the less it mattered. I just couldn't care enough to be scared or fight.

My present situation grew worse and worse by the second. I should have been tearing my way out the door. Hell, I should never have walked through the door. Instead, I walked hand-in-hand with a mass killer as if we were on a stroll.

But as my grandmother would say, 'shouldas and wouldas don't count.'

This was the biggest risk of my job—being caught. I'd known it. Life expectancy for bait was short. It's why they paid me the big bucks. I stopped planning to have a long life before I joined Colby's team.

Rurik kept his arm around my waist as we walked by his people and their thralls. Some nodded, but most bowed as we passed.

His people parted as a ravishing dominatrix moved to intercept us. She glided over the floor wearing a full-length, black, leather, strapless gown. Her straight auburn hair reached her waist, not a strand out of place. That much grace and perfection was unnatural, and unfair.

Rurik cursed under his breath.

She approached us and offered her hand. "Rurik." She rolled the r's of his name, making it sound exotic.

He kissed her hand.

"You're fashionably late again, naughty boy. You've left me here to entertain myself among this tiresome retinue." She ran her gloved fingers through his hair. "You know how I get when I'm bored."

With a devilish smile, he replied, "I'll have to make it up to you, Mistress Elizabeth."

"Please do, darling. Come, join me." She gestured to a seating area close to us. A gorgeous, young man lay sprawled among the cushions on the floor. He couldn't have been older than eighteen, just a boy by my standards. He lay so still. A bite mark at the base of his neck cleared up what type of entertainment she partook.

I stepped toward the boy to check on him but Rurik held me tight. Then I noticed his bare chest move with a deep, slow breath. At least he lived.

"Soon, Lizzy." Rurik gestured to me. "I need to deliver my gift to *him*. Do you know where he is?"

Rurik wanted to give me away, like a toy at Christmas. I glanced down at my dress and grimaced at my choice. It wouldn't take *him*, whoever he was, long to unwrap me. *Damn, damn, damn.* I feared this unknown vampire would be much worse than Rurik. Better to stick with the monster I knew.

She nodded in my direction. "She's a doll, so fresh and pretty." It should have been a compliment but she pursed her lips, like she'd bitten into something distasteful. "Give her to me instead, Rurik. It's been so long since you've offered me a gift." She looked me up and down. I had the ridiculous urge to laugh. Now I knew what a hot fudge sundae felt like when I looked at it that way.

The laugh died in my throat, however, as I saw the hunger for me bloom on her face. Unbelievably, I found myself trusting Rurik for my protection. I wrapped my arms around his waist and pressed myself against him.

She placed those long fingered hands on her hips. "He won't care if you give her to me instead. What's mine is his and what's his is mine."

"We both know it hasn't been that way for decades, Lizzy," Rurik whispered. "I can't risk his displeasure right now. If he wants you to have her, he'll give her over to you himself."

Her eyes narrowed. "He doesn't need any more distractions." Her sharp words carried power and authority. "Give her to me."

At the snap of her command, I fought the desire to obey and run to her arms. I must have tightened my death grip on Rurik's waist because he stroked my hair and smiled at me.

"Everything will be alright, Rabbit." His beautiful eyes offered me the reassurance I needed. He returned his attention to Lizzy and shook his head in denial.

"He barely has time for those worthy of his attentions." She pouted and made it clear that she was one of the worthy.

"You've never lacked my attentions. Soon none of this will matter." He pried my arms off him and gave her a chaste kiss on the cheek.

The way she looked at him left no doubt her thoughts were not chaste. Lizzy focused back on me as she circled around, inspecting all my little details, like

I was up for auction.

"She's plain."

Plain? At least I wasn't a scary-ass bitch. Rurik placed his finger under my chin and turned my face toward him.

"Connie is lovely. As the host of this gathering, it's traditional that I offer *him* entertainment." The slight shake of his head warned me to be quiet as he removed his hand from my chin. His attentions returned to Mistress Elizabeth. "Let me deliver sweet Connie to him so I can return to entertain you."

"When did you become a traditionalist?"

"I'm not, but he is." Rurik slipped his arm around me. His face remained pleasant but I felt his body tense.

"You shouldn't have picked such an innocent girl. It's so cruel."

"Isn't that what he expects me to be? Cruel?" He grinned at her. "Connie *is* plain in comparison to your beauty. Let me finish with this business and I'll return shortly." His charms worked enough to persuade her to return to the nest of cushions. She glided back to her young, foolish snack.

I glanced at the boy, worried for his fate.

Rurik whispered in my ear, "Don't worry. She won't kill him. It's not allowed, even for her."

She ran her hand along the boy's bare, lean chest. "He's towards the back, Rurik. Playing games with Tane and his kindred."

Rurik maneuvered me deeper into the hall. We passed more guests too busy amusing themselves to pay us any heed. They lay in a pile of tangled bodies on a nest of cushion, feeding. I imagined it would be different. Hands stroked through hair, lips met, and fangs pierced smooth skin. No one fought or screamed, just quiet sensual touching. *Almost erotic.*

I didn't notice that I'd stopped to watch until Rurik whispered in my ear, "We can sit and enjoy the show if you'd like. I'm really in no hurry to return to that bitch." His warm breath brushed against my skin.

"No." My voice sounded hoarse. The eerie scene made me morbidly curious, like watching at a car wreck. They all seemed to enjoy themselves, but the blood and the bites appalled me. "You said Lizzy wouldn't kill the boy because she wasn't allowed. What about them?"

What about him? We hunted Rurik for just that crime.

"Killing attracts too much public attention to our kind." He pressed himself against my back as he quietly spoke into my hair. I watched this intimate moment between predator and prey while I felt his warm breath against the nape of my neck. It gave me a flutter of confusing emotions.

His firm body along mine aroused me. When he continued his explanation, I almost missed it. "Our governing body has worked very hard over the centuries to make mankind dismiss us." His hands wandered down my hips, gathered the hem of my dress, and touched my skin. The brush of his fingernails along my thighs caught my breath. "We need to protect our obscurity, even if it is against our nature."

"You agree with this?" If he did, maybe Colby had mistaken his target and I could seduce Rurik to keep me for himself instead of passing off as a present. *Distract him long enough for my rescue to find me.*

"I don't have to agree with it, just abide by it. We are predators, Connie. We need the hunt..." He leaned in closer from behind so his lips brushed the base of my neck, running his fangs along my skin. "And the chase." He continued tasting me until he came close to my ear once more. "We all have our weaknesses, our favorite types of prey. You caught his attention at the hot springs last night and fit his tastes. He won't be able to resist you." Rurik took a deep shaky breath and stepped away from me. "It's why I brought you here."

I turned to face him and slid my hands along his chest to his shoulders. If I stood on tippy toe my lips almost touched his. "You could keep me." It wouldn't be all bad to let him have me, as long as I could get past the fangs and keep my dress with the tracking device close by.

His expression changed from a flirtatious playboy, to one of regret. "No, I can't." He stared toward the back of the basement then back at me and scratched his chin. "I'll make you a deal, though. If you do your best to please him, I'll help you survive the night."

My heart skipped a beat and I plunked back onto my heels. "How?"

"I'll watch over you."

"You won't dump me for Lizzy first chance you get?"

His cold stare told me his opinion of that action.

I got the impression Rurik didn't mean a little flirting when he said 'please him'. "What do I need to do?" How far would I go? I'd like to think I'd keep my dignity but knew I'd dance the can-can, naked in a pool of chocolate syrup, to save my ass.

"I need him to feed from you. It's what he'll want the most."

"You'll make sure he won't drink me dry?" I hated the insecurity in my voice, the sound of my plea.

Rurik stroked my cheek. "It's against our laws and we're at a public event. He should behave himself. I'll make an effort to stay close to you and intervene if he starts to harm you."

That didn't comfort me. Fighting was suicidal, nowhere to run, and no one to care about my cries for help. It came down to placing myself on the menu while I waited for my rescue by Colby. *Damn, I was screwed.*

I prayed the tracking signal could penetrate these stone walls. What was taking them so long? Could they even take on this many vampires? We usually ambushed one at a time, not a truckload.

The display of sensuous feasting next to us quieted. Rurik took my hand, then led us toward the music and my fate.

We reached a gathering of tall muscled vampires, more a gang of thugs in comparison to the refined guards who followed Rurik. My heart raced as some of them assessed me. Their eyes roved over my body, one of them touched my hair as I squeezed by him.

They laughed as I scurried away from him and almost ran Rurik over.

He looked over his shoulder and frowned. "Easy, Rabbit."

I rubbed my sweaty palms on my dress.

"Is that really her name?" Touchy-feely pointed at me. "We haven't done much but arm wrestle tonight. Maybe we can have a little game of chase?"

"I provided you with other sport for this evening, *gentlemen.* This one's for..."

"Rurik." A soft, commanding voice interrupted him. The group parted as someone approached. "It's about time you joined us."

My legs became rubbery as Rurik brought me to *him*.

"Master." Rurik bent down to one knee, offering up my hand. "I've brought you a gift."

CHAPTER THREE

"A gift? Why Rurik, you shouldn't have." The master's soft voice cut through all the background noise. His aura and presence made people hush to hear him speak.

He moved in closer and loomed over me. My eyes only came up to his massive chest, a buttoned up black leather vest barely contained it. His pale skin looked translucent, like it hadn't seen the sun in a very, very long time. A black tribal tattoo wrapped around his bald head, down his neck, and disappeared under the vest. Misshapen pointed ears sported a set of gold loop earrings.

I glanced into his black soulless eyes. Where Rurik made me think all kinds of naughty things, his master made me think all kinds of dreadful things. Most vampires could pass for human with some effort. Not him. I doubted he could ever blend in.

"I've never been courted by a man, Rurik. Then again, times have changed."

The surrounding vampires laughed.

Rurik's eyes narrowed but a slick politician's smile camouflaged his face. He gave a little laugh and nod but I stood close enough to hear him grind his teeth.

His master signaled for him to stand up. "Of all my Lords, you're the last I expected to offer such a gift."

"I know my duties, Master Dragos. If you don't like her then Mistress Elizabeth has asked for her."

I twisted and stared daggers at him. Even I understood Lizzy's relationship with this vampire was on the rocks. Why bring her up and piss him off?

Dragos frowned.

Then I realized Rurik's intention. Dragos probably wouldn't give me to Lizzy now that he knew she'd asked for me. Such a clever, devious vampire my quarry showed himself to be.

Rurik held himself with confidence against these hardened men. Where he was refined and sleek, they were coarse and frightening, like a panther confronting a pack of wolves. Yet they were both predators.

Then it dawned on me that Rurik had called Dragos, *Master*. I didn't know a city's lord could have a master. I'd been taught the cities were independent of each other, like little vampire countries. Unless this *Master* just took over Budapest. But that couldn't be it.

Rurik still wore the ring. When he spoke of a governing body earlier I thought he meant just Budapest.

What a horrifying theory. Colby *really* needed this information but my own incompetence had me trapped. It irked me to be so dependent on their rescue. I'd been in an emotional coma for the past year and never cared to accept Colby's offer to help me master some combat moves. In hindsight, it seemed somewhat suicidal, considering my job description. This experience defibrillated me of my indifference—I wanted to live.

Dragos paced around me. His eyes travelled up my legs, over my hips, and hesitated at my breasts, before glancing at my face. He examined me like a mare. He stepped close to touch my skin, my curls, then brought his face down to smell them.

"Lavender." His comment sent a jolt of surprise through me. It was my favorite scent to wear. He entwined his fingers with mine and drew me closer.

Rurik held me tight for a moment before he let me go. "Her name is Rabbit." He observed the surrounding men and I followed his gaze. Some were longhaired, some short, some bulky, some lean—they all looked like fighters. Among all this brawn, I felt very small and fragile, but I wouldn't give them the satisfaction of knowing it.

I ignored a quiver in my chest. There would be no crying, maybe some screaming, definitely no crying. I'd done all the crying I was *ever* going to do in the past year.

Creatures such as vampires liked to hunt the frail and weak. They probably smelled my fear. I couldn't help being frail but I'd make them think twice before they thought I was weak.

Movement behind Master Dragos caught my attention. Someone else came up to inspect me. He resembled Dragos more than the others with his bald head and very pale skin. He also had pointed ears and bore a similar tattoo on his neck that extended down under his torn red t-shirt. He and Dragos seemed more monster than men.

Dragos didn't even turn to see who approached. "What do you think, Tane?"

"I think slick and sneaky Rurik plays at politics too much of late, and forgets to tend to his own." He looked from me back to Dragos. "Beware of Greeks bearing gifts, Master."

"We've come to Budapest to make peace, Tane. To settle our differences." He glanced at Rurik. "I like her and I accept your gracious gift." He pressed me against his broad chest then stroked my hair. His finger entwined in my curls and he gently pulled my head back to examine my face. The pounding of my heart deafened me. It thumped hard against my ribcage in response to his cold touch. Long, sharp nails scraped my scalp as his fist tightened.

I usually dealt with small time vampires, like rogues or gang members, nothing at this level of power. It was like a rookie cop dealing with the mob boss.

I was speechless—I didn't know what to say to my

worst nightmare. 'Please don't eat me,' came to mind.

He smiled then said something in what sounded like Hungarian.

I tried to shake my head. "English?"

His eyes widened. "American? I assumed you were Hungarian all this time." He looked at Rurik. "I wondered why you spoke in English."

Tane stepped up quickly and whispered to the master. "She's heard too much, she should be destroyed. Feed from her and be done with it."

I tensed reflexively when I overheard. Struggling was useless, it was like going against *Superman*, but I couldn't stop my reaction.

Dragos shushed me by placing a finger across my lips and released my hair. He twisted to face Tane. "You're scaring my pet. When did you start fearing ... rabbits?"

Tane bowed his head and stepped away.

His smile grew into a grin. Sharp fangs glistened in the pale light as he returned to me. "I remember you from the hot springs on Margaret Island last night. Your presence is hard to forget." The Master cocked his head. "You're far from home."

No shit. I clenched my hands into fists, digging my nails into my palms. The pain drove back the sob that waited in my throat. "I'm on vacation." I still felt lightheaded from whatever Rurik put in my drink but it could be from fear as well.

"Budapest in spring is quite lovely. Are you enjoying yourself?"

The surreal conversation made my head spin more. "I wanted more adventure in my life."

"I think you've found it." He traced the edge of my dress' neckline. The smooth, icy sensation of his fingertips as they ran along my bosom reminded me of marble. It made me squirm with unease.

"Do you know how to dance, Rabbit?"

"A little." It wasn't exactly a lie, I could move to a beat. Rhythm lived in my bones but nothing trained or classical.

He released his hold on me and gripped my hand to lead me away from my so-called 'protection'.

I looked back at Rurik and he watched us with a scowl. Slick bastard turned the table on me so effortlessly—I'd gone from being bait, to being trapped. I wasn't the only one giving him the eye, Tane stood to the side observing him as well. I understood completely. Rurik was a clever, devious, jerk who better keep his end of the bargain and protect me. What could I possibly do if he didn't? Sue him?

We continued moving further away from the entrance. The crowd parted and kept their eyes on us as we moved. Tension filled the air as we passed Rurik's people. I could see fear in their eyes. They weren't alone. It was probably visible in mine, too.

We didn't go far before we reached the end of the basement. The dance area wasn't much, just a cleared section of the cement floor. Three women danced together. They left when they saw us approach.

Dragos left me at the edge of the dance floor as he

addressed the gathering audience.

"Our gracious host, your Lord Rurik, has offered us a gift." He gestured to me. "We will entertain him with a dance in gratitude." Applause and whistles followed this announcement.

This announcement hit me like a truck. I stepped back, my pulse pounded in my ears as my hands began to sweat. Not for the reasons you'd think. Not because vampires surrounded me, or I'd been given to the scary *Master of the Lord of Budapest*. No, I was about to be made to dance in front of *all* of them. When I danced on a crowded floor surrounded by other people, I could move to the rhythm as I wanted, and no one watched. Dragos and I had this floor all to ourselves.

I felt a hand support my elbow. Rurik stood next to me, a concerned look on his face. He'd followed us. A small surge of pleasure surprised me at his keeping his promise. Now I needed to keep mine and be a midnight snack.

My hand clasped at his. "I-I can't do this."

He smiled at me. "Do what?" He knew what, he just wanted to torture me.

"Dance in front of all these people," I hissed back.

"You see *us* as *people*? That's a good beginning, Rabbit."

"What?" I was too nervous to follow the sharp twist in the conversation.

"Most humans would have said *monsters*, not *people*."

Here I was in the throes of massive stage fright

39

ANNIE NICHOLAS

and I had *Dr. Phil* analyzing me. Who cared? People, monsters—they all had eyes pointed at me.

He chuckled. "You *are* entertaining." He lifted my chin to look into my eyes. "I can help by influencing your mind, like outside in the alley." His smile softened. "I swore to protect you if I could, but let him feed if he wants. This will make him happy. He likes to show off, especially in front of my people, so don't struggle. It excites him too much and he will hurt you more than necessary. Are you willing to keep your end of the bargain?"

I didn't see that coming. I took a shaky breath. "How much influencing are we talking about?" It would be nice to keep something in my head intact. No one knew the side effects of multiple mind invasions.

"Just a little, enough to get you through the dance," he whispered back.

"Okay." I wanted to get it over with before my anxiety consumed me. I expected something like earlier, a warm wave that made me feel carefree, but he changed it. Just a trickle of warmth flushed through me. My anxiety fled and was replaced by self-assurance.

I could do this—the dance we were going to perform was easy.

Dragos removed his vest and left it on the floor. The strong line of his back extended down to a slim waist. He filled his form fitting leather pants, leaving little to the imagination.

A local song I'd heard over and over in the bars thumped from the speakers.

I strutted out to Dragos.

"Are you ready, my little rabbit?" He placed one of my hands on his shoulder and we began a simple fast waltz. The tension in my arms and legs eased as he moved us around the dance floor. I flowed with the movement as he led us faster and faster with the music. My curls began to whip around my face with each quick turn. I knew where he wanted me to step as he spun us around and around, until I could only focus on him. He was power and control. Being in the center of it with him was as sweet and deadly as Rurik's fruit juice ambrosia.

He suddenly stopped to twirl me on my toes.

My breath caught as I wound down around his leg and rested on the floor by his feet. It must have looked great since everyone erupted in applause.

Rurik stood across from us. He clapped and laughed with the others but when his gaze met mine, I saw the amusement didn't reach his eyes.

Dragos lifted me to my feet and startled a little cry from me. He placed my hands on the solid expanse of his chest, while he put his own hands behind his back. He pushed me back across the dance floor, shifting us around with unnatural grace for a man his size.

We came to the edge of the crowd. He wrapped his arms around me and we started our waltz once more. This time he had us bending our torsos together with the spin. My back arched and pressed us together as he supported my weight with his hands. When had I become so flexible? I laughed out loud. I'd always wanted to be able to dance like this and given the situation, it was hilarious.

He grinned, exposing all his teeth. We slowed down to a stop in each other's arms. Then he bent me back slowly into a deep, deep dip that made my knees bend with the arching of my back.

He ran the tip of his tongue from my low neckline between my breasts up slowly to the hollow of my neck. Alarms and gongs clanged in my head. My stomach churned at his touch.

I was in *deep shit*.

He nipped gently at the sensitive skin along my collarbone and pressed me against him as his mouth found the pulse point on my neck.

I tensed with expectation. *This was it.* My first bite and I hoped I survived.

He suddenly dropped me on my head. It exploded with pain and stars danced before my eyes.

The next thing I knew Rurik knelt by my shoulders and guided me to stand. Dragos was gone and people turned to the entrance of the basement in alarm. Rurik shoved me behind his back and I wobbled on loose knees, so he kept one of his hands around my waist to help my balance.

There were cries of dismay and Dragos men mobilized as his voice barked orders. That's when *I* saw the first UV light grenade go off.

My cavalry had arrived.

CHAPTER FOUR

The music quieted and inhuman high pitched screeches filled the smoky air of the dimly lit basement. Sounds of a fight erupted toward the entrance but grew closer. Another UV grenade went off and the basement air grew thick with ash. They were like low intensity balls of sunlight but they needed to be on top of the vampire to be effective. If I got to close to one I'd have more than sunburn. Colby must be desperate to use them in such tight quarters.

Rurik herded me toward the stone wall.

I crouched to the floor and pressed myself against the cool surface while he towered over me to face the oncoming assault. His actions surprised me. I knew he promised to protect me but I was impressed a vampire would follow through on his word.

Tane appeared beside him. "It's a group of humans." He handed Rurik a handgun, which he stuck in his back waistband. "The gun won't help much with the fight if it's in there."

"I don't intend to use it unless forced to. Their bullets won't kill me."

"They've got those cursed sunlight weapons, they know what we are." Tane glanced down at me and winked while he showed off his fangs with a big smile.

Rurik elbowed him. "Leave her alone. How did a bunch of slayers find us?"

Tane's smile faltered and he shrugged. He pointed to the gathering mass at the entrance. "Go to the left and I'll flank them from the right. We'll corral them and keep them in a tight group so they can't use the sunlight weapons." Tane spoke without any of his earlier animosity. He'd given me the impression he hated Rurik, yet now they spoke to each other like good friends.

This switch made me more wary. These were more than just *creatures of the night*. Some of their human nature traversed the change to vampire. I always thought they mimicked our behavior to draw in prey but my experiences tonight changed my mind.

Gunshots startled us. Most of the crowd ducked and scattered. Rurik grabbed my arm and dragged me to the closest seating area. I gasped at the rough handling as he wedged me between a couch and a wall.

Tane shouted more orders to re-organize their

defenses and they left me. Dragos, the master, was nowhere to be seen.

Short bursts of semi-automatic weapons rebounded off what sounded like the stone walls. At least one shotgun went off, leaving me somewhat deaf. Although bullets wouldn't kill the vampires, they would hurt and slow them down. Unfortunately, they would kill me and any other humans in the crossfire.

Colby's resources were limited. He designed operations for single takedowns, not open conflicts. There was no way Colby and his men could take on everyone here, especially the strong, powerful vampires I'd met tonight. They wouldn't be able to reach me if I remained here at the far end of the basement. I gathered my dress around my hips and crawled on all fours to peek around the side of the couch.

A crowd formed around the sitting areas where the fight ensued. Others hid like me behind the scarce furniture, or stood by the walls to watch the action. The metallic smell of the UV grenades overwhelmed the room to a point I could almost taste it.

I didn't have many options. A back door would have been nice, the small blackened windows were too high for me to climb out of, so I decided to make a run for it. I huddled low and moved fast. Maybe I wouldn't get shot, stepped on, or crushed. Crouching on my heels beside the couch's arm, I sprung up to sprint but I didn't make it far.

Someone grabbed me by the waist and plucked me from the ground. I twisted around and prepared to gouge my assailant's eyes out.

Rurik swung me into his arms like a child, shielding me with his body. I thought he ditched me. Even caught in this commotion the touch of his hands on my body electrified me.

Tane followed Rurik and watched his back.

Rurik heaved me onto one of his shoulders.

I struggled to get loose but his iron strong arm clamped on my legs. "Let me go." I punched at his back, feeling helpless. Glancing up I saw Tane grin at me. I gave him the one-fingered salute and continued to wriggle out of Rurik's grip.

He carried me back toward the wall. I could see Dragos' thugs fighting. A glimpse of a tall man with short, blonde hair in army fatigues between these warriors caught my breath. Colby was about to get creamed.

The smash of glass breaking made me twist around. Rurik had broken one of the small windows. He cleared the big shards away with his hands and winced as they cut through his skin. They barely even bled. He lifted me up to the hole, shoved me through it, then shouted, "Run, Rabbit, run!" A hard slap landed on my rump and pushed me through the rest of the way through the window. It stung.

I rolled on the ground to land onto my stomach in a puddle of cold, mucky who-*knows*-what. The window remained empty as I watched for them to follow me out. No one came. I leaned forward to look back inside only to see the back of Rurik's neatly combed head as he made his way into the fight again. He defended his people. My eyes widened. *And he saved me.*

A shiver ran down my spine. I jumped up and pulled the hem of my wet, white dress down. It stuck to my skin and didn't want to cooperate.

The alley looked like the same one Rurik and I walked down, a dark, foggy, narrow space that would spook even someone with a limited imagination.

The gunshots would draw the local law enforcements so I needed to return to the team and disappear. Shouts near the mouth of the alley caught my attention, the voices sounded familiar. I scurried toward it and Rurik's car parked at the mouth became visible.

A window from the party basement, a few feet in front of me, burst out. It sent shards of glass flying. I threw my arms up to shield my eyes. I was so close to safety, I could taste it, but a body blocked my path to refuge. It could be human and could need help, but it could be a hungry vampire, too.

Battle noise engulfed my cries for help. The corner of the building was just a few feet away and Colby should have left a rear guard outside. I just needed to pass the body lying in the alley.

My hesitation saved me. If I had been any closer, it would have gotten me.

The creature snapped his head up. His pupils were so dilated they absorbed the whole irises, his nostrils flared, and drool dripped down his exposed fangs. The fighting must have excited him into a frenzy.

Stumbling back, I swallowed hard. I'd never faced a

rabid dog before, but it must be a close cousin to this. *'My, what great big teeth you have,' said Red Riding Hood to the Big Bad Wolf.* The thought flashed before I did what I always hoped I wouldn't do—I screamed like a little girl and ran.

Every documentary I'd ever watched on predatory animals instructed people not to run when confronted. I'd like to know what prescription drugs they took, because I needed some. In reality, thousands of years of instinct kicked in. Your forebrain shuts down and a second later you're running down a dark alley like a gazelle in three-inch stilettos.

A carnivorous growl rumbled behind me. The vamp must not like his meals on the go.

I glanced over my shoulder to see him vault up in one smooth motion and stroll after me like it was a Sunday afternoon.

The slam of my body on a six-foot-high chain link fence stopped me cold. It cut the alley in two and I realized why my pursuer took his sweet time—a dead end. I pivoted to face him.

Past his monstrous features, he was an average looking guy—short brown hair, less than six feet tall, pale skin. He could have passed for human. His black jeans and t-shirt were torn and dirty from crashing through the window.

"You dance beautifully. Now dance with me, eh?" He spoke with a heavy accent I couldn't identify. Maybe it was the fangs. He continued down the alley toward me at a leisurely pace.

Pressed against the barrier I grasped the metal wire between my fingers and watched him stalk me. A heavy sinking dread clenched low in my stomach. I was breathless from running and my voice shook. "Rurik-ik told me you're not su-supposed to kill, only taste." I hoped by dropping Rurik's name it would deter him from doing anything rash.

With his jaw clenched he growled, "Rurik is feeble."

So much for name-dropping. I desperately searched the alley for something to fight with. My vision adjusted to see an outline of a door. It hid in the shadows on the building across from where the party was held. I sprang at it and hoped no one locked it.

To both of our surprise, it opened.

He let out a howl that vibrated through my body as he charged at me.

I raced through the opening then slammed the door in his face. My trembling fingers fumbled the bolt lock into place before he rammed his body against the door. A small whimper escaped my lips as I stepped back.

His crazed attacks made the walls shudder. The solid wood, in spite of its strength, wouldn't keep him out for long, and I needed time.

I stumbled along in the dark against the walls, until I felt a door. It opened to what appeared to be, in the dim light, an abandoned store. Large picture windows at the front of the room faced the street, which had been on the other side of the wretched fence. Faint streetlights filtered in and contrasted with the shadowy empty shelves scattered throughout the room. I could make out an outline of a checkout counter by the front door. As I rushed to it, I noticed something sitting on the counter too small to be a cash register. It was a phone!

I grabbed the receiver to my ear and heard a dial tone. My eyes closed in relief. I wasn't a religious person but this was a *miracle* in my book. That or the Budapest phone system worked differently than the American one.

The banging at the door stopped and silence hung in the air like a guillotine. I didn't know where he was now.

I could dial the team's cell phone number blindfolded.

"State your business," was the gruff greeting.

"Red?"

"Connie? Where the fuck are you? Colby's tearing apart that hole you were in. The chip says you're in the area!"

"I'm close. I'm in the next building. One of them is hunting me, Red. Hurry, I'm in…"

The earsplitting sound of shattering glass in one of the back rooms startled me enough to drop the phone. In my panic, I rushed the front door and battled with it. My luck ran out, it was locked. I'd trapped myself. Pressed in the corner by the door, I slid down to my hands and knees then crawled away from the windows so he wouldn't see my silhouette.

His boots crunched the broken glass as he drew

closer to the storefront. Quietly, I crawled out of the room to what I thought was a closet. My breathing sounded so loud. I tried to take slow, easy, controlled breaths, but I felt like I was suffocating. My heart pounded hard against my ribs, demanding more oxygen.

I made it into the room to come face to face with a commode.

Not a closet—a restroom—with a 'Connie-sized' window just above me. It was an old-fashioned one that hung on hinges and swung inward. I'd have to use a stick to prop it open. I heard him make his way into the storefront. The hope that emerged at the sight of the window plummeted.

My time was up.

Sucking in a deep breath, I kicked the door closed, hit the lock on it, climbed up on the commode, and propped open the window with my body.

Once again, my pursuer slammed into the door with full force but this time the frame splintered. One more hit and he'd get that dance he wanted.

I squeezed and squirmed through the tight window like a worm in the dirt. My breaths came in short gasps as fear coursed through my veins.

I tumbled down into that nightmarish alley and stood on the other side on the chain link fence. I've got boobs and junk in the trunk, but I was still a slim girl. There was no way he could fit those broad shoulders through that small window.

A shout startled me. Red ran toward me from the

ANNIE NICHOLAS

other side of the fence. I stared in disbelief, I couldn't have worse luck. One of us would have to climb it.

The crash from the bathroom door echoed through the alley.

"Climb!" Red's voice snapped still halfway to the fence.

I started to reach for the wired mesh but knew in my heart I couldn't make it in time. "Follow my tracker." Red and the boys would have to scale the fence, I couldn't afford to waste any more time. The vampire would find me before I made it to the top. Who puts a fence in an alley?

I gritted my teeth, yanked my expensive heels off, and sprinted away from Colby, from Red, and from safety.

Soon I came out of the alley onto the Danube Promenade. A few cars drove by on the busy road. At this time of the night, this area was dead—just a few streetlights and trees lining the sidewalk to accompany me.

I must have looked like a crazy woman as I sprinted barefoot, my sopping wet dress clinging to my legs, wild curls flying behind me.

It wouldn't be long before the vamp made it out of the store to track me. I needed to get out of plain view. If I could hide, maybe he'd give up, or Colby would find me again with the tracking chip.

A heap of trash left out for pickup sat by the walkway against a red brick building. Gross inspiration struck. I shoved myself into the middle of the stinking pile and pulled some over my head. Retching at the unbelievable stench, I pinched my nose to block it out. Hiding in trash seemed like a good idea a moment ago.

Something sticky oozed onto my hand. It took all my effort not to wig out. It was probably something innocent like jam but my imagination was way too vivid for that. After everything I'd been through—by the skin of my teeth—I would probably catch some horrid disease from the trash. I squeezed into a tight ball and tried not to touch any more anonymous slime.

I heard fast paced footsteps draw closer to my hiding spot. My hands began to sweat and tremble. They slowed to a jog until they stopped nearby. He must have seen me hide. How else could he know I was close?

My legs tensed and I prepared to flee. I refused to go down without a fight. The fear of a vampire hunting me down like a rabbit rapidly turned into frustration. I wanted to jump out and attack him, but I didn't think I'd survive that stupid urge.

"I hear you heartbeat, Bobbit. It races." He stood so close I heard a snuffling sound, like a dog smelling a trail.

Vampires had heightened senses. They could see and hear better than humans. They were also stronger and faster. Following a scent trail like a hound and listening to my heartbeat were skills unknown to me.

"You so scared. It make you taste sweeter, you know." So he *didn't* see me hide but he knew I was close. His pronounced accent made his words sound more sinister. The trash became a good choice for disguising my scent, but the heartbeat thing gave me away.

The screech of tires coming around a corner interrupted the vamp's hunt. A short burst of gunfire spattered against the red brick building above my head. I shuddered with the rattling cacophony and covered my ears. The sudden deafening sound of the car and gunfire quickly faded away, leaving me scrunched up in my trash haven in an envelope of silence. I took some deep shaky breaths and waited.

He could still be waiting for me to come out. My limbs refused to respond. I was too scared to peek and kept thinking of horror movie victims. The ones who want to check out the strange noise in the backyard while you're screaming at them to stay inside the house.

The car had to be from Colby. There couldn't be too many people shooting it out with the local vampires. They knew I was out here being hunted. Colby didn't make a habit of shooting up neighborhoods, tonight was exceptional. Our plans went wrong in every way possible.

Things stayed quiet, if I waited for them to return it could backlash. My limbs trembled from the continued tension. There could be others who lurked around, looking for an exhausted, smelly snack.

After what seemed like an eternity but probably closer to fifteen minutes, I crawled out of the trash with my teeth chattering and began the long walk to my hotel. Soon the adrenaline wore off and left me wrung out like a dishrag. My knees felt weak as I wobbled on rubber legs, bare foot toward my goal. I fantasized about a long hot shower.

Somewhere in all the excitement, my sense of time got lost. I hoped it would be dawn soon so it would temporarily be safe enough to sleep. I wrapped my arms around myself. I had so much to do. I needed to reach Colby to tell him everything I'd learned tonight and get instructions on what to do next. Sending me home to America sounded good.

I was so absorbed in my own tired thoughts of hot showers and soft beds that *he* easily took me.

Silent as a nightmare he slipped his arm about my shoulders. His eyes were still dilated, but he'd gotten the rabid drooling under control. "Where you hide?" He sneered as he steered me away from the street into a dark corner between the buildings.

My struggles didn't affect him one bit. I sensed him test my mental shield. It smoked my mind for a moment but my shields held. He was either a weak one or whatever affected me before wore off.

He loomed over me with his head tilted back. "You stay quiet and I feed."

I barked a laugh at his command and did what every girl learns at one point or another in their life, the old knee jerk to the joy sack.

He let my shoulders go with a howl and stumbled back. Shoulders straight and legs apart I glared at him. I was through running. There was only so much abuse one person could take. If he wanted to feed on me, it came with some side dishes of kicking, gouging, and biting.

Before he recovered from my initial attack, I shoved my thumbs into his eyes as far as I could. His bloodcurdling screech satisfied something sinister and hungry in me. I poured all my frustration, anger and impotence from tonight into my assault.

"I may be prey but I've got bite, asshole."

He threw me off him hard enough that I was airborne when I hit the building. The ground broke my fall and all I could do was lie there, guppy breathing, and watch the stars spin around my head. I waited for him to take me.

Nothing happened. When my lungs learned how to function, again I rolled off my back to look around.

I was alone.

No way did I cause him sufficient hurt to make him run. He wanted me enough to return to hunt me after being discouraged by gunfire. I struggled to my feet and shuffled to the corner of the building. Peeking around it, I drew a shaky breath of relief. I stiffened and spun to look behind me. The alley was deserted.

Never releasing my watchful vigilance on the area around me, I wiped the eyeball gore from my thumbs onto my ruined dress. It made my skin crawl. My mouth became dry and nausea rolled my stomach. Where did he go?

I checked around the corner again but the Danube Promenade looked empty of monsters.

He was gone.

CHAPTER FIVE

The night clerk at my hotel gave me the fish eye as I walked up to the counter and confessed I'd lost my key at a party.

He handed me the replacement, taking in my torn dress and bare feet. "Must have been some party." I'd walked like this for six blocks down the Danube Promenade waiting for fang face to jump me again.

I rolled my eyes. "Yeah, you could say that." I took the elevator to the seventh floor.

Rurik astounded me. I flip-flopped between hatred and lust. At the club I would have staked him myself, but at the party... I fanned myself. He set me on fire. I never thought I'd meet another man who could do that. Then again, Rurik wasn't a man.

The doors opened onto my floor and I stepped out. Rurik rescued me, sure Colby provided a distraction, but Rurik could have left me stuck behind the couch with a mob of angry vampires between my Calvary and me. It should make no difference to him if I survived the attack at the party. *Or did it?* He'd come back for me.

I was too tired to think straight. Beautiful and heroic, didn't change the fact that he'd done something bad enough to merit Colby's hire. I opened my room door. The only thing I wanted to do was sprawl on top of my big soft bed and lapse into a coma. My stench overcame me in the closed quarters. The coma could wait until I showered.

A sliding glass door across from my bed overlooked the Danube River and the city's skyline. The need for fresh air drew me out onto the balcony and I admired the night view. A breeze brushed against my wet dress and cleared some of the smell from the hotel room. Whatever Colby paid for the room, this sight made it worth every penny.

The Buda Castle spread itself on the hillside across the river. It shone golden against the night sky, reflecting the spotlights that surrounded it, and was probably the largest Gothic palace in Europe. The city extended around its hill with a combination of medieval and modern architecture, all lit up for their nightly display. The rich lights danced on the gentle currents of the Danube River.

I leaned against the doorframe and watched the

ripples of the water warp the reflections. The soft wind made me shiver and I wished for a certain set of strong arms for warmth. Loneliness overwhelmed me. It hadn't always been this way, but it felt so achingly long ago, it may as well have been a lifetime. I saw no point in dwelling on it. Despair would just hook its claws into me and drag me back under its gray misty clouds.

Wishing wouldn't bring my husand back, nothing would.

I would call Colby again, but first, I needed to wash my hands of the dirt and vampire gore that still clung to them. Hopefully, the liquid-soaked dress didn't short my tracking device and they knew I made it back to the hotel. I would hate for them to cruise the streets searching for me.

My reflection in the bathroom mirror appeared pitiful. No wonder the night clerk gawked. I looked as if I'd been wrestling in trash, instead of hiding in it. A piece of potato peel hung from my hair and my lower lip split from being backhanded. I picked the peel out of my hair and tossed it into the commode. A hysterical giggle bubbled up. I clamped my hands over my mouth before it got out of control. *What a mess.*

The hot water ran over my hands, and all the little cuts I acquired in my adventures, screamed at the same time.

I hopped up and down from the stinging as I scrubbed with lots and lots of soap, getting every bit of contaminated gunk off me, then started on my face. Amazing how a little soap and water can rejuvenate someone. The split on my lip began bleeding from the scrub. I looked up at the mirror again to examine it.

My gaze met a pair of cool, blue eyes.

I gasped and my heart raced. "You!"

Rurik leaned against the bathroom's doorway and watched me. He moved with unnerving quietness. Somewhere between shoving me out the window and his arrival here, he'd lost his dress jacket. I appeared to have done more fighting than he did, not one of his hairs looked out of place.

I spun to point my finger at him. "How did you get in here?" Then marched up to him, planted my hands on his chest and pushed. "How dare you!" A bulldozer wouldn't have moved him.

His eyes widened at my unexpected assault and he raised his hands in a vain attempt to placate me.

I put my shoulders into the effort to move him out of my room.

He laughed as he backed out of the bathroom of his own free will. His hands reached to touch me but I slapped at them and knocked them away.

"Are you laughing at me?" I slapped his hands again and again, until he captured my wrists gently in his hands. I tried to pull away. "Stop it!"

He sported a huge stupid grin. "You're such an interesting woman, Rabbit. And what a vision." He choked on a chuckle, unable to contain himself.

I was supposed to be safe. I'd fought for my life and finally reached my room. My face and hands were clean, my shower waited, then my soft, cozy bed. He wasn't supposed to be here. I was supposed to be ... *safe*.

Tears welled up in my eyes. I tried to blink them away but they trickled out. He held my wrists so I couldn't wipe them away. Instead, I looked down at my grubby feet and tried to focus on what was left of my pedicure.

I wished he would leave me alone. His presence made my loneliness sharper, closer to the surface than I'd allowed it to be in almost a year.

The dam broke loose and the tears flowed in steady dismal streams. Pressure built in my chest. It ached to breathe. A big sob escaped.

"Rabbit?" He knelt down to look up at my face as I tried to hide my tears.

I turned away but it didn't do any good.

He released my wrists to wipe away the tears spilling down my cheeks with his thumbs. "Please don't cry."

I'm sure it was an ugly thing to witness. Heat spread across my cheeks as I got blotchy, my nose ran, and a fat, split lip didn't help. He pulled me down into his arms and pressed me against his chest. He felt solid as I sat on his lap and leaned on his shoulder to sob my heart out. Once I started, it became hard to stop. I hated it.

"I'm sorry," he chanted between my sobs, his voice soft and concerned. We sat on the carpet in the middle of my room as his hand stroked my hair and he rocked me in his arms.

When every pent up tear had poured from me, I pulled away to use the hem of my destroyed dress as a handkerchief.

"I didn't mean to make you cry." He set me on the floor with tender care and walked back into the bathroom.

I heard the water run. A few seconds later, he returned with a wet face cloth. He knelt in front of me and washed my tear streaked face. My temper cooled with each refreshing, gentle swipe. He was so careful with it, as thought unfamiliar with the act. His smile was gone. It surprised me, to find myself yearning for his touch. He kept glancing at my mouth as he washed my face.

He took my breath away, full soft lips contrasted with the hard lines of his jaw, the sensitive disquiet of his expression softening the edges. His face lowered to mine slowly, coming to within a hair's breadth of my lips. Our eyes met and he hesitated.

Who could blame him after my recent impersonation of a psycho? This man who kneeled in front of me, sweetly concerned, did not seem like a monster. I wanted to kiss him but my thoughts and desires warred with each other.

Rurik drugged me, then offered me up as a pet. I couldn't afford to be this naïve.

He continued forward, closing the gap quickly, and traced his tongue along my bottom lip.

I raised my eyebrows and reflexively reached up to touch where he'd tasted me. My fingers came away with a little blood. The split in my bottom lip still bled. Something squirmed inside my stomach. I remembered how I felt watching the feeding at the party—a twisted combination of arousal and revulsion.

He brought my bloody fingers to his mouth and delicately sucked on them as his gaze burned into mine.

I pulled them from his mouth and watched, fascinated, as a lazy smile curled his lips.

He sighed. "Thank you for sharing. I love the way you taste."

"Uhh, you're welcome?" Was that the right response? This was weird, even for me.

He folded the cool washcloth neatly and handed it to me. "Keep it pressed to your lip. It will help with the swelling."

I held the cloth to my mouth and hid the blood from his sight. "How did you find me?"

If he used some kind of mind trick to locate me, I needed to know. Dragos wasn't like Rurik. If he could find me in the same manner, I could kiss my sweet ass goodbye.

The lazy smile still graced Rurik's face. "I saw you walking along the street and followed you."

Relief flooded me—no tricks, just dumb luck. Something else disturbed me though. "How did you get into my room?"

"Do you always ask so many questions, Connie?"

That was the first time he'd used my name since we'd met. I'd graduated from being a main course to a person. I glared at him.

He relaxed back onto his hands and tilted his head, flirting with his seductive eyes.

I wasn't buying it, at least not for the next minute or so.

He reached over to remove an errant curl from my eyes. "I just wanted to make sure you weren't injured."

"Yeah ... but how did you get in my room?"

His fingers trailed down my arm sending a shiver up my spine. My resolve dissipated as well. "Is your lip the worst of your injuries?"

"Yes." I swallowed as his fingers moved back up. "Did you bribe the clerk? Use vampire mojo on him?"

His hand paused and his eyes flicked back to mine. "Mojo?" The lazy smile turned into a wicked, amused grin. "No mojo. I saw you standing on the balcony. You seemed so very sad." The silence grew as I waited for his answer. We stared at each other and Rurik's grin grew as well. "You left your balcony door open, so I came in."

"We're seven floors up!"

"I used my vampire 'mojo'."

"Oh." Seven floors up—that was pretty high—even with mojo.

He lifted my hand to his mouth and pressed a kiss against the pulse in my wrist. The soft caress against my skin made me long to have him touch those lush lips to my other pulse points. Similar thoughts seemed to heat up his stare but he released me. "It's almost dawn and I need to go. I had fun tonight."

"You have a peculiar taste of fun."

He stood from the floor in one fluid motion then came and plucked a scrap of paper out of my curls. "I can't remember the last time I laughed so hard." He kissed me on the top of my head and grimaced. "You need a shower, Rabbit."

"Really? I kind of like the stench."

He chuckled under his breath while he walked out to the balcony.

"Rurik?"

He turned and looked at me, the lights from my room reflecting off his eyes, making them swirl like black pools. The cool breeze played along his body while he stood outside the balcony doorway.

"I was attacked by a vampire in an alley nearby. Just as I couldn't defend myself anymore, he suddenly disappeared." I watched his face for some hint of recognition. "Do you know anything about that?"

He still grinned. "Maybe it was the smell."

"You followed me."

"I offered you my protection."

"If I pleased Dragos. I didn't do anything."

His grin softened and he blew me a kiss. "You pleased me." Then he was gone. *Just like that. Poof.*

He didn't go over the side, I would have seen that. Staggering to stand, I wandered onto the balcony, dumbfounded for the second time that night. I think he went ... *up.* The washcloth dripped water onto the floor, forgotten in my hand.

The shrill ring of the bedside phone shattered my wonderment. It made me jump as if struck by a cow prod.

CHAPTER SIX

I knew who it was before I answered the phone. "Colby?"

"Are you all right?" His voice dripped with anger.

"I think so. One of them followed me here." I regretted those words as soon as they popped out. Exhausted, my brain must have malfunctioned.

"Is it still there? We can be at the hotel in minutes."

A twister of emotions raged inside my heart. I didn't want to tell him it was Rurik.

"Connie? Are you there? Connie, if you're in trouble, this would be the time to use one of those code words I made you memorize."

"No need for the Double-O-Seven stuff. He's gone."

"Did he bite you?"

"No, I convinced him to leave ... I told him I belonged to a stronger vampire." Technically Rurik gave me to Dragos as a present. I wasn't lying. Colby would want to dissect every nuance of my conversation with the Overlord of Budapest. The details of vampire politics and laws I'd learned at the party needed to be shared but our conversation in my hotel room was private.

"What? That worked?"

"It's a long story."

"Tonight was a clusterfuck. Report in five minutes at the front entrance, there'll be someone waiting for you."

"But—" The dial tone cut me off. I needed a shower. He could use a lesson in phone etiquette. My ride could sit there and grow roots. I was taking a shower. I had unidentified alley fluid dripping off the hem of my dress, vampire saliva on my chest, and eyeball remains under my nails. Colby could park his mercenary ass and wait ten more minutes.

A driver waved me over and held the door for me as I exited the building. Sunlight chased the stars away with its nimbus of pink light in the east. My ponytail dripped warm drops of water onto my t-shirt as I climbed into the back of a cab. I finally felt clean and comfy in my sweatpants. Our destination was a mystery to me. As a rule, the bait never gets informed. Basically, it's a need-to-know relationship and a safeguard.

Good bait was hard to find. Can't exactly place an

ad in the classifieds. *"Vampire lure wanted. No prior experience needed. Great benefits!"* I snorted at the thought. Getting groped, chased, and then enthralled were not my idea of benefits. However, when a plan worked and a killer got dusted, it made up for all the other stuff.

Colby saved me from my first vampire encounter. It was a dismal time for me. The recent loss of my husband, Laurent, to cancer, cut a huge hole in my soul. Captain Morgan and I prearranged a date every night. I had nothing left and the prospects of joining my husband sounded nicer each passing hour.

Colby saved my life twice the night we met, the first time from the vampire and the second time from myself.

The cab stopped in front of a church and the driver looked at me through the rearview mirror. "When you get inside, go down the first set of stairs on the right."

I stood on the curb and watched the cab fade into the growing traffic. The church loomed above, a giant stone monstrosity from a time when religion ruled the people.

Inside the entrance, I found the stairway, but something drew me further into the church. An altar stood on the dais in front of an enormous stained glass window. The weak sunlight, the only light in the room, filtered down around the altar and made pretty patterns of pinks and blues on the floor. Tranquility filled me. A small island of peace after the storm I'd just experienced.

I knelt at the closest pew. "Thanks for the help tonight." Then I stood and did a little curtsy to the altar. That might not be the right way but I winged it. The appropriate formula for prayer was foreign to me.

When I returned to the stairs, Red blocked my way. He grinned from ear to ear, disfiguring his ruddy pockmarked face.

"That was so cute, Connie. Someone might mistake you for a lady doin' a curtsy like that."

"Stick it in your ear, Red." I brushed past him to make my way downstairs. Red was the size of a grizzly bear. People thought his size made him slow but they were wrong. He snatched me up like a doll and crushed me in his version of a hug.

"Breathe..." I swatted the back of his head with my free arm while stars flashed before my eyes.

He loosened his grip while setting me back on the ground. I gasped in air. "You big red-headed goof. Are you trying to break me in two?"

"Thought we lost you tonight, shrimp." He ruffled my hair, pulling strands out of my neat ponytail. "You added more white hairs on my head when you ran out onto the Promenade away from us." He leaned in close, meeting my eyes to make his point. "Next time, climb the damn fence. I'm too old to be sprinting after a lunatic."

"Have you ever tried climbing a fence in a dress and heels?"

"When we get back home, you're doing more training with me." He pointed his thumb to his chest.

Red's hair may be getting whiter but his body could still dent things. "I'll have you climbing fences in a clown suit."

I snorted but returned his hug. Red meant well. I could count on one hand the number of people who truly cared about me. Red was one of them.

We made our way down the stairs. He glanced at me from the corner of his eye. "I heard about the vampire who followed you home. You shouldn't play with strays, you might catch something."

"Har, Har, you're such a comedian." We continued further into the church basement.

"How come he didn't do anything to you?"

"I didn't—I mean, he lost interest and dawn was coming."

"You tellin' me this thing chased you three blocks, followed you to the hotel, and then lost interest?"

They thought the vampire who hunted me from the party followed me to my hotel room. "I reasoned with him."

His eyebrow rose. "How?"

My thoughts raced. How indeed? "At the party Rurik gave me to a pretty powerful vampire as a present. Everyone witnessed it. I reminded him of that." If I kept my lies close to the truth, I had a better chance of keeping them straight.

Red just stared at me, ridicule painted across his face. "That's it? How'd he find ya?"

"I don't know, Red. The subject didn't come up, kinda had my hands full, staying alive and stuff, okay?"

I could have sworn I felt my nose grow with each lie.

He opened his mouth then hesitated before shrugging. A huge duffel bag lay open on the floor. He picked it up. "Jump in."

"Why?" I peered into it. "Is this punishment for screwing up?"

"If we wanted to punish you, we would have left you at the party." He opened the bag wider, placed it back on the floor, and gestured to it. "It wouldn't be the first time I've carried a body in it." His face looked grim.

"I believe you, Red." I mirrored his expression. "How else would you get a date to go home with you?"

His grin re-emerged.

"I've always liked 'em small and quiet-like."

"Good thing I have a big mouth."

His laughter filled the room.

"Why couldn't we meet here, Red? Why do all this subterfuge?"

"Things went bad tonight and on top of that, you were followed. It may be daytime but what if one their humans trailed you here? Maybe they made a connection between you and our attack last night. We can't afford that." He gestured to the bag again. "Getting in?"

I stepped into it, humiliated. I fit but stopped Red as he zipped it up.

"Not all the way. I need to feel like I can open it." My voice sounded small, even to me.

"Okay, not all the way." He left it open a smidge

so I could see some light. Then heaved me over his shoulder and exaggerated a stagger. "Need to lay off those cookies."

I elbowed him through the bag and he rewarded me with a grunt.

"Red," I whispered quietly as he lugged me around like dirty laundry. "You're not putting me in the trunk of the car, are you?"

"As tempting as that sounds, no. I'm tying you to the back of my motorcycle."

"Red!" Suddenly I became weightless as he threw me onto the back seat of his car. Relief washed over me—I could be so gullible. The car's motion rocked and lulled me into a much needed sleep.

Colby assisted me out of the bag when I was placed on the floor at last. We were in a makeshift office. No pictures or advertisements hung on the walls, just a room with a desk, chairs, and a filing cabinet. He stopped my progress to examine my split lip then my neck. His piercing green eyes never missed a detail. "No bites. Good. Any other injuries?"

"Just bumps and bruises."

He released me and made his way to sit behind a battered wooden desk.

I pulled up a cold, metal chair to sit on and faced him. His dirty blond hair stuck out as if he'd been pulling at it. Thin strips of medical tape held a cut over his right eye together and a bruise along his jaw line was surfacing. "Was any of the team killed?" No matter how many times I explained this to myself, I still felt responsible when someone got hurt trying to protect me. Thank goodness it didn't happen often.

"None. Three sustained injuries, enough to merit a hospital, but it appeared like most of the vamps held back from the fight." He rubbed his bruised chin.

"From my angle at the top of the stairs, I could see some of the vamps fightin' among themselves. Mother fuckin' weird, if you askin' me." Red leaned against the wall by the door with the duffle bag at his feet.

"What happened at the club? Why did you let him lead you out a side door instead of the main one like planned? I figured he didn't know you were planted since he didn't kill you in the alley." His soft commanding voice gave me a chill. It reminded me of Dragos'.

I leaned forward against the desk. "Things were going smoothly. He finally made a pass and offered me a drink. We flirted a little and I got him to agree to leave the club with me, but he slipped something in my drink. I had trouble focusing on what we were doing. He took me to the side door instead of the main entrance. A car waited for us when we got outside then he pulled a whammie on me." I glanced at my clenched hands and relaxed them. "The drug affected my mental shield more than anything else. I had no power over them. They just ran through my control like sand. He took me."

Red cleared his throat. He stood by the door, guarding it. "He ... uh ... *do* anything to you?" His crossed arms over his chest, which bulged with contained tension.

"No, at least not what you are implying." I shifted self-consciously on my seat. "He helped me into a car and told me he wanted to introduce me to an important magistrate. I have to point out here that Rurik's powerful. He's not fresh-outta-the-grave, he's old and strong. Some of the vampires at that party were even stronger."

"We noticed." Colby ran a finger along his injured jaw.

"Rurik offered me as a 'gift' to a real bad ass vampire he referred to as *Master* Dragos." Colby and Red exchanged a quick look.

"Describe him."

"Tall, bald, pointed ears, skin so pale it looked transparent. He had an intricate black tattoo on his scalp that extended down his neck. I can't express how much he frightened me. Power just oozed from him. He was—" I searched my vocabulary to find the right word "—compelling."

Colby sat back in his chair, fingers steepled under his chin. "Did he like you?"

"What?" The question threw me. "I mean, he accepted me, and made me dance with him." Heat crept up my cheeks. Red would use this to tease me. I could hear the wheels turning in his head from here.

My boss' green-eyed gaze stayed clear and direct. He never looked tired and he never looked happy. "Dragos." He ran his fingers through his messy hair once more. His eyes never left me. "Can you work him if I find him?"

"Colby!" Red's voice snapped across the room and made me twist in my chair.

They glared at each other as if having silent communion. "Never mind, Connie." Colby pulled at his hair again. "We decided earlier you're in too much danger. These aren't the kind of vampires you're used to working with. Red will get you on a flight home."

Red picked up the duffel bag and approached me.

"Now wait a moment there, big boy." I waggled my finger at him. "I'm not done reporting. This has been a tough night for everyone." Turning back to Colby I met his steely stare. Hints of strain showed around his eyes. He didn't tell me everything. He never did. "Rurik told me about a vampire government. It sounded like something more global than territorial. I think Dragos is part of that."

He opened his mouth.

"Wait, don't interrupt me yet." I held up my index finger. "He also told me they have a 'no-killing-people' policy. It attracts too much attention to their kind and they want to remain obscure. If this is so, why have we been hunting so many killers?"

"He sure told you a lot for a first date."

"I know. It struck me as odd. Is he lying to me?"

"He's just playin' with your head," Red commented from his post by the door. "He has his own agenda and he's usin' you."

"It wouldn't be the first time. He makes my head spin." I rubbed my hands across my face and tried to stay awake.

"Don't discount all this yet." Colby's comment did a better job at waking me. "Something has stirred the vampire community this past year. It's true, Connie, the killings have been increasing. We've never been so busy. I just assumed it was because we're in America, where control is still being fought over. Things settled in Europe centuries ago so the vampire communities have been stable. Until now." Colby spoke quietly to himself. "I wonder what is stirring them up. We're missing something." He rubbed his temples. "None of this makes sense."

"Maybe if you told me more, I would know what to listen and look for."

He raised an eyebrow at me and leaned forward. "Then you're interested in going back?"

Red muttered under his breath behind me.

I shifted in my seat under Colby's scrutiny. "Maybe. Depends on what you're about to tell me." This would be a milestone in our working relationship. We had a need-to-know agreement and Colby didn't think I needed to know much.

"I hate it that Rurik got past your mental shield. Do you know how deep he went?"

"N-no. How could I tell? Each time felt different."

"Each? How many times did he touch your mind?" His shout made me jump and my cheeks got warmer.

"Three." I looked at the edges on the worn, wooden desk. The varnish peeled in places but the areas were smooth with age.

"I wonder if he had time to glean any information from you." He leaned back in his chair and clasped his hands over his flat stomach. "Or enthrall you. Your behavior will be suspect from now on." His stare traveled to Red. "Maybe we should send you home."

I wouldn't argue with him. He was right. It wasn't just my behavior I worried about but my judgment too. I wanted to go home, but then the team would have to go to vampire territory to complete their contract. Not have their quarry brought to a battleground of their choice. Could I live with my cowardice if say, Red were killed because I ran away with my tail between my legs?

My decision to withhold the information of Rurik following me *was* suspicious. Did he do something to my mind? I didn't sense anything different, except I think I liked him. Yet, I still held my tongue. If I couldn't trust my own thoughts I'd go mad second guessing myself. *I am who I am.*

"If you send me home, you'll be endangering yourselves. I can lure whomever you want to you safely. Have I ever failed you?"

"It's against my better judgment, but I want Rurik bad, and I wouldn't mind a meeting with his Master." He watched his own hands and avoided me. "I saw the way he looked at you at the club. Rurik would follow you again." Colby continued to think aloud. "Would Master Dragos?"

"No, I get the impression he'd eat me on the spot if I ever encountered him again."

"Hmm, figures. I think he might be a *Nosferatu*

vampire. They're much more volatile."

"We don't know for sure what he is, Colby." Red stepped away from his post, bag forgotten in his hand. "He could be just a freakin', big, bald vamp."

"You saw him before he escaped the building. He had the markings on his head. We both did. Connie's description fits."

"There hasn't been a sightin' of a *Nosferatu* in centuries. They're a myth, like the Loch Ness monster." Red almost never argued with Colby. He was his right hand man, his enforcer.

"Red, most people think vampires are a myth and look what we do for a living."

I felt left out. "*Nosferatu*? As in the movie?"

Colby gazed at me. "We don't know much. There are some drawings and vague descriptions in our oldest records. They're a species of vampire, probably the source of their kind. To sum it up, they're hairless, powerful, vampire warriors. Uber-vamps."

"Uber-vamps, sounds like Dragos." I remembered the power and confidence that oozed off him. I also remembered the fear in the eyes of Rurik's people as Dragos approached them.

"I wonder why you're still alive." The softness in Colby's voice didn't match the hard look in his eyes.

"I really thought I was riding on an express elevator to the afterlife until you showed up."

Red stepped up to the desk. "Is it possible Dragos enthralled Connie? Used his power to track her here?"

"I thought you didn't believe in them?" I couldn't

help myself. Red was so fun to tease.

"Wise ass."

I curled my lip at him playfully. "We shouldn't go down Paranoia Lane just yet. If *we* were followed, we'd be waist deep in trouble by now."

Colby still leaned back in his chair, thinking about my information dump. "I live on Paranoia Lane, but you have a point. We don't know enough to make any decision presently. Something big is happening. I can sense it." He leaned forward, drawing our attention. "I've changed my mind. Connie, you stay."

Red took a step forward, his mouth open, but Colby held his hand up. "No, Red."

Colby pointed at me. "She's doing well. She's kept her head and collected more Intel in one night than we have all year." He looked to me. "We'll take you back to your hotel. Pack and move to another one. Red, get her a new identity. We don't want to make it easy for them to find her. Connie, I want a detailed list of who you met and descriptions. Anything you can remember, even if it seems insignificant. If anymore vamps contact you, call my cell before taking action." He stood and walked to the door. "I'll get in touch when I need you."

Red held the bag open for me. "All aboard."

CHAPTER SEVEN

Red transported me back to the church in his stinking duffle bag then released me to climb in their cab with a set of orders and a new identity snug in my pocket. It took a while for me to get the instructions straight. I read and re-read them. Not because they were complicated, I was just too tired to absorb anything.

First—move to the Rudas hotel. Second—don't attract attention, then wait for Colby's phone call. They would find out the vampire communities' reaction to last night's fiasco before making further plans.

It didn't take me long to get my stuff together and switch hotels. Working for Colby taught me how to get my ass in gear. When he wanted you to 'mobilize', you worked fast and carried your own stuff, or you lost it.

I took one last look at the beautiful river view from the balcony. My curiosity got the better of me and I couldn't resist examining the building above. Maybe Rurik jumped up and climbed the building when he vanished last night. I could see there were handholds someone ridiculously strong and nimble might use. Since it was so dark last night, my eyes probably tricked me.

The riverfront entrance of the Rudas hotel divulged a drab, late 19th century industrial building, but these architectural impressions proved to be misleading. Hidden inside this retro-modern hotel lived a well-preserved ancient bathhouse built in 1578. At least, that's what the brochure stated.

I set it back on my new desk. This place oozed with luxury. Red would have to stuff me back into that duffel bag if he wanted to send me home. I crawled onto the down filled bedding and basked in the puff of heaven.

There were so many unanswered questions swirling around my busy head. The foremost being—why did Rurik save me? If he hadn't drugged me, I may have allowed my attraction to grow. The visit from Dragos masked something bigger brewing in Budapest. He and Rurik obviously didn't like each other. Maybe Dragos knew of Lizzy's attraction to Rurik. Could they be having an affair? When out of earshot, Rurik expressed his dislike for her. I decided Rurik had his fingers in too many cooking pots and was going to get burned.

I cracked my jaw yawning and rolled over to allow

the sunlight to warm my face. It offered me security. No big bald *Nosferatu* would crawl from under my bed to suck my blood in the daylight. I smiled and watched the geometric shapes dance behind my eyelids.

I'm not sure what woke me first, the aches in my body or the urgency to use the toilet. Both were equally uncomfortable. Injuries always hurt worse the day after. My back groaned with stiffness as I made an attempt to roll out of bed. It was to be excepted when you've been thrown against a stone wall like a rag doll. My legs tried to cramp while I shuffled to the bathroom. I caught a glance of myself in the mirror and grimaced at what looked back at me. People with naturally curly hair shouldn't fall asleep when it's damp. My ponytail resembled a huge, fuzzy pom-pom on the back of my head. Rurik would appreciate my rabbit tail. My grimace transformed into a grin at the poof. When had thoughts of Rurik start making me smile?

His tenderness last night caught me off guard. It made me aware of how affection-starved I'd been. He started the evening so cold and malicious then grew into someone charming. Would the real Rurik please stand up?

The odd incident with the disappearing alley vampire bothered me. Rurik did some interesting physical feats—like getting into and leaving my hotel room, seven floors up from the ground. He could have defeated my attacker while I got the wind knocked out of me, then followed me back to the hotel.

Now Colby wanted to use me as bait for Rurik

again. We both knew he'd respond, except I didn't want to hurt him. I never dealt with an internal struggle like this. Each contract I helped Colby complete, the vampire *always* tried to hurt to me. None of them charmed me, attracted me, or wiped tears from my face. Seeds of doubt bloomed. How could I find out the truth?

My gut told me Rurik was different. I sighed and fluffed my pom-pom tail. Maybe I confused my libido with my gut. I wish I'd been given the chance to peel him out of his suit last night.

A growl came from my neglected stomach. I'd slept through the day and most of the evening. After I flipped through the menu and ordered room service, I picked up the hotel brochure depicting the other amenities once more. A hot, steaming bath with a massage at a genuine Hungarian bathhouse sounded right up my alley.

The entrance to the ancient section of the Rudas came through a portal arch pinched at the top like the toe of a genie's shoe. The wooden door to the bathhouse lay at the end of this narrow corridor.

I looked forward to a long hot soak and a well-deserved night off. When I pushed at the door to enter, it remained immobile. A little sign beside it showed the hours of operation.

They were closed.

I leaned against the rough, solid, wooden door

and banged my forehead on it. I shouldn't have paused to eat. Sometimes I forgot not everyone lived on a vampire's time clock. Now, I had to be satisfied with a stupid hot shower.

The door swung open and for a second, I became weightless before falling forward to sprawl onto the floor. I jarred my already sore body hard enough to rattle my teeth and groaned at the sharp pain.

"Rabbit! You're not who I expected."

The silken, sexy voice sounded familiar. I rolled onto my back to stare at the source.

A set of widened, pale, blue eyes looked down at me. I sat up, the quick movement sent spasms down my back. The muscles quieted after I stayed still.

Rurik squatted next to me. He turned his charming smile on. "I'd happily accept your company instead." He wore a blue muscle shirt that accentuated his eyes, and a pair of faded jeans.

Instead of who? The pang of jealousy that accompanied the thought amazed me. I scrabbled up to my feet. "I thought the bathhouse was closed."

Fluidly he stood with me. "To the general populace it is. Those of us who are—" his grin grew, flashing fang "—daylight challenged, come here after-hours."

Even dressed casually he was easy on the eyes. He reached to lay a bare touch to my forehead where I felt tender from knocking my head. "It's an odd way to knock on the door. Most people use their knuckles." He lifted my hand to exhibit the correct tools for the job.

My eyes narrowed. "I read somewhere, that's how they knock here. So, when in Budapest, do as the Hungarian do."

His startled laugh at my wiseass remark made him seem more human. He lowered his face, laughter still shining in his eyes. "I'll remember that the next time I knock at your door."

"Next time? I don't remember you knocking last night." The huskiness of my voice made it a whisper.

"No, I didn't." He stood so close I could smell the mild spice of his cologne. His face was almost too handsome to look at.

A thrill of anticipation ran through me right down to curl my toes.

"How did you find me, my little surprise?"

I placed a hand against his chest, reluctant to keep him from closing the gap. "I wasn't looking for you." No breaths or heartbeat moved against my hand. Only warmth radiated from beneath his shirt. He must have fed. "I'm sore from running last night. I wanted to soak in a hot bath." His heart may not be beating but mine drummed.

"So you knocked to come in?"

I chuckled, feeling the heat of color rising to my cheeks. "Well ... I was, actually, banging my head in frustration. It didn't occur to me to knock."

He stepped forward to touch my frizzed out ponytail. His proximity caused me to step back against the door, closing it. "Scary hair."

"That's an understatement."

"Such frustration should not be left unfulfilled, especially if it will lead you to bang your pretty head." He pulled me from the door and stepped in behind me.

A middle-aged, plump woman watched us from across the room. She wore her dark, gray streaked hair pulled back into a tight bun. She wasn't much taller than me. The bulk under her dress gave me the impression she could wrestle me down and tie me into a pretzel without breaking a sweat.

He spoke Hungarian to her, then to me in English. "Pembe will bring you to the bathing room."

"Rurik, I'll come back in the morning. That way I can get a massage afterward." I reached around him for the doorknob but it wouldn't budge. He'd locked it.

I didn't want to stay. Rurik stirred up desires I thought dead. It mixed with conflicted emotions from my job and lost loved ones only to make me miserable. For once, I needed to feel good. Not happy, I don't remember happy, but tranquil, like at the church yesterday. That one of the walking dead could raise lust or more from me made me cringe.

It wasn't a recipe for a relaxing night.

"Pembe is an excellent masseuse. Please, I see you're sore and feel responsible for your pains. You have my protection, once again, while in this bathhouse."

I'm such a sucker for a pair of pretty eyes. He batted his thick lashes at me and my resolve to leave crumbled. Good thing he wasn't human, I'd probably throw myself at his feet. *Oh yeah, I already did.*

Pembe snapped her fingers at me then pointed at

a hallway entrance. "Follow," she ordered in a thick Hungarian accent.

I walked through the reception area and glanced back at Rurik. "Quick,"She snapped and made me jump.

His amused smile curled even more.

Pembe led me down a hall and handed me a canvas slip she pulled out of a basket. The changing area consisted of curtained off cubicles, each with a small cot for resting after the bath and massage.

I changed into the slip. It came down to my knees, one of the advantages of being short. I carried out my folded clothes but she took them from me, scolding as she placed them back in the cubicle. Maybe she thought the louder she spoke the better I'd understand.

She led me into a little slice of heaven.

Inside the main bathing area, green marble columns supported a low dome. It rose above an octagonal pool at the room's center. Each step through the dimly lit roseate granite hall swallowed me deeper into a steamy fog. Cut into the dome overhead were small hexagons, plugged with blue, yellow, and red stained glass.

These people knew how to live. The grin spreading across my face made my split lip ache. Bet Colby and the boys weren't having half the fun I planned on having.

The air cleared a little around us so I could see that we weren't alone. Others soaked in the pool. The daylight-challenged kind of people, I assumed.

Pembe stood next to me. She waved to the pool.

"Go?"

I needed to express to this Hungarian speaking, assertive woman there was no freaking way she could get me into a pool full of vampires.

I pointed to the pool. "Too many people."

She shook her head, not understanding.

I placed two of my fingers by my own teeth like make shift fangs.

Her eyes widened before the room boomed with her laughter. She thumped me on the shoulder in good-natured way but nearly knocked me off my bare feet. Maybe she didn't know. Then she either thought I tried to joke, or I needed to be placed in a crazy-house.

I glanced around looking for inspiration on how to explain what I wanted. My communication skills lay back in my suitcase, in the form of a Hungarian/English dictionary. We needed a translator. "Rurik?"

Pembe glanced at the pool then at me then raised an eyebrow.

"Rurik?" I repeated.

She shrugged and led me to a secluded sitting area.

I sat there alone in my canvas slip, disappointed in the turn of events. It never occurred to me there would be other vampires here. Rurik offered me protection but how did that work when he wasn't around? Either way, I didn't come to socialize. It would be in everyone's interest if I just hunted down my clothes and escaped.

Pembe peaked around the corner and ordered, "Follow."

She brought me further into the bathhouse and

led me to a room with individual marble tubs. Hot, steaming water brimmed to their edges and a drain in the middle of the floor took care of the excess water if it should spill. Warm mist filled the air. We were alone.

This was what I wanted.

I smiled gratefully. "Koszonom." *Thank you.*

She nodded and gestured for me to use the center tub. "Towel." Then she left.

I hoped she meant to go get me one. All this wonderful, steam filled luxury caused my muscles to cramp in anticipation. I couldn't wait to dive in. The canvas slip pooled at my feet then I hurried to the hot water. I eased into the tub and experienced what a lobster must feel when sliding into a pot.

Once immersed in the tingling water I stared at the colored glass set into the ceiling until I entered a blissful trance.

The door opened behind me. Someone passed me to place towels on a table by the tubs. I turned to thank Pembe.

Rurik stood there instead with a stack of fluffy white towels folded nicely in his arms, wearing nothing but a smile. Strong, muscular arms set the towels down. A lean, long waist met the rise of his firm ass.

I shut my mouth before I caught flies and checked for drool.

He glanced a shy look over his shoulder but the shy was pretend. "May I join you?"

Chapter Eight

Rurik's voice dripped with enticement. Delight twinkled in his eyes as I continued to watch, forgetting to answer. He gave a purely masculine laugh that conveyed his pleasure more than words ever could.

He strode to the tub next to mine and stepped in. Water sloshed over the edges as he made himself comfortable. He rested his head back against the edge and he gazed across at me. The heat of his stare reminded me of my own nudity. There was only a sheet of water covering me and I ducked down further, thankful it was deep.

"Ask me a question, Rabbit." His voice caressed me like the steam, warm and moist.

"Why?"

"I make you uncomfortable. Ask me a question, it'll make conversation easier."

I didn't need to think too hard on what I wanted to ask—it tugged at my mind all day. "Why did you drug me?" It's one of the things that kept me from believing his innocence—that horrid act and giving me to Dragos.

He made a rude noise. "You're so subtle." His grin softened his sarcasm. "I am trying to lighten the mood, and instead you make me uncomfortable, too." Rurik's quiet chuckle echoed off the tiled walls. His broad shoulders hunched slightly and his chin dipped to his chest as he avoided my direct look. "It is regrettable but I had no choice in the matter. Dragos is traditional in his rule. His people insisted on a gift and I am not powerful enough to deny him anything. When he commented about your presence at the hot springs I knew you'd be perfect. I noticed you myself a few nights ago at the concert." Finally he met my gaze. "I wouldn't have let him kill you."

The comment knocked me in the chest. Would he have let him hurt me? Either way, he never had to make that choice and he did rescue me from my own Calvary. "I actually understand being forced to gift me but why drug me and not just mesmerize me?"

He leaned forward and rested his arms on the tub's edge. "I tried. You're not as susceptible to my mind, and stronger than most prey. I needed the drug to break down those walls." He sounded sincere and I wanted to buy into it. "Dragos is not easy to please. I did all I could to protect you. Please tell me you forgive me."

I didn't know what to say. There had to be a way for me to find out who the real Rurik was.

He sighed. "You confound me, Connie. You came into that club looking for trouble, now you act betrayed that I found you."

"Looking for trouble?" He was closer to the truth than he knew. It made me more wary but if he suspected me as the source of last night's attack I'd already be dead.

He leveled his gaze at me and quirked an eyebrow. "Someone who wears a dress like that is asking for attention."

"Fine." I looked away chagrined, and changed the subject. "Will Dragos be hunting for me?"

"Why would he?"

"Don't I belong to him now?"

Rurik relaxed deeper into the hot, steamy water. "He won't waste the resources on you. There are other things occupying his attention at the moment. For your own safety, forget last night—and forget vampires."

The reflection of the colored glass danced on top of my bath water, over and around the ripples. "You too?" My whisper was so soft it was barely audible to my own ears.

"It's my turn to ask a question." He didn't hear my question, or he ignored it.

I smiled to myself, pleased he didn't answer. "Okay."

"Where are you from?"

"Didn't you ask me this last night?"

"You can't answer a question with a question. That's cheating."

I looked away from the colorful reflections in my tub to watch him. He still lay back, enjoying the wet heat with his eyes closed.

"Presently I live in a hotel room in Budapest, I was born in America."

"And your heritage?"

I wasn't sure what he wanted. My silence must have mirrored my puzzlement.

"You have some Romanian in your features."

I nodded. "Yes, Romanian and French."

"Your skin is too dark for either of them. There is something else."

I'd had some of the oddest, yet most interesting moments with this man. I rested my chin in my hand and watched him soak. "There is? I didn't know my parents, they died when I was young. My maternal grandmother raised me. Pictures showed my father *was* dark. The Romanian comes from his side."

"A dark Romanian." He continued to soak quietly while he mused over this. Then quick as lightning, he leaned way out of his tub toward mine. "Let me see your eyes again."

I put my hand up to stop him from getting more of a view than I was ready to share. "Whoa there, buddy, that's close enough. You can see my eyes from there."

His amused grin returned.

I placed my chin on the tub's edge and opened my eyes wide.

He laughed at me. "I'm not giving you an eye exam, Rabbit."

I retreated to my comfy spot. "What's the prognosis?"

"I think it's gypsy. It would account for your sweet olive skin and your beautiful gray eyes."

"You know, my grandmother told me she was a gypsy. I thought it to be a lifestyle, not a nationality."

He leaned back. "See? A few questions and already we begin to know each other. Nothing to worry about—I don't bite—not unless you want me to."

Thick lashes made dark half moons under his closed eyes. He feigned disinterest. The steam beaded on his pale smooth skin. Some of those beads slipped down his face, tracing a line from his jaw, to his neck, then along his well defined chest.

I wanted to do bad things with him. I wanted to reach over and lick the beads off his chin then work my way down. I wanted to stroke my hands along...

"Rabbit?"

"Yeah?" My gaze rose from tracing the streams into his blazing stare.

He enjoyed my admiration. "Would you like me to ... bite you?"

"Not yet. What? I mean, no. Thank you." Thinking was hard enough with Rurik fully clothed. Now it was impossible. I could tell I entertained him to no end. "Are you hungry?"

"Yes, but not for your blood." The edges of his eyes crinkled with his grin as he showed fang.

I was tired of him taking the lead in our rapport. My job dealt in seduction, yet since I'd met him, I'd lost control. He teased me with his flirtation and his body but two could play this game.

Self-confidence stirred back up, I turned away from Rurik and reached to get a sponge from the table. My movements exposed the length of my spine and a little more, just enough to make him think he got a peek.

His eyes burned along the curves of my hips and shoulders. They left my skin scalded with his desires. It's been a long time since I dared play this game with such stakes on the table. Did I dare collect the pot if I won?

I knelt in the water, still facing away from him, and shook my hair free of its ponytail. The sponge spilled water as I squeezed it over my head. Warm and delicious it ran down my heated skin. I repeated this over and over until my hair was soaked. The tangle of my frizzed out poof tamed to soft curls once more.

"Why do you insist on calling me Rabbit?" My question floated on the steam in the room across to him.

"Rabbits are soft, quick, sweet creatures. You bring to mind a favorite poem." The hunger in his voice made it deeper, almost sensual.

"*Run, rabbit, run*
Try to get away.
Run, rabbit, run
I've come out to play.
Run, rabbit, run

For it's the end of the day."

The poem sent shivers down my spine. *'Run, rabbit, run'* was what he shouted as he shoved me out the window. Another shiver followed. Soft, quick, and sweet. He described me as prey. This was not a man but a vampire. If he liked me, did that make me safer or more tempting?

The splash of water landing on the floor caused me to look over my bare shoulder. Rurik retrieved a bottle of shampoo and paced back towards me. Bodies like Rurik's were made for fantasies. Lean, long muscles moved under his skin, his actions graceful and strong. His heavy lidded glare made me feel like his thoughts could travel places his hands hadn't touched.

"Let me wash your hair."

I looked at him, cynical of his offer.

"So wary."

"Can you blame me?" I didn't know if I was ready for this, I wanted to be. It had been a long time since I was intimate with anyone. The need in my body encouraged me along this path of seduction. Rurik represented most women's wet dream but a heaviness in my heart held me back, twisting me up inside like a knot. Sex could never be just a physical thing, my heart always got dragged into it, and in the end, it was broken.

"It's good to be wary. I am a *predator* after all." He knelt by my tub. "Indulge me. I like to do this." For a fleeting moment, a touch of vulnerability peaked through the veil of intense, blue eyes. A yearning for my acceptance. It flashed so quickly, I doubted if it was real.

"Lean your head back and put your hair over the edge."

"The water will spill onto the floor."

"That's what the drain is for. Take it easy, I won't mislead you ... again." A soft smile touched those full kissable lips.

My hair did need a wash. Who was I kidding? I wanted to feel his touch. It had ignited an inferno when he held me last night. I gave in to my dark side and did as he asked.

He took the sponge and squeezed more hot water over my hair, making sure it was saturated. He then worked the shampoo through the tangles of curls. His strong fingers massaged my scalp, my forehead, and down behind my ears. They made firm, confident circular motions.

The tension in my neck melted away where he applied pressure, kneading those sore tight knots. Tingles ran along my nerves wherever our skin pressed together. The spark of desire grew more intense.

The strength of his hands caressed the tender muscles of my shoulders. My moan echoed in the room as the pleasure bordering pain pulled from my injuries.

The floor ran slick with steaming water and soap as he began to rinse my head. He abandoned the sponge to use his hands to scoop water from my tub over my hair. His fingers ran through the curls, gently tugging them. It felt wonderful. This was the first time I allowed a man to do this. The pull on the strands increased with each pass of his hand, pulling me up out of the water, arching my back in response to the delicate pain.

He gathered a handful of my hair and pulled forcefully trapping me with my back arched against the edge.

He whispered in my ear. "Run, rabbit, run, try to get away." He slowly moved to the other ear. "Run, rabbit, run, I've come out to play." He pulled harder on my hair making the pain a little sharper. I cried out in surprise. "Run, rabbit, run, for it's the end of the day."

He sipped at the water running down my neck making his way to my shoulder. The pulling eased but he didn't release me. "Sweet, sweet, Connie." His cool breath flowed down my skin raising goose flesh, making my exposed nipples harden. Only then did I realize how shockingly far out of the water I'd raised myself. I tried to cover up with my hands but the tension on my hair increased.

He released it but I felt his hands run under mine to cup my breasts as he continued to rain kisses down to the hollow of my neck. His teeth dragged along my skin as if to test my skin for tenderness. I had almost forgotten how it felt to have someone touch me. A fire built inside of my chest where his hands kneaded me. I took all my loneliness and grief then shoved them into this inferno. It burned.

Lifting me from the tub, he pressed my back to his solid chest. He was hard against me. His hands explored my skin and his mouth consumed mine.

My body screamed 'yes' but my soul wasn't ready. The passion dissolved into guilt, as similar memories were dragged from the corners of my mind. An old familiar hurt twisted my heart as a vision of my dead husband returned.

I sobbed.

Rurik misunderstood it for desire. He laid me on the soapy tiles and crawled onto me. "Oh, Rabbit." He moaned as he tried to press his lips to mine.

I turned my head, hiding the tears that trickled from my eyes. Stupid of me to allow things to get this far, I should have known I wasn't ready.

His weight no longer bore down on me instead he hovered over me and tipped my chin back toward him. "Connie?" His gentle tone caressed me. "Did I hurt you?" The concern in his voice sounded genuine.

I reached up and touched his handsome face and traced those well-defined cheeks. "No, but I'm not ready. I-I haven't been with anyone but my husband in years."

His eyes widened. "You're married?"

I tried to sit up but he still pinned me. "No, I'm widowed."

He sighed and rolled off me. "You shouldn't tease a man like that."

It felt like I'd been slapped. "Tease! You invited yourself in here."

He raised his eyebrows at me. "Pembe said you requested my presence."

I sat there on the wet, soapy floor, naked looking

like a fool. "But..." At the pool! I'd asked Pembe for Rurik because I'd been afraid to get into a pool filled with vampires. "I... Oh, Rurik, I didn't mean..." Getting up I rushed over to the table and wrapped a towel around myself. I felt horrible and embarrassed. "It's a misunderstanding."

Rurik watched as I tucked the towel securely in place. A frown marred his features. "I've already seen your breasts." He fluidly stood and sauntered over unfazed by his nudity. He reached for a towel as well and began to dry off. He glanced at me with a wicked smirk. "And fondled them."

The tub room lacked places for me to crawl into. I couldn't look up from my feet. Rurik had his little revenge.

He wrapped the towel around his hips. Patiently waiting for me to get over myself.

I looked up at him.

His face softened. "How long since he passed?"

I wrapped my arms around my body. "Eighteen months."

He nodded to himself and gazed at the tubs. For a moment the seductive, confident vampire dropped his mask. Grief remembered reflected in his conflicted eyes. Just as quick as it came, it disappeared.

Twisting sinuously, he caught my chin, lifting it up to his face. A slow sensuous smile graced his face. "Vampires know grief well. I can wait, Connie."

Stunned, I nodded. Pulling my towel tighter, I left the private tub room in search of my clothes.

CHAPTER NINE

The next morning I woke disappointed in myself. The sexiest man I'd ever met wanted me and I flaked out.

I left the bathhouse last night in a flurry of quickly applied clothes, assisted by a distraught Pembe.

Rurik made me cry twice in twenty-four hours. I needed to get away from him. The temptation to succumb combined with my unresolved grief made me crazy. To add to my confusion, Rurik kept giving me the wrong impressions. For a murderer, he treated me well and with compassion. It produced too many doubts.

I trusted Colby and his judgments. This time my instincts fought against it. I didn't know what to do.

Colby would send me out to lure Rurik in for the kill, I won't be the one holding the stake but the responsibility felt the same.

After breakfast, I called Colby's cell but only got his answering service. My instructions were to sit and wait. So I did. I feared missing his call.

———

The late afternoon sun soaked into my skin while I lay on the hotel bed. I flipped through another brochure for a tour of Budapest, this one featured a haunted cemetery. With a wistful sigh, I threw the pamphlet on the floor, which had become littered with them. My cell, which sat by my hand chirped, I snatched it up and knew it would be Colby finally returning my call.

"How are you holding up?" His voice sounded like crushed gravel.

"I'm bored beyond belief."

His low chuckle carried well over the phone. "I have something to alleviate your boredom. We have a place for you to go."

"Okay." I'd spent the afternoon rehearsing what I'd say to him but it all evaporated. "Is Rurik still my target?"

"Yeah. Who else would it be?"

My heart fluttered with the realization I wasn't going to tell him about the bathhouse. He already threatened to send me home after the club screw up. If he found out about our impromptu date he'd start to doubt everything I did. I walked a tight rope between these two men, and my balance sucked. "You spoke about Dragos yesterday," I snapped. "Where do I go?"

"The A38 club. My sources tell me Rurik is supposed to be there tonight."

"Colby, what if Rurik's not guilty for killing those victims? I mean, you're planning to kill him tonight, right?" This dilemma tore me up. What if we killed the wrong vampire? What if something worse took over Budapest because of it? We could be doing more harm than good. The silence from the other end of the line continued. "Colby?"

"Tell me what's bothering you."

"*I've* met with and spoken to Rurik. He's not the same as the others we've disposed of. My gut tells me we've got the wrong vampire."

"Your gut?"

"He's the one who followed me to my hotel room. He's the one who shoved me out the window, at the party, to help me escape. I'm sure he's the one who saved me from the vampire that chased me through the damn alleys. Doesn't that say something?"

"Yeah, he's trying to seduce you and doing a good job at it."

"What?" Colby's perception annoyed me. "All that to get into my pants?" Rurik almost accomplished it last night. Even though I sat alone in my hotel room my cheeks still got warm but from anger not embarrassment.

"He's entered your mind deeper than I suspected. I'll be honest, I'm starting to agree with Red on this one. Maybe you should sit this one out. Once they breech your shield, Connie, it gets easier for them to manipulate you. He drugged you then took you as a meal for his master. Does that spell 'nice guy' to you? Has there been any other ... contact with him?"

"No," I lied. "At the party he offered me protection— he wouldn't allow Dragos to kill me." I omitted my part of the bargain. It wouldn't help my case to investigate this crime some more before executing the wrong vampire.

"If he's such a hero, he shouldn't have brought you to the party in the first place."

"I didn't say he was 'nice.' Just he may not be the killer." I rubbed my forehead. A migraine brewed. "Colby, I've never questioned your judgment before. You must have some kind of hard proof."

"No, you've never doubted me. That's what worries me the most. You *know* I always get proof. But I'm not giving you details. Especially now I think you've been compromised."

I could hear him breathing over the line.

"Red is right about this. They're too powerful to use live bait. You'll get hurt."

This wasn't going according to my plan. It never occurred to me he'd start doubting *me*. "You need me, Colby. If you really want Rurik, I've got him for you. He'll come to me, but I need some piece of hard proof, for my conscience."

He was going to send me home. I could picture Red breaking down my door and stuffing me in a box with an express stamp to the U.S.A.

This job suited me. It gave me purpose. Ever since watching Colby stake the vamp who had attacked me in a Las Vegas club bathroom, I knew it was for me. I didn't want to go home. Alone with no distraction but my own pathetic thoughts, I'd be romancing Captain Morgan within a few days.

He sighed. "Connie, I'm sending you a package. It will contain your assignment and your proof."

I silently did a little happy dance.

"Stop dancing and listen. Don't make me regret this."

How did he do that?

The package contained a sheet of paper with directions to a jazz club on the Danube River.

It also contained pictures.

They showed a kiss of vampires feeding on a pile of victims. I counted over fifteen dead, pretty young things in their twenties. The bodies were posed in gruesome, horrendous displays for the camera, like they wanted mementos of the event.

One of the close-ups was Rurik. His eyes gazed into mine from the picture.

I sank to the floor. My heart wrenched at what I'd almost let him do to me last night. Nausea rolled the dinner in my stomach.

Nightmares haunted me at night sometimes but these images would make sure I never slept again. I picked up my instruction sheet and looked over their directions.

Time to get this bastard.

CHAPTER TEN

"Hold still, Connie. You're going to make me drop this down the front of your dress." Brad's hands trembled as he tried to attach the chip inside the cup of my bra. If he pulled the material any further from my skin it might snap off into his hand.

I stopped tapping my foot and watched his face as he concentrated on his job. A five o'clock shadow that never seemed to thicken or lessen accentuated his strong jaw.

Brad functioned as the team's gadget man and didn't like the way the chip's signal worked the other night. They got intermittent readings and almost didn't find me. He thought it got damaged when I fell on the dance floor steps at the club where I met Rurik. So he decided to place it somewhere less likely to be crushed.

I would have accused him of coming up with this idea just to cop-a-feel, but the blush and flutter of nerves he radiated changed my mind.

He glanced up and met my stare, his fingers accidentally brushed against my cleavage. His blush deepened to a lovely shade of scarlet. "Sor ... sorry."

Red came up behind him. He winked at me. "Keep your hands to yourself and attach the damn chip already."

The chip tumbled down the front of my neckline to rest between my breasts inside my bra. Brad's shoulders slumped and he hung his head in defeat. Rurik would never see this as a loss but an opportunity. I chuckled to myself before the memory of those terrible pictures returned. It wasn't fair. He shouldn't be in my head, I hated that I still caught myself thinking about him.

I sent a glare of hot, smoking daggers at Red. "I'll fish that out myself. Thank you for your help, Red." I wore a spaghetti strap, mid-thigh length, black dress. There wasn't much material to work with, which led to the tracking chip being clipped to the cup of my strapless bra. The chip proved to be elusive at first. Brad needed to assist me with his penlight to find it.

The jerk, Red, leaned against the wall, arms across his chest. His shoulders shook with contained laughter.

This only stoked my anger. I couldn't stop thinking about Rurik. The raging, hot steam those pictures generated produced a pressure in my chest and I couldn't wait to release it. My revenge would taste sweet.

BAIT

Brad finished setting the chip into the lacy material. "All done." He grinned at me, a thin sheet of sweat beaded on his forehead, under the disheveled mouse brown hair. Why couldn't I be attracted to a sweet, shy man like Brad? Instead I fantasize about a bloodless cold monster. I needed therapy.

The laptop on the bed blipped and Brad turned his attention to it. He tapped a few keys. "The readings look fine. Why don't you move around. Maybe jump up and down."

My mouth dropped open.

Red stepped forward and smacked Brad upside the head. "Behave."

"I didn't mean ... I wanted to make sure it'll stay in place." He shook his head while the scarlet color returned to his cheeks.

I laughed. "It's okay, Brad." For a hardened soldier he sure could blush. I shimmied and jiggled for him. Shy men may not stoke my libido but they did bring the devil out of me.

"How are the readings?" Red maintained his stoic expression but his unheard laughter produced a shimmer of tears.

Brad pulled his eyes from me. "Yeah, great signals."

Red loomed over me and stopped my antics by steering me from Brad's view. "Stick to the plan." He handed me a small black purse. "The ticket for the concert is inside. Colby's tried to get someone in there with you but the show's been sold out and the club's administration is being difficult."

"How did he get my ticket?"

"From a source. This plan stinks. You should both wait for another opportunity and more back up."

"There may not be other chances. Don't worry, Rurik will follow me home. Be ready for us." I squeezed his beefy bicep. After the bath house, I'd be shocked if Rurik didn't.

"Watch your back."

I nodded. The devilish side of me finished teasing Brad by pecking him on the cheek and watched another bloom of scarlet grow on his face. Time to bring in my target, to meet the real Rurik, and get some answers.

The A38 club was the reincarnation of a Ukrainian stone-carrier ship. It started a new life on the Danube River as one of Europe's coolest clubs.

I arrived at the refurbished boat's mooring beside the Petofi Bridge. It stood two stories above the water, made of solid, thick iron and full of bright lights. Fresh paint and windows made it shiny but the ship's design enhanced its age. A wonderful medley of new and old. The doorman held the door and allowed me in.

The club subdivided into three floors of revelry: the roof terrace on the deck, the restaurant by the galley, and the lounge with club in the hull. I made my way to where the concert would be held in the lounge. Its interior furnished in brown leather and dark wood in a modern style provided a warm and elegant atmosphere.

I forced my fists to unclench as I stood at the entrance. I'd find him here. Rurik. The images of those photos still haunted me. They clung to me like tar.

We would start with him, their leader, and then work our way to find the others who had participated in the massacre. I took a deep breath and pulled myself under control.

Tables surrounded a stage where the band played a smooth tune. I gave my ticket to the vendor and entered the dimly lit room.

Private booths lined the walls. The lack of lighting made it difficult to see, all I could make out were dark silhouettes. But I was confident Rurik's vision would be able to see me.

A touch to my elbow caught my attention. I smiled to myself. That didn't take long. As I twisted toward him I pasted my best sultry smile on my face.

A gentleman with long blond hair and a casual gray suit stood next to me. He held up his glass, even though I didn't have a clue what he said, the gesture made it clear. He wanted to buy me a drink.

Damn, I flirted with the wrong guy. I shook my head. "English?"

His eyes traveled up my body back to my face. A sugar coated smile appeared as he lifted his glass once more and pointed at me.

I shook my head again. "No thanks." I pivoted to leave but his hand snaked around my elbow.

His hand caressed my skin until it reached my shoulder, his intentions painted on his handsome face.

I ground my teeth and glared. Apparently he wasn't used to being refused. If shaking my head didn't translate maybe a right hook would. Taking a deep breath, I counted to ten. I couldn't afford getting kicked out of the club. Then again, it would get Rurik's attention and relieve some of my pent up tension. I eyed my amorous new friend and sized him up.

Before I could decide what action to take, a set of long, pale fingers wrapped around my unwanted flirt's wrist and removed it from my shoulder.

The man's grin disappeared, replaced by fear.

I stared at the inhuman hand that replaced his. My heart sped up as my eyes trailed from the hand, up the arm, to the face. I hoped to see a set of icy, blue eyes but instead met black, soulless ones. "Tane." His name was barely audible as I choked on it. I saw him last at the party, one of Dragos' kindred. He had stayed with Rurik to fight off Colby's men.

A fedora covered his bald head and pointed ears. He released the man's wrist and in a calm voice told him something. My assailant lost interest and left us.

Tane's attention returned to me. He wore a short sleeved shirt with a buttoned up vest and matching black, pin-striped slacks. His tattoo scrawled in an intricate fashion down his neck to disappear under his collar. In the dim light, he could pass for human.

His stony expression didn't change as he gripped my shoulder like steel. "You're the last person I expected, Rabbit." His voice blended with the soft jazz music. It soothed my raw nerves and allowed him to catch my gaze as I continued to stand in shock. His power snapped against my mental shields and rung them like a gong. It weakened them enough to daze me.

His arms clung around me as if supporting a drunken friend. Tane's power made Rurik's wane in comparison. Where Rurik needed to drug me first to control me, Tane just mentally bitch slapped me and took me by force.

We made our way back across the lounge to a secluded booth in the corner. He settled me on the bench and slid me further in. We weren't alone in the horseshoe shaped booth. A man in his late thirties with short salt and pepper hair waited for us. He sipped a drink as he watched me with his crystal green eyes.

I sat trapped between them.

Tane grinned and flashed his fangs, like a saber toothed tiger that just caught a rabbit. He removed his hat and flipped it onto the table. "Rurik's little rabbit. I'm so pleased." He gestured to the other man. "This is my ... companion, Eric." Then he gestured to me. "And this pretty morsel is Rabbit. Rurik brought her to Dragos' welcoming party. As a gift for our Master if I recall."

"More like entertainment than a gift. He wasn't supposed to keep me." I giggled like a nut too terrified to think straight. "I mean who keeps people. Nice hat by the way." The babble came out in an uncontrolled torrent. It left me breathless.

Tane ran a finger along the hat's rim. "Thank you, I do make an effort to keep up with the changing styles, and Dragos *always* keeps what he likes."

Eric raised his eyebrows. "Quite an end to the evening though. Parties are always more fun when they end with a brawl."

I faintly remembered Eric as part of the group of men playing daggers. I swallowed with a dry throat. "Are you going to take me back to him?" Over my dead body, with no back up and only a tracker as help, it may come to that.

He shrugged. "No, I don't think so. As long as you don't attract attention. I need you to be calm and to behave now, right?"

A flash of metal slipped from Eric's sleeve to reveal a fine, sharp blade.

My heart skipped a beat.

Tane waved his hand at the blade. "There's no need for threats. Rabbit is going to be our new friend. I do love it when a plan changes unexpectedly for the better." He reached over and petted Eric's hand. "It was such a good idea of yours to use that ticket as a lure. The results are not what I expected but this truly pleases me."

Eric beamed like a good pet.

"Leave us and enjoy the concert. Rabbit and I have business to attend." Eric stood to depart. He came close to Tane and hesitated to glance my way before planting a quick kiss on his lips.

We both watched his departure for different reasons, Tane with his heart in his eyes, me for a possible escape route.

Before I could move, he laid his hand on my arm and turned to me with a small smile. "Don't make this difficult. I won't hurt you unless you make me."

I looked from his large hand that gripped me tight to his face. "You kind of are now." My heart would soon burst from my chest if it didn't decelerate. If Dragos was a Nosferatu then so was Tane. They had similar traits. That meant an uber vamp held my arm.

His clasp lessened. "I had hoped Colby would be the one to use the ticket and come to this concert. I wanted to meet him in person. Very resourceful of him to use you as bait, something tasty and sweet, instead of deadly and hard. No wonder his kills have increased." He released my arm to lean his chin on his hand, smile still present. "I'm such a fan of his." He spoke like he followed Colby's career as a slayer.

I tried to control my breathing but I may as well have tried to control the weather. A trickle of sweat made its way down my back. He associated me with Colby. How? Did we have an informant on the team? The fact he knew Colby existed and what he did for a living terrified me. Where was Rurik? I could use my hero again. The irony of my needing rescue by the vampire I wanted to kill was not lost on me.

"Who?" I did my best to lie.

"Let's not play games, Rabbit."

"I'm not." My palms got clammy. He implied he'd used the concert ticket as a lure to trap Colby. Who gave Colby the ticket and what did Tane want with him?

I glanced at the band and feigned interest in the show but checked out my exit options instead. The main entrance was across from us, but a crowd of people in the lounge blocked my way. There were two exits by the stage, one on each side.

Tane slid a little closer and spoke in a quiet voice. "The attack at Dragos' private party surprised us. I know Colby hunts Rurik, I saw him in the fight, but I couldn't figure out how he found us. Until now."

I turned to glance at his pale, sculpted face. His eyes were the color of a dark, bottomless ocean. He must have been beautiful as a man.

As if committing the way I looked to memory he stared at me. "Is it a coincidence you arrived at the party shortly before the attack? Then arrive here, to a concert bearing a ticket *I* gave Colby? I must admit, I am a little disappointed in not meeting the legendary vampire killer."

I couldn't trust myself to speak, fear paralyzed my thoughts. Tane figured out everything. I didn't think I could charm my way out of this considering he chose a male companion.

He leered at me. "The bath house attempt was brilliant, by the way, but I don't understand why you didn't complete the assassination. Why did you leave so suddenly? Rurik wouldn't tell me."

"He wouldn't?" It touched me that Rurik didn't speak about our misunderstanding on the tub room floor.

"I enjoy the *Rudas* when I visit here. You truly frustrated Rurik. Maybe that was your purpose? So he'd be more determined to pursue you."

My mouth became drier than a popcorn fart.

"I hoped to ... ensnare Colby but this may turn out to be a better situation." He leaned back against the bench with his arms over the top. "I can't allow him to run about Budapest unmonitored. He may break into the wrong gathering and kill innocent, law abiding vampires. I expected an attack on Rurik but not that soon, foolish of me to have under estimated Colby." Tane eyed me.

My charade ended, I couldn't figure out how to deny it. Colby did the team's thinking, including mine. Tane knew too much. I didn't like his game but I had no choice but to play it. "Colby wouldn't help you."

Tane's grin grew into a smile. "Maybe not of his own free will but I too can be ingenious. Who do you think hired him?"

His revelation felt like a punch to my gut. My breath caught in my throat and I pounded my fist on the table once. "Bull crap. He wouldn't work for a vamp."

Tane's eyebrows shot up at my explosive response but his body remained relaxed. "He doesn't know since Eric did the actual hiring and he's not a vamp." He sneered the last word.

I stared at the table top as this information seeped in. Colby worked for a Nosferatu vampire and didn't even know it. The irony almost killed me, literally.

"Your mental shields are stronger than most humans. Better than when I first met you."

I blinked. "You broke through them easily enough a few moments ago."

He laughed softly and shook his head in disbelief. "At my age, Rabbit, there are few who keep me out. I think Dragos is the only one left stronger than I."

I jumped when what I could only describe as a caress brushed against my mental shields. A shiver ran down my spine. "Rurik drugged me before he brought me to the party. He said he needed it to bring down my shields."

Tane gave me a sly smiled and rubbed at his chin. He glanced around the room before returning his attention to me. "How well did it work?"

"Totally demolished them."

He sat so still, he looked made of stone. "Rurik is more resourceful than I'd estimated. I begin to understand how he obtained this territory at such a young age."

The band began to play a more up-beat song and someone in the crowd whistled their approval. This drew Tane's attention to the stage. His long fingers tapped the table to the beat of the music.

I began to inch my way around the horse shoe shaped bench away from him.

He continued to watch the show. "Rurik won't be here tonight."

Thanks, Sherlock. I guessed that by now. "You're Colby's informant. The one who tells him Rurik's whereabouts." That would tie Colby's underpants in a knot. I crept to the edge.

"Do you have a point?"

The pictures Colby sent me came to mind.

Something didn't fit. You'd think vampires would be more hands-on with their version of justice. Rurik himself told me of the vampire law against killing, so they had some kind of system. "I know about the evidence you gave Colby and your people's laws to not kill. Why hire someone else to punish Rurik?"

He smirked. "Why, indeed? You don't really expect me to answer, do you? It's not your business. You just need to follow orders, Colby's and mine."

I ground my teeth and turned to look at the band. *Orders my ass*, I cooperated if things made sense and until recently they had been. My legs swung free from the bench when I twisted to watch the show, they now rested free of the table. The tension to get up and run made them ache. Tane didn't protest my movement, he watched the stage as well. I understood the concert being sold out. The band was good. On any other night I'd be up there dancing with the others.

A waiter approached with a tray full of drinks. An idea popped into my head and I allowed my instincts to direct me. I sprang up to collide into him. With a tug at his jacket, I maneuvered him to spill the tray onto Tane.

I glimpsed his wide-eyed, open mouth expression before running for my life. If I survived the night I'd be able to cherish that moment later, there would be no mercy if he caught me. I shoved my way through the crowd toward the stage. The exit sign over the door shone like a beacon, the glow cried out to me as if telling me to hurry. As I reached for the push bar on the door I slammed into a solid, wet mass. It felt like I just ran into a wall. My brain rattled in my skull and little lights flashed in front of my eyes.

A voice spoke to me over the ringing in my ears. "I don't remember giving you permission to leave."

My vision cleared enough to see Tane reach out to steady me by my elbows. A slice of lemon clung to his vest. "Stop being such a bitch, Rabbit. That was unnecessary." He smelled like alcohol and fruit juice. The lemon slice slid off his vest to flop on his polished black shoe. He looked down and shook it off then gazed back up at me with a small growl. With a yank, he pulled me through the exit door, grasped my upper arm and climbed the flight of stairs. "I told you I wouldn't hurt you."

"Why should I believe you?" I tried to keep up, his long legs took the steps two at a time.

He stopped and looked down at me. "I have a use for you." We climbed to the terrace where only a few lovers strolled along the deck. Tane dragged me to the rail and wrapped his arm around my waist to pull me closer. "Now, my little bait, I have an assignment for you."

"I won't work for you."

"Battle lines are being drawn across Budapest and you, my dear, are caught in the center. You'll have to choose a side soon, and you have a better chance to survive if it's mine."

Trapped in the arms of this demon I had an epiphany. If Tane hired Colby then it must have been him who sent the pictures. I didn't like that. It made me suspicious of them and of Tane's motives.

I couldn't do anything to warn Colby or help Rurik if I coerced him to kill me. He stated he needed me so that meant I'd get off this boat alive if I agreed to do as he asked. I sighed and hung my head.

"What do you want?"

He placed a finger under my chin to tilt my face up to his. "First, I need you to keep me informed on Colby's plans. I won't tolerate being surprised by him again. Second, I want the vial of the drug Rurik used on you."

His touch made my skin crawl. I twisted in his arms to pull away but they were made of steel. "How am I supposed to do that? Colby never tells me anything except where to go and when. I don't even know how to find Rurik."

"You're a clever girl. You'll figure out a way."

"If I refuse?"

An evil smile spread across his pale, in-human face. "I wonder how either Rurik or Dragos would react to find out it was you who lured the attack?"

"They'd kill me." My voice was a bare whisper. I glared at him and wished my thoughts could burn him alive. "I could inform Dragos you're trying to kill Rurik."

He chuckled and ran a hand down my hip. "That would be foolish, child. *Dragos* is the one who ordered me to dispose of Rurik in an indirect manner. He also regrets losing you. I think he'd be happy for your return."

Nothing on this planet scared me more than Dragos. I'd rather spend a night in a cave of rabid werewolves than spend it with him. Colby would freak when I told him about our boss.

He slid his hand under my bottom and pulled me closer to whisper in my ear. "Don't tell Colby about me and Eric." It was as if he could read my mind. "If you do, I'll expose Colby to the vampire community. Neither he or his team would escape Europe alive."

I couldn't stop the shudder that shook me. That would be real bad. "How do I contact you?"

He slipped a business card into my hand. Only a phone number was printed across it. "Do you see that pier over there?"

I looked up from the card. A short dock jutted from the main pier that moored the A38. Small boats were tied to it and a ladder led into the water. "Yes." Maybe he owned one of the boats.

"Can you swim?"

I faced him and quirked an eyebrow. "Yes. Oh no! Wait..."

He picked me up and threw me overboard.

I plugged my nose before the water engulfed me. Reflexively, I kicked to the surface. The water spilled over my face as I gulped air and sputtered. I treaded water and looked up to see Tane, whose eyes crinkled with amusement. "Bastard." My voice echoed across the water.

He leaned forward on the rail with a huge grin on

his face. "That's for dumping a tray of drinks on me."

CHAPTER ELEVEN

I watched Tane walk away as I coughed and sputtered in the river. On-lookers began to gather and point at the silly woman in the river. No one offered to help. They just stood and waited for me to drown.

I didn't lose my purse to the dark waters; it remained grasped in my fingers. Lights from the A38 reflected off a small white rectangle of paper that floated by my face. Staying afloat occupied my mind, not flotsam, until I realized Tane's card was not clutched in my hand any longer. I did a frantic search of the immediate area for it.

The river's gentle current pulled it away from me, my only tie to contacting Tane. I paddled, like a dog, to catch it in my grip but something brushed my leg and a startled cry echoed over the river.

It came from me.

The dark water held secrets I didn't care to know. I envisioned fish, eels, and two-headed monsters. It increased the efficiency of my strokes and I caught the damn card.

My heart, ready to explode, pounded against my ribs as I raced to the small pier. The sensation of being chased by those dark secrets fueled my speed. I pulled myself out of the black water to collapse panting on the dock.

I hate vampires.

When my heart calmed and my lungs no longer billowed, I stood to assess my situation. This small pier connected to the main one but I'd have to pass a guardhouse at the only exit. The street wasn't too far from there.

I sighed when I looked down at myself. *One more dress ruined.* At this rate, I'd be returning home with empty suitcases. Yet, I still managed to keep a shoe, not that it mattered. I slipped it off and flung it over my shoulder, back into the river to join its sister.

Carefully, I opened the delicate, wet card Tane had given me. The phone number appeared faded but still present. At least I didn't lose my handbag. I placed the soft paper in between my credit cards, then made my way to the exit.

The short, round guard at the booth opened his mouth to speak but nothing came out as I drew closer. He rolled his eyes and waved me though the gate, apparently more concerned with those breaking in than breaking out.

I smiled my gratitude and took the stairs that led to the street.

The first taxi driver took one look at my dripping hair and hem, shook his head, and pressed the gas pedal. I waved a second one to stop soon after and got a similar response.

I shook my fist at the retreating vehicle. "Paranoid money-grubbing fascists who eat children." Just like my grandma taught me.

The rendezvous point with Colby was a mile away. How would I explain my being half drowned? I tripped and fell overboard? He already distrusted me, this would make it worse. I couldn't blame him, I was about to lie my ass off to him.

I passed a gas station and spotted a pink pay phone. A desperate idea emerged. I made my way over to it and dialed a number.

"Hello?"

"The gigs a bust, Colby. Rurik won't show up and I'm going to bed."

"Your signal disappeared. My men should be there looking for you." His tone told me more than his words. He was pissed.

"Someone spilled their drink on it." Kind of the truth if you considered the river drinkable.

"You barely arrived. What makes you think he won't show. My source seemed certain he'd be there."

"Trust me." I wanted to tell him everything. I

wanted to jump up and down while I spilled the beans. I wanted his men to whisk me away back to America so I could hide in my apartment with a week's worth of DVDs and chocolate chip cookies. "I've been following him to clubs all over Budapest. This place won't be to his taste." I couldn't risk the team's life so I'd do what Tane wanted. Not like Colby told me much.

He didn't respond.

"I'll catch a cab and talk to you tomorrow."

"Fine."

"Colby, I wouldn't listen to that source anymore." Tane never said I couldn't hint.

He grunted and hung up.

I leaned my forehead against the booth. It would be a long walk to the *Rudas* but I could use the time to think. Tane told me so much, my head spun with the possibilities. He hired Colby to execute Rurik. I assumed he provided the pictures but he never mentioned the crime tonight. This smelled bad.

He wanted me to snitch on Colby's movements. It didn't bother me so much since Colby kept me in the dark. After my appearing to bail out tonight, I'd be lucky if I ever heard from him again.

The drug was my problem. Why the interest in something like a Roofy? To get it, I'd have to find Rurik on my own. Even if I could steal the drug from him, should I entrust it to Tane?

This was not going to end well for me. I could feel it.

The crunch of tires on the pavement as it pulled

along side me caught my attention. I palmed a vial of pepper spray from my handbag. It didn't work on vampires but worked great on humans.

I looked over my shoulder as a powder-blue microcar pulled up to the curb. They built these tiny cars in the 1950's yet some Hungarians still drove them. The driver leaned over to open the rust bucket's passenger door.

"Rabbit, did you take a swim?"

I almost wished it was serial killer. Rurik, the last person I wanted to see, gave me his sexiest smile. I didn't have a plan formulated yet and I needed to make a decision on his fate. "I fell off the terrace of the A38." I grinned as I examined his small, two-passenger tin can. "I imagined you drove something more sporty and fast, like a Jag."

He flinched. I didn't know Rurik was capable of looking embarrassed. "My car's getting repaired. This one belongs to a friend."

We exchanged small lies and both of us knew it.

He twisted to glance at the on-coming traffic then back at me. "Need a ride?"

I did, but those pictures showed me a possible side of Rurik I didn't care to meet. "You can't expect me to believe that you just casually drove by and saw me walking."

"Rabbit, please. Someone's bound to notice us soon. Get in, we need to talk."

"Then you'd better answer quick."

He growled. "I followed Tane here, then saw him

toss you in the river."

I felt my mouth drop open. "Why would you..."

"Rabbit—" he interrupted, and gestured to the vacant car seat "—get in."

I swallowed my questions and climbed in.

He accelerated from the curb. The little, vintage vehicle's engine whined from the effort.

I needed an ally and I wondered if maybe he needed one too.

We drove in silence back to the Rudas. He parked the rust bucket on a side street, not trusting the valet with it.

When I tried to open my door, the hinges stuck. I pulled at the handle and heaved with all my strength.

"Stop, you might break it." He got out and pulled it open with a metallic squeal.

I unfolded to get out of the compact vehicle. "This thing's a death trap."

"Not for me." He had to put his shoulder against the door to push it closed. "I don't think we should open this door again until I get it fixed." He gave the microcar a sad look and patted the roof. "It's my first car. An Alba Regia, I bought it after the second world war."

"I thought it belonged to a friend." I grinned to myself amused by my suave, elegant vampire's eccentric tastes.

"And I thought you tripped into the river." His eyebrow quirked up.

I struggled not to laugh and bit my lip with the

effort. Vampire or human, deep down inside, men were the same, in love with their cars. I took his hand and tugged him towards the hotel. "Come on, no one will steal your rust bucket."

I rolled my eyes at his behavior but it dawned on me that this was something vampires always dealt with. They could never really keep anything. Everything around them changed, aged, died but they never did. Rurik tried to explain this to me the other night when we bathed together.

Vampires knew grief well.

I flashed him a gentle smile over my shoulder and squeezed his hand. Unbelievable how easily he made me feel comfortable and at ease. I knew grief well too.

He pulled the hood from his sweatshirt over his head, leaving his face in shadows. He wore baggy jeans and faded cracked sneakers. "You look like a street thug." *A really yummy one.*

He chuckled. "That's the point. I'm in disguise."

I gave him a silent 'oh' and lead him to the hotel. Why would the Overlord of Budapest be hiding? Maybe he didn't want to be seen with me, or worse, maybe he didn't want anyone to identify him later. I gulped and glanced back at him.

This was it. I had to make a decision, killer or not a killer. Without the pictures I believed him innocent but that evidence probably came from Tane which made them suspect.

We arrived at the back entrance and I pivoted to face him. Our eyes met, grey storms versus blue ice. I didn't know what I looked for but I wanted something, anything to clue me in on what I should do.

He picked at a wet strand of hair stuck on my cheek. His fingers hesitated on my skin as if enjoying the touch. "You're freezing, let's go warm you."

I nodded and opened the door. My gut instincts won over my rational thoughts. We climbed the stairs. Once we entered my room I tossed my hand purse on the night table. "Okay, spill it. What do you want?" A shiver shook me and made my last words tremble. My cold, wet clothes clung to me and sucked any remaining heat.

He wandered around my bed and plucked the blanket from it. "Take your clothes off and wrap up before you catch your death."

I reached behind me to undo my zipper.

"Whoa." He spun to face away.

"What? It's not like you haven't seen it before."

He chuckled. "No, and I wouldn't mind seeing you again but we've important things to discuss. If we start out like this, I can guarantee you there will be no talking. And I promised you I'd wait until you were ready. Are you?"

I slipped out of my sopping dress and took the blanket from Rurik's out stretched hand to wrap around me. "No."

He sat on the edge on the unmade bed, with a slight heave; he was up against the headboard, his feet crossed at the ankle. He patted the space next to him.

I shook my head. "I'll take the chair."

"Why were you at the A38 with Tane?" I could feel him watch me cross the room to sit in the chair. A tinge of jealousy colored his voice. "One vampire in your life isn't enough? Or does his power draw you? The power hungry are always drawn to him."

"Tane frightens me, not attracts me. Anyway, I don't think I meet his crazed, knife wielding tastes."

"Eric accompanied him? He usually doesn't like to share his master." Rurik's smile grew.

"They surprised me. I didn't expect them."

"Who were you expecting?"

"You." I looked at my blanket bundled lap, unable to make eye contact. The comment wasn't suppose to come out so personal but it did. We needed to change the subject before things went where they couldn't go. "Why were you following Tane?"

He stared at me for a moment longer before he sighed. "I think you're keeping secrets."

I sat straighter in my chair and crossed my arms. "Ditto." A manila envelope sat next to me on the desk. The temptation to pull out those horrid pictures and throw them in his face almost overcame me. It would reveal me as a potential threat though. Even *if* I believed he wouldn't kill me, it would be difficult to ever wipe their memory away.

The only reason Rurik didn't get introduced to Colby tonight was a niggle of suspicion created by Tane. He and Dragos didn't strike me as humanitarians. Hiring Colby's mercenaries to take out a rival seemed more plausible. Unfortunately, the pictures told a different story.

Rurik's gaze bore into me. "My compound was attacked this afternoon. They specifically looked for my place of rest. They destroyed it, and my home."

My heart thumped and I tried to control the sudden rush of adrenaline, but I may as well have tried to control a wild horse. Was it Colby? "How did you survive the attack in the middle of daylight hours?"

A small smile touched his lips. "I'm not without resources, Rabbit." He held up the hand that bore the Overlord's ring and tapped it. "Someone informed me there would be an attempt."

That ruled out Colby, since no one knew what he planned to do until the last minute.

"My people have been evacuating the city in small numbers since Dragos' arrival. A few have volunteered to stay and keep up pretenses. Most think the attack on the party was after Dragos but I know better. I think someone hired a slayer to kill me and he found my kiss." Rurik moved so fast, when he wrapped his fingers around my wrists I felt the sensation before I saw him do it.

I jumped in my chair but his eyes held me so I poured what concentration I could muster into my mental shields.

"Tell me, Rabbit, what were you doing with our charming Tane tonight? Is your grief so easily forgotten?" His grip tightened. "Did *he* catch your eye at the party?" He pulled me close, pressing my hands against his chest. "Why did your heart speed up when

I told you of today's attack?" His eyes began to dilate, absorbing his irises.

Curse his hearing! "T-Tane lured me there." My voice shook, I couldn't help it, but the fury it ignited helped me control the fear and come up with a plausible story. "I thought you sent me a ticket for the A38 jazz concert."

Rurik's grip loosened and he released me. He heard my words through the rage that boiled in his face.

"Tane wants to use me. He heard what happened between us at the bathhouse." I rubbed my wrists where he'd gripped them. There would be bruises in the morning.

"Of course he knows, I told him."

I startled. "Why?"

"He's been my friend for centuries."

"Your *friend* wants me to spy on you."

Rurik sat on the floor at my feet. He stared at the ring on his finger in silence. "Why would he want that? I hide nothing from him."

"Tane said a bunch of terrible things to you at the party. What kind of friend is that?"

Twisting the piece of jewelry around his pinky he didn't even look at me when he answered. "A secret one. If you didn't notice, Dragos barely tolerates my presence. It places Tane in an awkward situation."

I went to the other side of the room. Not that the distance really made a difference if he attacked but I needed the space. I thought my lack of friends pathetic but next to Rurik I was Miss Popularity. My wrists ached and my skin itched from the dried river water.

He still didn't look at me. His shoulders slumped while he lost himself in thoughts. The Overlord of Budapest, confident playboy deflated and vulnerable on my hotel room floor. I needed to decide whether to trust him or not. Things were over my head and I was drowning. It looked like he was too.

The role of judge and jury weighed heavily on my shoulders. "Look, I'm going to take a quick shower and change. Then we'll talk some more."

He looked up with sad eyes and nodded.

When I returned, he had taken off his hoodie while I showered. The tight white t-shirt clung to his shoulders and outlined the muscles of his torso. It didn't leave much to the imagination.

I needed to grab reins of my libido. The urge to rush over and run my hands over his chest grew. His loose jeans hung at his hips and I remembered what they hid. One small tug and they'd slide to his ankles. I should have taken a cold shower.

"Can you forgive me?" His eyes pleaded.

"You need to stop grabbing and scaring me like that. It doesn't help build trust."

He came to stand next to me. His fingers hooked into the belt loops of my jeans to draw me in closer. "After I followed Tane, I wanted to find you and ask for your help." He bent down to rest his forehead against mine. "But then I saw you together. I couldn't think rationally."

"He threw me into the river."

Rurik chuckled. "Yes, well, you can be infuriating." He lifted my chin to press his soft, full lips to mine. Whatever I wanted to say evaporated. This tender kiss did not resemble the previous heated one we'd shared yet it still provoked a tidal wave of carnal desires. The feel of his mouth slowly exploring mine, not demanding more than I gave, curled my toes. Something vulnerable unfurled in my chest and my loneliness called out to him.

I couldn't resist fulfilling my desires anymore and ran my hands over his well-developed chest. Hard plains of muscles met my hands with only a thin layer of soft cotton between.

He pulled away from the kiss but kept me pressed against him. "The night's still young. What do you want to do with it?" The heat in his eyes told me exactly how he wanted to spend it.

I wanted to agree with him and push him on the bed to live out each of my fantasies. Earlier today, I kicked myself for flaking out last night. How many second chances would I get?

If we started this, I needed to finish it. There hadn't been enough time for me to reflect on my attraction to Rurik. He was the first person to arouse these inclinations in me since Laurent died. Not just physical cravings either. I liked Rurik. He made me at ease with myself, he'd taken care of me, and, I mentally kicked myself in the ass, he possibly killed a bunch of people.

We weren't going to do anything until I had my answers. I stepped back.

BAIT

A flash of disappointment skipped over his face. He pulled a chair closer while I sat on the edge of the bed. "You never told me why you are visiting Budapest, Rabbit."

Colby made me memorize my cover story until I could recite it without a flinch. "I've been sent to investigate Budapest nightlife. I work for a travel company that wants to invest in a singles tour trip here."

The awe in his face made the lie priceless. "They pay you to do this?"

I laughed. "Yes and it's usually fun. But getting abducted, then Dragos, now Tane. Well, you can understand I'm anxious to leave even though I haven't seen a single tourist attraction." The bitterness in my voice came from reality. I really did want to see the city and its history. How many times would I get to visit Eastern Europe?

"Then let me take you somewhere special tonight."

CHAPTER TWELVE

"What about the attack on your home? There must be a search for you?"

Rurik laughed. "Yes, but not for a street thug with his girl driving a..."

"Rust bucket."

His smile faded. "I would have called it a love bug." He leaned forward and drew me into another gentle kiss. It lingered, neither of us wanted to pull away. The bed I sat on invited us to crawl in.

So lost in the sensation of his kiss, I somehow ended up on my back with him on top as he kissed his way down my neck. His hands slid along my sides to my waist.

I couldn't help but arch my body against his. We

needed someone to hose us down.

"Why do you think it's a vampire slayer who attacked your home?" While Colby did slay vampires by trade, I never would have used that term to describe him. It sounded better than mercenary but I knew he took care of more than just vampires.

Rurik ignored me as his fingers found their way under my shirt. He traced his tongue along my collarbone to the hollow of my throat. Once there, he sucked on the skin and gradually increased the pull.

I moaned at the feel of his hands and mouth on me but I kept my wits. "*I* think Tane did it."

He stopped seducing me then sighed before he gazed up at me. "Do I bore you?"

I snorted and then ran my fingers through his thick, black hair. "You set me on fire but, I'm not ready. If you think it's safe, I'd like you to take me someplace." I needed to get out this room before I took off my clothes and did things I could regret.

He pushed some of my crazy curls from my face. "*Tane* is the one who warned me."

Touché. I shrugged. "How did he know?"

Rurik rolled off to stand next to the bed, his eyes lingered on me with a speculative light. "He has followed this group of slayers actions for some time. They don't realize if they succeed in killing me they'll be hunted down and slaughtered for the crime by my people." He shook his head and a flash of regret crossed his face.

"You don't want the slayers dead?" The repercussions

of assassinating an Overlord never came to my mind. Guilty or not, we weren't the vampire police. Rurik's people may not know of his supposed crime. What the hell did Colby get us involved in?

"Of course not, it's like being angry at the gun instead of the shooter. I have uses for slayers and these ones appear efficient. I need to figure out who is trying to kill me and deal with them on my own."

Tane. It sat there on my tongue, a lead weight waiting for me to spit it out. Creepy bastard was right, battle lines were being drawn and I'd have to pick a side. Rurik thought him a friend. What a mistake. If I told Rurik what I'd learned, my fate would be tied to his. I didn't completely trust him. Not yet. I wondered if Colby really knew what he took on by accepting this contract since we've only done small time vampires on American soil.

Shit.

Rurik offered me a hand. "Come on, I'll take you somewhere special."

"This is one of my favorite places."

We stood at the bottom of a stone staircase. It led up to what looked like a medieval rampart. Its worn projections and turrets rose above us, with the full moon behind them in the clear night sky. A light fog rose from the river as we climbed the stairs through a forest of silhouetted branches, they were full of spring blossoms, and a cool crisp breeze flowed through them.

BAIT

My breath puffed out in little clouds as I tried to keep up with Rurik.

He turned to wait for me. No mist emerged from his mouth. "This is the Fishermen's Bastion. The surrounding suburb used to be Fishermen's Town and they held their market behind the ramparts." He grinned and his eyes sparkled with the moonlight as he spoke. His hand found mine and we climbed the rest of the stairs together.

The top of the Bastion opened to a flat ambulatory-like gallery that offered a panoramic view of the city. Rurik led me to the wall and leaned out to watch his home. The fog swirled by the lit areas and we watched their patterns dissolve into one another. He appeared lost in his memories and a slight frown marred his forehead. They didn't seem like happy ones

"I grew up here, in Fishermen's town, with the Bastion guarding our home. So much has changed since then." He glanced at me then pointed out across the fog-veiled river. "Margaret Island is hidden in there. The Romans used the thermal waters on the north side of it. Now a modern spa occupies the area."

I stepped closer to peer at his face. "You were here with the Romans?"

A grim smile appeared. "They stole me away from my home to work at the springs. Some of them liked pretty, young men."

I tried to hide the horror that fought to surface. "That must have been horrible for you."

Our eyes met and I couldn't help but flinch at the

sight of the embedded pain lingering there. "My maker saved me from them. Brought me over and gave me a chance for a new existence. I left Budapest for a long while." A wicked and familiar glint returned to his forlorn eyes and he chucked me under the chin. "Not before I got my revenge." He turned and gave his back to the island as he leaned his elbows on the solid, stone wall. "This place always feels like home."

Revenge, Romans, and vampires; sounded like a new movie release.

"Tane mentioned that he thought you were young to have become Overlord of Budapest. You must be a few hundred years old if you were around with the Romans." Centuries. The word settled on my shoulders. He looked so young and I treated him like he was my age.

He laughed and it rang out against the empty surroundings. "Compared to Tane, I am young. Creatures like him and Dragos have been around for millennia. But he's right, though. Budapest is a major hub in Europe, a powerful place to rule. An ancient master, like them, used to rule here before I took over a hundred years ago."

"What happened to him?"

"Elizabeth."

"Scary Lizzy from the party?" The arrogant dominatrix who tried to convince Rurik to give me to her instead of Dragos.

He looked down at his worn running shoes. "Dragos has ample reason to be angry with both of us."

The wheels began to creak in my head. "Why *is* he in town?"

"Who?"

"Dragos. I get you're not best friends. Why the visit?"

"There has been a lot of animosity between our people since my rule began. Incidents have occurred and we are trying to make amends." He reached out and massaged between my eyebrows with his thumb.

I felt the tense small muscles there relax. Even that small touch electrified me.

"I didn't bring you here to make you think so hard, Rabbit."

I sighed. "I'm tired of these games. You said you wanted my help."

He wrapped me in his arms. "To ask for a safe place to hide for a day until my people can gather at a safe haven tomorrow night. Not for you to save me from a millennia old rival." He kissed the top of my head.

I melted into his embrace. It felt right to be here. "You call me infuriating."

His chest vibrated with his chuckle. "What makes you think this is the first attempt to destroy me?"

I stiffened. That was an excellent question. It never occurred to me that there had been other attempts. "Well ... you're still here."

"Your opinion of me is that low?"

I regarded him. His beautiful, masculine face with ice blue eyes topped with his thick jet-black hair. "You obtained your power by seducing Lizzy."

His eyebrows rose and he tilted his head to stare at me. The cocky smile faded.

I suddenly wished we were on the deck of the A38. The Fishermen's Bastion was high enough that I would need to know how to fly to survive that fall.

He looked away and shook his head.

I gripped him tighter, afraid he'd let me go. "I'm sorry." The words surprised both of us.

He leaned towards me and met my lips with hot passion. My ambivalence weakened with each touch and kiss. I never doubted he'd seduce me and maybe that's what I needed, someone to pull me away from the past since I couldn't let it go.

Still in each other's arms, after the kiss, we looked out over the city. He whispered close to my ear. "I obtained and kept my power by being smart enough to stay ahead of my enemies. Don't judge me with what little you know."

Likewise. I was trapped in the center of Rurik, Tane, and Colby. Of the three, Rurik showed the most concern for me. "I need you to show me the real Rurik."

"Sweet Rabbit, that would take a lifetime. Are you offering to stay with me that long?"

I thought he teased me but the loneliness I'd glimpsed at the bathhouse returned. This time he didn't bother to hide it. My heart turned inside out. I didn't know what to say so I did the next best thing and kissed him.

I molded my body to his. The touch of his full lips never lost their thrill. His hair felt as soft as it looked and I ran my hands through it, determined to mess it up.

My tongue caressed his lips and his mouth opened to invite me in. I explored each sharp, delicate fang with care yet still managed to nick myself.

A low growl purred in his throat and he crushed his lips to mine with the small taste of my blood. It caused him to lap at the little wound, to suck on it until it bled no longer.

He pushed himself away. His hands trembled on my shoulders.

"Are you okay?"

He nodded. "That's the first time *you* kissed *me*." He gave me a small, shy smile and this time the shy was for real. "Let me show you something else."

CHAPTER THIRTEEN

Rurik gave me a wonderful gift, something I cherished. We toured the Fishermen's Bastion and he told me of its history. Details I don't think the official tour guides knew. I finally got to see a part of Budapest that wasn't vampire related, not counting my guide. A place so old it made Rurik seem young. The history of this city made my bones ache with curiosity.

We stood in the middle of the promenade and he pointed to the seven towers. "Each one symbolizes the seven Magyar tribes that came to Hungary in Eight Hundred and Ninety-Six." He glanced at me. "You don't mind my telling you all this? You're not bored?"

I laughed. "That's the third time you've asked me. Now finish the story."

He crossed his arms over his muscular chest. "I don't mean to annoy you, Rabbit. This modern age has bred a generation uninterested in their past."

I pursed my lips in thought and noticed the amused twinkle in his eyes. "I'll admit listening to North American history puts me into a coma but we didn't have Romans and Huns."

"Unfortunately, we'll have to finish this another night. I can feel the dawn approaching." He took my hand and we walked to the stairs. Before we descended he turned to me. "I can stay with you?"

"I'll hide you for the day." My libido was going to get me killed. After I'd spent time with him tonight, I realized I enjoyed more than just looking at him. I liked to talk to him as well.

I didn't get the 'killer' vibe from him. He'd been given endless opportunities to do-away with me. Yet, instead he saved me, seduced me, and took me on a personal history tour. Yeah, that spells 'mass murderer'. Hell, I spent less than an hour with Tane and he threw me in the river.

Rurik was innocent, I was sure of it. Now, I needed to find the proof.

We stood in the center of my hotel room after a quiet drive from the Bastion. I didn't have a spare coffin to lend him. "I don't think these curtains will keep out all the sunlight." This may not have been the best thought out plan. How much light could a vampire take?

"The bathroom has no windows. I'll just block the

light from under the door and lay in the tub. I've done that before. You'll have to find an alternative place to use for the day."

"I can use the public restroom in the lobby, that's not an issue, but the tub sounds uncomfortable." I grabbed a pillow and an extra blanket from the room's closet then followed him into the bathroom.

He pressed himself against the sink as I pushed past him and laid them out in the tub. I turned to quirk an eyebrow at him.

He watched me in silence, an odd, soft look on his face.

I'd rather have had him in my blankets on my bed instead of in my tub. That tender look disturbed me. "I'm not Betty Crocker or June Cleaver. Don't get used to this."

His eyes wandered slowly down my body and back up. "I would never make such a mistake." There wasn't anything in his tone but I could read the subtext. What would he do if he knew that I was more like *Buffy the Vampire Slayer* meets *Legally Blonde*? He rubbed at his jaw as he glanced at the door.

I took my cue to leave. As I passed him, I stole a quick kiss, just a press of my lips to his soft, sweet ones.

He reached out to me but I retreated from the room. Always leave them wanting more, my grandma gave me that piece of advice. She was a smart woman.

I huddled in a cocoon of pillows and blankets to watch the sunrise. The creep of light behind the thick curtains grew until it brightened up the room to look

BAIT

like twilight. I couldn't keep my eyes from wandering to the bathroom door. Each time I snagged them away they eventually made their way back.

No howls of torment came from behind it. That comforted me. I wondered if he slept like humans did or went into another state of unconsciousness. Rurik's taken care of himself for centuries, he knew his own limits.

Why did I worry? I understood my attraction. He was a striking man. But my affection bothered me. Last night I would have staked him. The manila-envelope-of-trouble sat on a table across the room. If I could delete the memories of those pictures, I'd burn them and be done with it. Unfortunately, it could never be that easy.

Something told me to keep them safe. Tane's involvement in this confusion tainted the picture's validity and my growing attachment to Rurik tainted my sanity.

A little over a year ago, life had been simple. No vampire hunts or being chased through dark alleys. I didn't even know they existed. Then Laurent's stomachache turned to cancer. The Connie Bence I'd been disappeared with his death forever.

At least I thought she had. I think she may have peeked out last night. Rurik did that to me, drew out the person I used to be. He gave me genuine smiles, laughs, and cries.

Something knotted and twisted deep down in my heart loosened its grip. I never knew it could do that. My grief, my dirty little obsession, didn't seem so constricted.

Laurent must be disappointed in me. He'd made me promise to move on afterwards, to find someone to love and continue living. I would've promised him anything. Instead, I nurtured and grew this demon inside of me. Fed it alcohol and drugs so it would blind me, make me forget. It taught me not to feel.

Colby helped me tame it by giving my life purpose but it never went away. Until now, I didn't think it could.

Rurik was a man who couldn't get sick, who couldn't grow old, and was difficult to kill. Someone who appeared to care for me.

All I needed to do was let go of my past.

A knock on my door made me jump and squeal like a greased pig at a country fair. I struggled with the blankets tangled around my legs so I could stomp out of bed and check the peek hole. Would I ever get some sleep?

"Delivery for Ms. Bence."

That stopped me in my tracks. Only two people in Budapest knew my real last name and one of them lay asleep in the tub. My heart dropped. I felt like a kid who got caught stealing money from her mom's purse.

Another knock echoed through my room. "Ms. Bence?" Yeah, that was his voice, all right.

Colby.

He wouldn't even have to stake Rurik, just open the bathroom door and let the sunlight in. If I didn't answer soon he would break the door down. In my over-sized, teddy bear printed PJ's, I cracked the hallway door open. A man in a navy blue uniform with a matching cap stood looking at his feet. He held a bouquet of white lilies.

He raised his piercing green eyes to glare at me.

"What are you doing here?" I hissed.

Colby placed his hand on the door and pushed it open then scanned the room behind me. Meeting his clearance, he brushed past me as he entered and laid the flowers on the manila envelope across the room.

I closed the door and leaned on it. Without its support, I think my knees would have given out.

"I wanted to check on you. You sounded strange last night when you called." He stared at the envelope, his back to me, and traced a finger around it. "Like you had other things on your mind."

"What do you expect? I'm hunting vampires with *Nosferatu* lurking in the shadows."

He spun around. "You saw more?" His eyes shone with excitement, almost the way Tane's did when he spoke of Colby.

"I saw Tane, Dragos' sidekick, at the club. That's why I left early, before he saw me."

He pointed his finger at me and raised his voice. "You should have brought him to me. That's your job, remember?"

"My job was to lure Rurik." Who, by the way, lay in the bathtub. I had to swallow a hysterical giggle and struggled with it until it became just a grin. "I'm not

Tane's type. He likes men—maybe you should check him out yourself."

That took the wind out of his sail. He dropped his arm to his side. "He's gay?" His voice returned to a normal volume.

"I don't know, maybe he's bi, but his date was a guy named *Eric*." I tried to hint. Maybe I could lay it on thicker but Colby could catch on and make me tell him everything. Then we'd all be dead.

He nodded, his expression lost in thought.

I stood away from the door confident my legs would support me now. "I'll admit, I feel like I'm over my head. You've pitted me against some pretty strong monsters. It's one thing to take on street thugs and small timers but this is beyond me. They're going to get me if we're not more careful."

"I agree. The tension level in this city is high. Things are about to explode." He leaned against the table and crossed his arms. "I'm thinking of bailing out."

"Really?" Colby's never given up on a hunt as far as I knew. Hope made me lightheaded. With him gone I had one less thing to worry about. This would solve half my problems.

"The contractor has offered to pay triple our price to finish the job. Most of the others want to stay. What about you?"

"He tripled the offer." Damn, that bastard, Tane. What was he up to? If he wanted Rurik dead, all he had to do was not warn him of the attack on his resting place yesterday.

"Who said it was a *he*?" Colby's voice sounded strained.

I shrugged.

He stalked up to me, backed me against the door, and then loomed. "I can't help you if you keep secrets. I know you, Connie. You've been hiding something since Rurik took you from that club."

Colby's stare pierced mine and I glanced away. I've faced centuries old vampires who were less intimidating. The memories of his ruthless training returned, of spending nights with him building my mental shields while he used his small psychic abilities to pound at them. Drunk, exhausted, starved I learned to defend my mind or pay his price. It gave me chills and my stomach clenched.

He placed his hand against the door and leaned down to my level, then lifted my chin with his free hand to look at both sides of my neck. He found it clean of vampire bites and sighed, letting go of my chin, but he didn't back off. "Do I need to search other body parts?"

"No!" Horrified at the thought. "I'm clean. I'm nobody's meal ticket."

"I'm worried about you."

He should be. I was worried about me too.

"I-I'm in trouble." I caught myself about to look at the bathroom door and stomped on the urge. "That's all I can tell you, I've *told* you everything else I could." I tugged at the hem of my PJ top and looked at my bare feet, corralled by his size twelve boots.

He stepped back allowing me to take a deep breath. I watched him as he took his hat off to run his hand through his blond hair, disturbing the neat part. By the end of the day his hair would be all over the place like Einstein's, as always.

I couldn't help but smile at the gesture and realized there was something I could impart to him. "Rurik's lair got attacked yesterday."

His eyebrows rose up to his hairline. "Who did it?"

"I thought it was you." From his reaction, I would guess not.

He shook his head. "Is he dead?"

"No."

"Yeah, you're not in mourning."

The comment rattled my already confused morals. I stepped forward and slapped his face without thinking. Colby knew me and how Laurent's death affected my soul He shouldn't have crossed that line.

He rubbed his chin and nodded. "I deserved that." He reached into his back pocket and pulled out a white envelope to place in my hand. "Plane ticket home. Leaves tonight."

I stared at it, not sure what to do. This was what I wanted, wasn't it?

Colby nudged me out of his way and opened the door. "Take the plane, Connie. Get out. Red and I will take care of things here." Then he left.

I sat on the bed with Colby's present in my hands. The battle lines drawn across this city were taut with tension, ready to explode. I assumed it to be just between Rurik and Dragos, but Tane seemed to be playing both sides and Colby was the wild card.

Tane told me I'd have to pick a side. Forget Dragos, he'd just eat me. Rurik wanted me but could he protect me? Tane needed me and had the power to protect me but I didn't know what he would do with me once I outlived my uses. Then there was this plane ticket home. If I took Colby's offer and left all this trouble behind, I'd live.

But at what cost? Rurik framed for a mass murder and no one believed his innocence but me. Colby and his men hired by Tane and didn't even know it. If they succeeded in killing Rurik they'd be hunted down by his people and if not, I think Tane would go after them anyway. The city of Budapest would be taken over by a new unknown Overlord chosen by Dragos.

The thought sent a shiver down my spine.

Did I think I could stop all this? *No.*

If I left and those I cared about got hurt because I kept my mouth shut and did nothing, I'd be responsible. That was unacceptable. I'd already had to sit back and watch one person I loved die. Not again, never again.

This little rabbit was about to draw her own battle line and cross all of theirs.

CHAPTER FOURTEEN

"Rabbit." A seductive, silken voice caressed my consciousness. "Rabbit." It got louder. I tried to ignore it and go back to sleep. Something smoothed my hair from my face. A light touch brushed my lips and sent a smoldering shockwave through my body.

Rurik. No one inflamed me like he did.

He pulled away from the light kiss but I reached out for more and trapped him in my arms. His deep, low laugh shook his body and I peeked at him from under my eyelashes.

His clear, cold sapphire eyes sparkled a few inches from mine. They searched my face and settled on my hair where he fingered a wayward curl. "There is nothing I'd rather do than spend the night in your warm bed but duty calls." He tugged at the curl. "Wake up." He rolled out of my arms to sit on the edge of the bed.

I groaned as I crawled from under the covers and onto his lap. "I don't have any duties. Why do I need to wake up?" It was mid-afternoon when I finally fell asleep, barely five hours ago. He felt solid and strong when I leaned into his waiting arms. The thin white t-shirt he wore stretched across his shoulders. I indulged myself by sliding my hands under it to feel along his narrow waist. The warmth of my hand disappeared against his icy skin.

I sucked in a surprised gasp and looked closer at him. The pale skin on his face appeared transparent and waxy. His pupils began to dilate and it reminded me of the vampire who chased me down the alley.

I swallowed the ball of tension that suddenly developed in my throat and scooted off his lap.

He smiled, flashing fang. "No fear, Rabbit. I've got control over my hunger."

The memory of him, as he enjoyed the taste of my blood, returned fresh in my mind. Maybe he did have great control but I wasn't going to test it.

I noticed my small, red suitcase laid on a stand by the door and a stack of folded clothes sat on my night table. "Did you pack for me?"

He nodded then gestured at the pile of clothes. "Get dressed and we will check out of the hotel."

I'd planned on doing all of this, but after Rurik left. It both pleased and annoyed me that he assumed I'd just go with him. "Where are we going?"

"To safety. An old friend has opened her home to us. At least until matters with Dragos are settled. I can't leave you here by yourself. If he found out you harbored me for the day it would go bad for you. I need to meet with my people and make plans."

I carried the clothes to the bathroom and noticed the manila envelope no longer lay on the table. I glanced over my shoulder at Rurik. Did he go through them? I didn't think so since I still lived. He must have respected my privacy enough not to look inside and packed it with my stuff.

Once in the bathroom I closed the door. I'd never had a man pick out an outfit for me. He'd chosen my black silk blouse, gray slacks, and matching black undergarments. The thought of him touching them gave me goose bumps. I sent a silent thanks to heaven I'd decided to leave the granny panties at home.

The outfit was not what I would have chosen to wear for tonight. Jeans and t-shirts were my preference. After I dressed I stepped out of the bathroom and shoved my PJs into my suitcase. The wastepaper basket stood next to it with the remainders of my shredded plane ticket visible. I should have hid it better.

My last pair of heels rested by the door. "Are we going somewhere else first?"

He walked up to me as his eyes traveled from my face to my bare feet. "No."

"Then why am I dressed up?"

"A women should always try to look her best." He smiled when my eyebrows shot up. "I'm very concerned at your lack of wardrobe."

"I've destroyed two of my best dresses since I met you. Are you sure this outfit won't get wrecked? It's one of my last ones. You may get stuck with my jeans and sweats." I stepped into my red heels. The extra height brought me closer to his face. His lips wouldn't be so hard to reach now. Maybe the outfit wasn't such a bad idea.

He picked up my single piece of luggage and opened the door for me.

"Are we driving in the rust bucket?" I couldn't help taunt. The Overlord of Budapest drove a fifty-eight year old micro-car that belonged in a museum, not on the road. "What happened to that nice black sedan you kidnapped me in?"

"That was a rental, Rabbit."

It took a few minutes to arrive at the lair—a small house nestled in one of the suburbs. The locals would never guess a kiss of vampires rested in their quiet haven. No traffic passed us as we parked on the sleepy street. Most homes in this city were spaced close together but this neighborhood oozed of old money. The stone fences and the moderate gardens said it all.

He led me through the front door where one of the guards who accompanied Rurik at the club greeted us. He watched me with a stern expression as we continued through the foyer.

Rurik handed him my suitcase. "Samson this is Rabbit. She is my companion. Please escort her to my room." The guard started up the stairs and stopped when I didn't follow.

"Where are you going?" A sense of unease settled on me. I knew Rurik but not these other ... vampires. If he wanted me to be alone with a stranger, it wouldn't happen. That's wasn't in my definition of 'safety.'

My face must have expressed my discomfort since he sighed and signaled Samson to hand the luggage back to him. "Follow me, Rabbit." He climbed the stairs.

The guard made room for us to pass. He leered at me, pearly fangs exposed, as I pushed by him.

The way Rurik used the word 'companion' made it sound like a title. It gave me a squishy sensation inside, as if he'd said 'girlfriend'. I probably read too much into the statement and disliked that it even occurred to me. If Red or Colby had said it, I would have reacted differently but Rurik nurtured relationship vibes from me.

The upstairs hallway led to a moderate sized master bedroom and attached bathroom. Rurik set my suitcase on the floor by a huge wooden sleigh bed. "I have some things to attend to. Stay in here for now until I have time to introduce you to my remaining clan. I won't be long." With that mild warning he left.

Things had gone better than I'd planned. Who would have guessed he'd invite me to one place I needed to find? Originally, I'd hoped Tane would inform me of Rurik's hiding place. I was so happy I didn't have to deal with that monster. He probably would have demanded my soul in exchange for the info.

I opened my suitcase and found the manila envelope within. It still contained the photos. How could I tell if he saw them? Rurik thought I worked for a travel agency. Maybe he thought the contents paper work.

His room held a dresser that overflowed with clothes and a chest at the foot of the bed. I eyed the mess of jewelry, papers, and socks that cover the dresser top. It looked as if things were dumped there in a hurry, as if they'd just moved in.

Where would I hide a drug capable of rendering my mental shields useless? A corner of a black lacquer box stuck out under a pile of ties. I felt under them to get a better idea of what hid there and was rewarded by pricking my finger. I yanked it out and stuck it in my mouth.

That's all I needed, to be bleeding in a house full of hungry vamps. I examined my wound but found just a dent, no blood.

The ties shifted in my haste to rescue myself and exposed the culprit, a letter opener. It lay next to the lacquer box, which contained nothing of interest. I did a quick search of the area. Under the bed, behind the dresser, and in the bathroom but I still didn't find anything which resemble a drug. Was it a pill, a powder, or a liquid? I ingested it in a drink so I assumed a liquid.

I knelt next to the battered wooden chest at the foot of the bed. The only place I hadn't explored and it was locked.

The mechanism looked old. If I could just slide something under the lid to pry it open. My finger throbbed and I remembered the letter opener. I retrieved it from the dresser and used it to pry at the hook-like lock under the lid. At any moment Rurik could return and walk in me. My heart drummed with each failed attempt until something grated and the letter opener slid between the spaces under the lid with ease.

I scrambled to my feet and returned the nicked implement to the dresser under the pile of ties. The bedroom door opened and I swiveled as Rurik stalked in.

He raised an eyebrow when he saw me by the dresser. "Find anything of interest?"

I smiled. "You're a terrible housekeeper." I gestured at the mess behind me.

He laughed out loud as he crossed the room. His skin color had improved and I bet he felt warm to the touch.

"Did you just feed?" The stab of jealousy surprised me and made the comment come out sharper than I intended.

He removed his sweatshirt and tossed in a corner. His voice became soft as he eyed me like a dangerous animal. "Yes, I need to feed, Rabbit. If I knew you were willing, you'd have been my first choice." He turned away and took off his t-shirt. The fine muscle of his shoulders and back moved under his skin with the motion.

"That's not the point." Hell, I didn't know what my point was anymore since he started to undress. The man knew how to unplug my brain.

He undid his belt. "Should I have asked your permission?" He turned his attention away from the belt to glance my way and grin at me.

I crossed my arms and tried to stare at the bed but that made my desires worse. My imagination played havoc on my concentration with ideas of what I'd like to do with him in that bed. My traitorous eyes returned to Rurik who just stepped out of his jeans.

"What are you doing?" I felt heat rise to my cheeks as I stared. Rurik apparently went commando.

"I want to shower." His grin never faded as he walked into the bathroom. "There's room for two." He called out.

I tried to remember how to exhale. The temptation to join him teased and poked at me. Of course his shower would be big enough for two. I laughed at myself. I wanted to take on Budapest's biggest and baddest monsters. All they needed to do for me to lose cohesive thoughts was get Rurik to undress for me.

Monsters. Tane. The recently unlocked chest at the foot of the bed. I raced to it. The lid weighed heavy in my hands as I pulled it open. The contents struck me with awe. Inside, a nicked, bronze short sword lay on top of an old, gray wool soldier's uniform. Some ancient foreign coins sat in a jar and a framed aged photo of him smiling with a new micro-car was among other things that distracted me from my quest. I fingered the dull edge of the weapon, a piece of Rurik's past, and wondered.

A red velvet jewelry case drew my attention. It stuck out of the uniform's pocket. I opened it to find a small vial of blue liquid inside. Could this be the drug? I hesitated to listen for the shower. It still ran. For all I knew it was perfume. I twisted the cap and smelled it. No sent rose from the vial.

This was as far as my plan went and why I needed someone like Colby to run my life. I sucked at this. My choices were to place it back in the chest and forget it, stick it in my pocket and find out later it was mouthwash, or to try it.

Crap. I twisted the top then dabbed a drop on my tongue. To err with less sounded safe.

The shower noise stopped. I stuck the vial into my pant pocket and closed the chest lid. My knees wobbled as I stood, probably from squatting too long.

Rurik came out with a towel wrapped low around his hips drying his hair with another one. "We will introduce you to my people so there are no misunderstandings." He approached me, beads of water sat on the skin of his chest. "You'll have full access-"

I licked at one of beads.

His head came up like I'd staked him.

My head fuzzed a bit, my mental shields still held but barely, and my inhibitions apparently flew out the window. I stepped closer to fulfill one of my bathhouse fantasies and sipped the water from his skin. It tasted warm and clean. No doubt about it, that vial contained the drug Rurik used on me, and I didn't give a damn.

He dropped the towel he used to dry his hair but

164

still didn't touch me.

I glanced at his eyes to see them full of fervent fire. His mouth parted a fraction while his hands hovered by my shoulders. I licked a solid line to the hollow of his throat.

As if coming to a decision he grasped my shoulders and lifted me to within an inch of his face. "No teasing this time." He glared into my eyes. "You need to say the word 'yes' or this won't go any further. Once we start I won't stop. Not this time."

I stepped back and his fingers trailed down my arms.

A hurt narrowed his eyes until he realized why I pulled away.

I undid the buttons on my blouse one at a time and watched as his eyes widened and were drawn to what I revealed. He picked out the undergarments I wore but they were empty and lifeless when he did it. Now, I filled every lacy tidbit. As the last button came undone I whispered, "Yes," and allowed the blouse to slip off my shoulders to the floor.

His eyes drank me in.

I yearned for his touch again. For that wicked desire he awakened in me. I slid one red heel off.

"Leave the shoes on," he ordered, his voice deep with passion.

Chapter Fifteen

I slipped the red heel back on.

Rurik crossed his arms over his chest with a crooked smile on his face. "Please, don't let me interrupt."

A nervous laugh escaped me. My mental shields no longer protected me but I didn't need them with him. He wouldn't hurt me. After all the opportunities he'd had to harm, he never did. Why would he start now? I felt wild and free, like a huge weight lifted from my heart. Rurik did this to me, not the drug. It may have affected my defenses but not my soul.

I undid my pants and let them pool around my ankles. The cuffs were wide enough I needed only to step out of them. I shook my head to send my bouncy, blond curls to fly wild around my face and turned in a lazy circle. His gaze never left mine. It waited for me as we lost contact for a moment when I completed the turn. Full of hunger, he absorbed my presence, but his eyes never wandered lower.

Mine did though.

His body's reaction under the towel told me he liked what he saw. The crooked smile on his face turned salacious as I advanced toward him.

I ran my fingernails down the sculpted ridges of his chest muscles until they reached the towel and gave a tug so it fell from his hips. It was hard to believe someone so sensuous could be real. That he wanted me.

His hands caressed my shoulders and he pulled me against him. I felt a potent snap of sensual awareness at the feel of his hard length along my stomach. Drips fell from the tips of his wet hair and rolled over his chest to rest on his hardened nipples. They summoned my lips.

I knew of the darkness in Rurik and his potential for ... evil, but I trusted he wouldn't do it. Use me, feed from me, and kill me even though I stood before him helpless. It was a lot of trust to have. More than I'd ever thought possible.

His chest rose with heavy breaths as my mouth moved lower. I kissed the smooth pale skin to his navel then nipped at the short hairs that grew in a line to more delicate bits.

He nudged my chin with his tip, asking for more attention. Fingers brushed through my hair before I blew a gentle breeze over his hot and needy end. He clenched his hands, entwining my curls in his fingers. I slid my mouth over him. A moan echoed in the silent room. Hard and stiff, I fought to take in as much of him as I could and swallowed him. My instincts cried out something this big shouldn't be coming down my throat whole but I found if I didn't struggle I could still breathe.

When my lips felt the solid touch of his base, I knelt lower to change the angle so he could watch as he slid from my mouth. Breathless, I was pleased with the results.

Rurik stared at me with carnal urgency. Maybe I wasn't as rusty at this as I'd worried. Almost a year and a half had passed since I'd been with a man, almost two since I had a wild one. I bent my face back over him. It was easier to take him in, harder, faster.

His short gasps filled the room and he gave gentle thrusts, trying to hold back so as not to hurt me, while griping my hair. It felt good to have him in my mouth, ripe and firm, to hear him make all those enticing sounds. The skin was so soft and silky as it rolled over my tongue. I took him deeper and concentrated on relaxing my throat so not to choke but it convulsed around him as I reflexively swallowed my saliva.

His breaths were frantic now, making everything from his abdomen to his shoulders move. He stumbled back. "Enough. I don't want to come this way. Not our first time together."

On tiptoe, I stretched my body along his torso to come eye to eye with him.

"Connie." A bare whisper fluttered from his mouth before he crushed his lips to mine. The kiss woke a fierce yearning and sent a shiver of anticipation down my spine.

His hands slid around to my back and with an expert's grasp he unclasped my bra. The butterflies in my stomach took wing. I gave up to his kiss in sweet surrender and opened my mouth to invite him in. His tongue swiped a sure stroke inside, he left no spot unexplored.

I felt him graze the underside of my breasts as he slid his hands under my bra to cup them. My nipples hardened when his palms brushed over them, he then pinched them between two fingers to twist and pull. A flood of reckless desire flowed from me. I returned his kiss with as much fervor as he gave. I grasped his broad, strong shoulders and jumped to wrap him in my legs. I wanted to be part of him, to be as close as possible, to feel every inch of him.

My action broke our kiss as he caught me. He gave me a shameless grin before he pressed me to the bed and removed my bra, tossing it over his head.

There was no way to describe the intense effect he had on me. He shouldn't have felt so familiar, as if I'd known him all my life instead of just a few days. I wanted so much for things to work out for us but our worlds fought against each other.

He pushed himself against the thin lace of my panties to remind me only this separated us.

I laughed at the hint and scooted out from under

him to crawl further onto the bed.

He chased and trapped me on the pillows. One hand pinned both of mine above my head and the other teased along the edge of my underwear. "I'm not usually a gentle lover, Connie." His husky voice whispered in my ear. "If I get too rough stop me."

For a fraction of a second, it seemed as if my heart stopped beating. At the bathhouse he was far from gentle but it had excited me. I stared into his clear honest eyes, with my mental shields useless, I never once felt him reach out to influence my mind. It supported my confidence in him. I knew with an unknown surety he wouldn't hurt me. Not unless I let him. I nodded. I belonged to him.

With a feral growl he tore the panties from my hips with a sharp tug. They followed my bra through the air. His body pressed along mine and his free hand wrapped itself in my hair. He pulled back to expose the line of my throat where he ran his sharp fangs gently over my increasing pulse.

A heated tremor passed quickly through my groin. I couldn't believe how much I delighted in this. Being at his mercy and held down for our pleasure. A new me flowered in this experience.

The teeth turned into kisses and I was thankful he'd just fed.

Then he entered me.

I gasped a sharp intake of breath. Things felt tight with disuse but I was wet enough that I didn't need gentle.

He thrust with an urgent rhythm while I lay pinned. I writhed under him unable to control the greedy passion he elicited from me. My breath came short and quick with each steady plunge. Deeper, harder he drove small cries from me. The pleasure built. It wanted to overwhelm me. I'd forgotten, forgotten how *good...*

He released my hands and hair. The sudden freedom caused me to open my eyes. It surprised me they'd been closed.

He lifted his weight off me and pulled my hips toward him at a steeper angle lifting my ass off the bed. His pale, blue eyes burned into me with such tormented hunger. At that moment I would have let him do anything he desired to me.

I ran my hands over his hips to clutch his firm behind.

He grasped the headboard of the bed for balance as he continued with his own beat to rouse both of us. The sight of his body pounding into mine was enough to throw me over the edge and make me scream my ecstasy. I felt Rurik give one last hard push before his body spasmed over mine. He kept his grip on the headboard as his head rolled back, eyes closed, as a shudder coursed through him.

My limbs refused to respond. They rested on a tangle of pillows and sheets, too exhausted to listen to me. I couldn't describe what Rurik and I had done as making love. More like fucking my brains out. It was dynamite. I wanted more but he said I needed to build stamina gradually or I'd regret it once the endorphins wore off.

He was right. I lay in his bed and just breathed.

The drug wore off sometime during the night. I didn't feel any regrets about my lowered inhibitions, just happy that I'd only taken a drop. My mind felt clear and strong but tired.

The bedroom door swung open, Rurik balanced a tray in one hand as he walked in. He placed it on the wooden chest at the foot of the bed. "Breakfast is served, my lady." His sweet, sexy smile warmed me.

"It's the middle of the night." I groaned as I made a half-hearted attempt to sit up. The silk sheets sat tangled at my feet and I pulled one of the corners to cover myself.

The smell of bacon made my stomach growl.

He chuckled at the sound. "You haven't eaten today." He stuffed pillows behind my back and placed the tray across my lap then removed the silver lid covering the meal. A plate of scrambled eggs, bacon and muffins spread before me. The bed listed as he sat on the edge to take the spoon from my hand. He scooped up some eggs and fed it to me.

I couldn't help smile at the gesture but removed the spoon from his hands, determined to feed myself. The food tasted wonderful. "I didn't know you could cook."

His eyebrows shot up as he gave a sharp laugh. "I can't. The cook made this." He watched as I took another bite. "Is it good?"

"Give him my complements." I mumbled around a mouth full. My empty stomach gurgled with joy.

"Why would you need a cook?"

He picked at imaginary dirt in his fingernails. "To feed the humans we care for." Though the words came out in a casual manner, his shoulders tensed and he glanced up once before continuing to examine his perfect manicure.

I took a sip of orange juice to help swallow the muffin caught in my dry throat. Obviously, other vampires lived here but the fact that other humans did surprised, maybe shocked, me.

He placed his hands on his lap and gave me gentle smile.

Anger started to bubble up inside of me. "Are they like cattle?" Even to me, my voice sounded strained.

"No. It's not like that at all. Not anymore." His smile grew. "They choose to live with us and in exchange we take care of them, like a family."

"Families don't use each other for food."

He sighed, his smile faded. "You're being judgmental." His became stern. "How would you have us live? Hunting the streets at night for victims?" He crossed his arms over his bare chest. "We cherish and care for our humans. In return, they cherish and care for us."

These heated words justified my cause to prove his innocence even more. "I don't know what's right anymore, Rurik." I shook my head and felt lost. Maybe I *was* being judgmental. What other conscientious way could they feed? "They're here of their own free will? No mind tricks?"

He chuckled and shook his head. "No mind tricks. No, how did you phrase it? Mojo. They're here like you are, of their own free will."

"Is this how most vampires live?" I picked up my fork again to resume my meal. This action seemed to calm him and he relaxed his arms.

"I can't speak for the world, Connie, but in Budapest it is. There are those who still like the old ways. Who speak against our new philosophy to live in this way."

I looked up from my plate. "Dragos?"

He touched my hair. "Perceptive. Dragos is very powerful, very old, and very insane. He frightens Tane." He hesitated. "And me."

"Is that why he attacked you? Because you chose to live this way?" I guess discrimination wasn't only human based. It transcended to the monsters too.

Rurik massaged between my eyebrows with his thumb. "You're thinking too hard again. Don't worry. Every little thing will be all right, Rabbit."

The scrape of my fork against the plate surprised us both. I'd eaten everything he'd brought except what was in a small cup by the juice. "What this?" I held it up and emptied some pills into my hand. They looked like vitamins.

"Iron supplements."

I glared at him. "You've got to be kidding."

"By your earlier reaction after I'd fed, I thought you'd want to be my main ... ahh ... well."

"Meal? Feed? Main course?" I laughed at the absurdity of it all. Rurik ran a vampire commune. They were paranormal hippies, who gave their 'family' iron supplements. Tears spilled from my eyes. "Are you sure I'm organic?" The juice cup rattled on the tray from my laughter and Rurik saved it from spilling.

He frowned. "I don't understand the joke."

I wiped the tears from my cheeks. "No, you wouldn't."

"I hoped you'd want to join us and be with me." The disappointment in his voice sobered me.

"You're not what I expected." I tried to explain but how could I without telling him everything. Our relationship was based on lies, my lies. He'd been nothing but protective, kind and loving. Who was the *real* monster in this bed?

I popped the pills in my mouth and washed them down with the last of the juice. It made him smile again. I needed to tell him the truth, all of it, even if it drove him from me, but I feared that the most. My heart couldn't bare another assault. It was held together by threads Rurik had just sewn to mend the tear.

He returned the tray onto the chest. "Where are you going?"

My foot dangled over the edge of the bed. "To shower."

He pushed me flat to the bed and slid me back up to the pillows. "So I could just dirty you again?" His smile spread wide to expose the dainty, sharp fangs. He yanked the sheet that covered my body to the floor and crawled over me.

My heart raced as he ran his hands over my skin.

"Where to begin?" He brushed his face against my left breast, over my hammering heart. His tongue made contact with my skin.

I closed my eyes and arched my back. A sense of pressure built around me like the air compressed itself. Then I felt him brush against my mental shield. A flood of panic filled me. I didn't understand what he wanted and pushed at his shoulders so he'd get off.

He never noticed or pretended not to. His power surrounded me, tried to lure me into submission, and lay down my defenses. I'd forgotten how strong he could be, he never tried to touch me mentally since we first met.

I panted, not from passion but fear. I didn't want him to find out what I was. Not this way.

The power shifted, like a weight off my chest, and I could breathe. I looked down at Rurik who gazed up at me with curiosity.

"Why do you fight so much? It will hurt worse."

"What the hell are you doing? I don't want you poking around in my head." The sharp words were out of my mouth before I could edit them.

"I got that impression the first time we met. I didn't cross the line then. I only influenced you, never went deeper. Why would I now?" He rubbed his cheek on my breast. "You're always so closed up. It's like a prison in there, with stone walls and barbed wires. You're painful to touch."

I closed my eyes so he wouldn't see the tears. *Painful.* I believed it, I lived in that prison. Colby taught me to build those walls to protect me from being taken, but I'm the one who added the barb and never opened the door.

"Let me in, Connie." He whispered the words into my skin. "Trust me. I just want to influence you so I don't add to your pain."

I took a shaky, deep breath. "I don't know how. You drugged me the last time."

I felt him smile. "I could again, if you wanted."

"No." The vial hid in my pants pocket, no longer in it velvet jewelry case in the chest. "No more drugs."

"It was a joke. I'd be affected by it as well after I've fed." He pulled himself up my body to meet my eyes.

"You would be?" This surprised me. "Drugs affect you?"

"No, just this one." I opened my mouth to continue my interrogation but he pressed his finger to my lips and hushed me. "Slow deep breaths, trust me."

I felt the pressure again. My instincts screamed to struggle with Rurik's invasion.

"Deep breaths," he whispered.

I inhaled and trembled with the effort. A visit to the dentist would have been less stressful. A sense of euphoric indifference filled me, just like our first date. The thought made me giggle.

Rurik moaned at my reaction. He liked it when I acted this way, all giddy and happy. Where did that thought come from?

I gasped when I felt the sharp stab over my left breast. It hurt for a moment but I didn't care. He squeezed that breast and enjoyed the feel of it in his palm. My eyes widened with that sensation, *his* sensation. I grinned. The link he used to influence my perceptions worked both ways. I got little snippets of his thoughts. Such as, he thought I tasted like champagne.

His power made me feel wonderful and free. I giggled again which only elicited another moan from Rurik. He pressed the hard bulge in his jeans to my thigh.

I guess waiting to shower was a good idea.

CHAPTER SIXTEEN

The hot shower pounded all my well deserved aches away. Some pains could be classed as good, exercise and well, sex being among them.

I toweled myself dry then wrapped it around my body, anxious to return to Rurik. The soft fabric rubbed on the tender bite mark over my left breast. I saw it in the steamed up mirror, peeking over the towel's edge and touched the spot, thankful for another chance at happiness. Two little puncture holes over my heart. The symbolism wasn't lost to me, though he hadn't said it, I suspected Rurik more than liked me. Never would I have hoped I'd be able to let Laurent's memory fade enough to allow someone else an opportunity into the fortress of my heart.

Elated emotions that soared through me during the past few hours vanished when I walked into the bedroom. My suitcase sat opened on the bed with a set of clothes Rurik must have chosen for me folded next to it. They weren't the only thing he removed from my luggage. The manila envelope lay empty on the floor and the pictures were in Rurik's hands.

He examined them, holding the photos close. His temple twitched as he clenched his jaw. The concentration on his face made the fine cheekbones stand out against his lush lips, which had just finished kissing me before I escaped to the shower. They thinned out in a frown.

I felt empty. My heart dropped and I was surprised not to hear it rattle like a coin inside the hollowness.

His eyes narrowed as he noticed my entrance and nailed me with their icy coldness.

I tried to make my mouth work but my vocal cords froze. I wanted to apologize, I wanted to explain those terrible pictures, and I wanted to tell him about my job. Instead, like an ass, I grabbed the jeans and red t-shirt then dressed, pretending innocence.

He placed the photos onto my open suitcase and I watched as his angry face melted into a soft, seductive smile. "So, Rabbit, what's this game you're playing?" He stepped closer to me, the ice in his eyes never melted.

This was the Rurik I'd met four nights ago in the club. The one who drugged me, who gave me to Dragos. The dangerous Rurik. I recognized the empty gaze he gave me and moved away until the wall came against my back. Anger or even violence I could have handled, but this scared me more. It made me think I was wrong about him. That he was guilty.

"Please..." I didn't know what I pleaded for. A mix of things, not to be the killer, not to hurt me, and not to break my heart. The pain stabbed me so sharply I couldn't catch my breath. Tears burned behind my eyelids.

"Interesting pictures." He gestured with his long fingered hand at them in the suitcase. "How did you manage to come by them?"

"I-I." The one time I needed to spill the beans and I had lockjaw.

"Doesn't matter." He sauntered toward me and leaned in close to my face. The tick on his temple returned and I could hear him grind his teeth. He broke my gaze to look down and set his hands on the wall, trapping me in between his arms. "They're such good pictures, *I* almost believe I was there." His stare returned to me. "What could you possibly want with those? Blackmail?"

I felt my eyes widen with the shock of the truth. He really was clueless. The thought raised my spirit. "They're not real?" I wanted to wrap myself around him and kiss the anger from his face. No matter the evidence, I believed his innocence, I needed to.

He hit the wall by my head with his palm. It creaked with the assault. "Of course not!"

I jumped with the bang. The suicidal urge to kiss him faded fast. "They were given to me. Someone is trying to frame you for those murders. They wanted me to believe you were guilty."

"My guilt?" He stepped back. The look on his face made me feel as if I'd turned into a slime creature from the Black lagoon. "Even if I'd done this crime, I would be held to vampire justice not human."

"Sometimes these matters fall into gray areas between our worlds. Some of those humans who live in that gray area are hired to fulfill that justice." I could barely hear my own voice but his sensitive hearing would have picked it up. "We haven't seen any evidence of vampire justice for this crime."

"You live in this gray area?"

I nodded, afraid if I spoke, it would turn into tears.

"If you wanted to slay me, you had ample opportunity. Why attack my people?"

I took a step forward. "We're not the ones who attacked your lair. We never found it. *I* don't believe you're responsible for this crime. I want to help prove your innocence."

An eyebrow raised in disbelief. "Then who attacked us?"

"Dragos, maybe Tane."

"Dragos would be crazier than I thought to attack me in my own city and Tane is my strongest supporter. He even keeps a companion in the same manner as we do."

I nodded. "Eric."

A look of surprise graced his face. "You know this?"

"Remember the A38, when Tane tossed me

overboard? He admitted to hiring us, through Eric, to hunt you. It was after that meeting I realized the pictures could be false and started to believe in your innocence. I've been trying to help you."

"Only after that? The bathhouse? The club?" He covered his mouth with his hand as if to block those questions. "The attack at the party. I knew they were slayers but not that you'd lured them there." His eyes narrowed and pierced my heart. "Such a clever little Rabbit."

"We need to discuss this. I've been—"

"Only now you want to discuss this? Not last night, before you seduced me or when we were at the Bastion? But after I find these pictures." A small growl escaped him. "You weave your way into my life, collaborate to kill me, try to turn me against my friend, and worst of all, you steal my heart." His voice choked on the last confession.

I couldn't defend myself. He was right, on all counts. "You stole my heart too." It's all I had to offer.

He shook his head, not listening. "Get out." When I didn't move he grabbed my arm and shoved me toward the door. "Get out," he yelled as his eyes dilated, absorbing the irises.

I didn't need to be told again. I ran.

In my rush, I slipped on the stairs and slid down the last five steps on my behind. A gray haired woman hurried from the living room to my aid. "What's going on?" She looked over my head at the top of the staircase. "Rurik!"

I turned to see him, his eyes blackened and fangs exposed. He hissed then retreated back to his room. The sound of the heavy wooden bedroom door slamming vibrated through the house.

The woman touched my shoulder. "Are you injured?"

I felt stunned. He hated me. My barbed wire soul should have protected me, it's why I kept to myself and never opened my heart, but I lowered those defenses. I swallowed the pain. It burned as I locked it up with all the rest. The ache almost unbearable in comparison to rest since it was shiny and new. I deserved it.

"I'm all right." The banister felt solid in my hand as I used it to stand. "You have a phone I can use to call a cab?"

Everything I owned sat in Rurik's room including my wallet. Someone else would need to get them for me. No way would I go back in his room.

She glanced at the landing above and I resisted the urge to do the same. "I will call one for you but first come sit with me. I have a fresh pot of tea and we can talk." She gave me a reassuring smile before leading me to the living room.

"It will be dawn soon." She sat on the sofa and indicated for me to join her.

"I think I should go. He's pretty angry."

She raised an eyebrow and pointed for me sit. "They don't kill and they're not petty enough to injure others. I wouldn't tolerate them in my house otherwise. Though I have to admit, I've never seen Rurik so upset."

A twinkle of curiosity lit her eyes.

It annoyed me. I sat next to her, not answering the unspoken question. Rurik's distraught face kept popping in my mind. Each time I squashed it down it returned. He hated me. How could I ever be able to make this up to him?

She sighed and passed me a cup of black tea.

The next thing I knew, my cup was empty. I drank the tea without tasting it. She sat next to me, quiet and still, to offer a refill. My opinion of her changed. She hadn't tried to pry but to offer an opportunity to talk. My cup rattled as she filled it. She reached out to steady my hand. "Thank you." I tried to smile but my face felt dead.

"Marie."

I nodded. "Rabb—Connie."

"It's dawn." She stated. The birds sang outside the dark windows but the eastern sky lightened to hide the stars. "Let him sleep the day. Tonight it will be better. You can work out your differences."

"I don't think so, Marie. He's got good reason to be angry." I was so stupid. I should have confessed to him earlier, before I crawled into bed with him. Now he thinks I did it for a job. That I came here with the intention to help would be of no consequence.

"You are the first woman he's brought to the clan in my lifetime." She smiled and patted my knee. "Trust me, he'll forgive you."

Her words sank in. "The first?"

She nodded. "It's a strict rule. Lovers are not to be

brought home unless they're to be accepted as part of the family. You're the first he's brought home."

This made me feel worse, not better. The pain I tried to lock away was too strong, it broke out and attacked. I thought it would rip me apart. A tear spilled from my eye, it traced its way down my cheek to drip into my tea. He hated me.

What should I do now? I tore my plane ticket home to pieces. The last thing I wanted to do was phone Colby. I still needed help. I had Tane, and probably Dragos, looking for me. My silent tears flowed freely now.

Marie made a sound of dismay. She set her cup down and hurried from the room while she called back. "I will get tissues."

I didn't want any freaking tissues. I wanted a cab. I wanted out of this nest of heartbreak.

The teacup bounced as I banged it onto the table and decided I'd walk until I found a pay phone. I marched back to the foyer, opened the front door only to surprise a young man about to knock.

I wiped my tears and nose with my sleeve. "What do you want?"

"I'm looking for Rabbit."

My eyebrows shot up. "That's me." He stood only a few inches taller than me, short for a man. Mouse brown hair neatly combed framed a freckled handsome face. A set of hazel eyes scanned me head to toe then glanced behind me.

I twisted around expecting to see Marie but the

foyer remained empty. A white cotton cloth covered my mouth as this stranger pulled me against him. It smelled of heavy medicine. He half carried me, half dragged me out of the doorway.

I kicked and struggled, trying to hold my breath to no avail. The chemical soaked cloth won the fight. Its fumes finally made their way to my lungs when I gasped in desperate need for air. I heard Marie cry out but my vision tunneled, all I could see was the stranger's face as he laid me on what felt like a car seat.

CHAPTER SEVENTEEN

I really needed to lay off the sauce. My mouth tasted like a hamster crawled into it and died. Industrious elves hammered in my head, which only got worse when I rolled to my side. I opened my eyes and sucked in a yelp. A rub to the sockets didn't change anything.

I was blind.

On my hands and knees I rolled to touch my face but no veil covered my sight. I groped around the unfamiliar area where I'd passed out. My heart fluttered and panic clawed at my throat. I crawled forward and tried to feel for something. Anything.

The soft threads of a carpet met my hands as I scurried aimlessly until I caught the corner of a solid piece of furniture across my forehead.

It cleared my thoughts. I sat back to squat on my heels and pressed my hands to the bump on my head. My poor brain throbbed in time with the hammering elves but the pain over-road the panic.

I gave up the bottle over a year ago. What the hell caused me to fall off the wagon? After a few deep breaths I blinked my eyes to make sure they were really open. Damn. The darkness sat heavy on my shoulders. This wasn't a hangover. I'd been drinking tea not alcohol. Why did I feel so horrid? A vision of a handsome freckled face came back to me. I'd been at Rurik's hideout. We'd been in his bedroom. The memory of Rurik's last words stung and I flinched. He'd scared me and I ran. It all came back, my opening the door, the stranger, and the drug soaked cloth.

Primal instinct prey had to sense danger awoke in me. I needed to get out of here. One inch at a time I explored the space surrounding me. I felt my way around what must be a sofa when I saw a faint line of pale light that traced along the floor. It looked like the bottom edge of a door.

Angels sang in my soul and rose up in a chorus of joy. I could see something. After I scrambled to it, the doorknob refused to budge as I wrenched it.

A deep, low chuckle rolled over the room. It came from behind me and sent an ice cold-jolt down my spine. I spun and stood, pressing my back to the locked door, ready to face whoever hid in the dark.

Light from an igniting match flared within a set of long, red nails. Those well-manicured hands lit an oil lamp and adjusted the flame.

My eyes adjusted to the light and my heart skipped a beat.

Lizzy sat at a small square table, the oil lamp next to her. Her long auburn hair pulled tight into a French twist. The flicker of shadows played on her stern face and a set of tarot cards lay face up in front of her. She smiled and exposed her fangs.

"Hello, Rabbit." She gestured to a chair across the table from her. "Would you like me to read your fortune?"

I didn't need the tarot cards for that. Pain and death looked inevitable with Lizzy. "Do I have a choice?"

"We can skip the pleasantries if you wish." Her smile widened.

I made myself walk slowly to the table and take a seat so as not to appear eager to please her. If we skipped the pleasantries I feared we'd go straight to the real reason she brought me here. Dinner. A cold sweat trickled down the side of my face. I wiped the beads that formed on my forehead with my sleeve.

On the table, the tarot cards sat face up in a cross shape. They were pretty to look at. Each had an individual colorful picture. Lizzy traced a bright painted nail around the card closest to her.

"What do you want with me?" I took pride in the fact my voice sounded confident, even though she made me as nervous as a rabbit in a fox den.

She admired the card. "I would think that is obvious." Then she lifted it to show me, a knight who brandished a sword while he rode a warhorse. "Rurik." With a swift flip of her wrist she turned the card and stared at it. "Strange, he used to be represented by the Page of Swords in my readings. Recently, he comes up as the Prince of Swords. He's grown since I've met him."

Lizzy set it down next to a card with a skeleton dressed in a suit of armor and pointed at it. "This card has begun to appear with Rurik's recently."

Something clenched my heart. "The death card?" I glanced up at her sparkling emerald eyes.

She nodded. "That's what the modern world calls it, but that's not what it truly means. This combination of cards represents something connected with Rurik is certain to come to an end."

"That's rather vague. It's probably his car."

She laughed. "Under different circumstances, I think I would have liked you." The laugh and smile faded. Her eyes narrowed as she pointed at two other cards, one of a woman holding a chalice and the other of a wheel. "This set appeared three days ago. I have discerned the Queen of Cups is you, Rabbit. The Wheel of Fortune has been following you."

"What does that mean?"

"You are approaching one of those moments in life when fate takes a hand in your affairs. Strange coincidences, fortunate meetings, and lucky breaks can all shape your destiny." Her eyes burned with zealous belief. "Too bad I plan to change all that."

I swallowed hard. Destinies were for heroes, not for lost souls. Although I'd had my share of strange these past few days, I couldn't believe what she said. Fortune telling belonged in fun fairs. Lizzy's parlor didn't resemble anything fun.

The other cards puzzled me and I scratched my head, causing my loose curls to tangle, while I looked at them. A devil card sat in the center of the cross with what looked like a King carrying swords. Below them a card showed a naked couple holding hands.

"This—" she lifted it "—is why I brought you here. The Lovers."

So, she'd already heard. I barely crawled out of his bed and the vampire witch knew. It never once occurred to me I'd have issues with Lizzy if I got involved with Rurik. She made her desires for him at the party clear but she also expressed her preference for Dragos. It didn't matter. Rurik hated me, anyhow.

I shifted my sight from The Lovers. A hollow space expanded from my heart and encompassed me at the thought of losing him. Am I really just going to let him go so easily? I deserved to lose him if I didn't ever try to win him back.

"I've heard Rurik has taken an unhealthy interest in you."

I glared at her. "Unhealthy?"

"Rabbit." She tsked. "How long before your mercenary friends find out about your relationship and destroy him?"

I blinked. Colby's clandestine skills were slipping. Then again, Tane could have told her his plans. I shrugged. "I'm protecting him until I can prove his innocence."

She gave a low chuckle. "Not very well. The location of Rurik's 'hide out' at Marie's home will be leaked out for your friends. They'll be too angry to care who it comes from."

A cold claw of fear clenched my spine. "Why?" I whispered.

"They'll be so upset after finding your broken, empty body."

The claw tightened and my mouth went dry. I scanned the dim room for an escape but I couldn't see past the nimbus of pale light from the oil lamp.

As if reading my mind she reached over and clamped my wrist in her red painted talons, preventing me from flight. "Naturally, they'll assume Rurik drained you of your life's blood." She pulled my arm and drew me against the table's edge, closer to her face. "In their fury they will slaughter his whole clan."

Her grip held me like iron and my hand went numb. "I thought you wanted to keep him safe." My mind raced over the methods of killing a vampire. I could stab her with a wooden stake but I'd have to break a piece of furniture to get it. The strength needed to pound one through a vampire's chest was considerable and I didn't think I could do it.

Lizzy yanked me to my knees by the table. The cards fluttered to the ground in a rain of large confetti as our arms swept them from the surface. She loomed over me in her thigh high, black leather stiletto boots. Her black silk blouse shone with the flame light. "I will swoop in to save my darling. He will be distraught and vulnerable with the destruction of his people at your hands, Rabbit. I wonder what level of pain he'll experience when he finds out you were the bait planted by these mercenaries."

More methods of monster killing ran through my thoughts. I'd been told with enough faith a holy item could vanquish a vampire, but I didn't have either. The pain increased as her hand applied crushing pressure on the bones in my wrist. I couldn't hold in the moan it caused. "He already knows." I gritted through my teeth.

Her grip lessened. "What?"

"I said, he already knows." Though her squeezing eased, the pain continued and I choked on a sob. I wouldn't give her the satisfaction of making me cry. "He found out just before you kidnapped me, Lizzy."

"Why should I believe you?" She tangled her fingers into my hair and snapped my head back. "And that's *Mistress Elizabeth* to you," she hissed with her face inches from mine.

"I have pictures that placed him at a mass murder. He discovered them in my suitcase. He knows I played a part in the attack at the party and hates me for it."

She smiled and laughed. The scent of decayed blood floated from her mouth, I gagged at the putrid stench. Her iron hold on my wrist disappeared as she hugged herself, bent over with laughter.

Even though emotionally I felt scattered, my mind cut through the fear and panic like a sharp ax. I focused on the locked door while I stumbled to it. My left wrist could move but in agonizing jerks. When I examined the locking mechanism I saw it needed a key to open.

"How did you ever get those pictures?" She wiped a tear from her eye.

I twisted and leaned against the door, my sore wrist cradled in my right hand. "I'll tell you if you give me the key to this door."

She fingered a chain that hung on her neck, the key dangled between her breasts. "Come and get it."

"*Lizzy*, are you making a pass? I'm really not attracted to crazy."

Her smile turned feral. She turned the knob on the oil lamp to increase the flame and lit the room then sauntered to a desk in the far corner by the window. Thick red drapes blocked the view to outside, and inside the top drawer she pulled out a thin stack of photos.

Suddenly, I felt foolish for ever believing in those cursed pictures Colby gave me. The flame flickered in the lamp. I should have burned them.

Lizzy returned to the table, shadows played on her face and helped me remember another way to rid myself of a bitch vampire. She wanted to steal Rurik, kill his coven, and worst of all murder me. If this worked, there'd be no regrets. If.

I approached the table as she displayed the images face up. They were duplicates of the ones in the manila envelope, except no Rurik. A different vampire replaced him. "I don't understand. Why frame him for this massacre?"

"Dragos hates Rurik and everything he represents with a passion. Your band of mercenaries wouldn't take the contract without proof of some kind of misdeed. Dragos had the pictures made and then Tane's pet, Eric, convinced them one of the dead girls was his daughter." She chuckled. "Vampire slayers hired by vampires to do their dirty work. Quite poetic, even for Dragos."

"He had those people slaughtered just for that. Why didn't he just go after Rurik himself?"

"You do not understand our politics. Rurik has a great deal of supporters. If Dragos were foolish enough to kill him, it would cause an uprising. All those centuries of power gone for one little city."

"I take it Dragos is more than an Overlord."

"Oh yes, he rules them all." She swept my hair from my face and tucked it behind my ear. It gave me the creeps. "Don't worry your pretty, little head. I'll take care of Rurik. Once his clan is destroyed, he'll be powerless and Dragos will let me keep him."

I couldn't stand the way she spoke of Rurik. It made him sound like a pet. My blood boiled at the thought this dominating witch touching him. She reached for me again but I stepped back. "Why did Dragos attack Rurik's original lair two nights ago?"

"He did what?" She growled. "That impatient fool! No wonder Rurik hides in Marie's home. No matter, Rabbit. I will see if you taste as sweet as Dragos dreamed you would."

Before she moved, I lifted the oil lamp from the

table and smashed it at her feet. Her eyes widened when the oil splashed on her legs and caught fire. The flames spread up her limbs with forest fire speed. Her ear splitting screeches filled the room as did a foul, rotten smell.

I pressed my hands to my ears and back peddled to the far wall. Heat scorched my skin and smoke choked my lungs. The fire ate at the furniture as Lizzy flailed around the room. I could have planned this better. Instead of being eaten by her, I'd burn with her.

She managed to tangle herself in the long thick red drapes behind the table. They flashed into an inferno that licked the ceiling. She cried out again and burst through the window pulling the curtain with her. She didn't fall very far. The room sat on the first floor.

I grabbed what remained of the scorched pictures and climbed out after her.

She flailed on the ground but her movements became weaker.

I allowed myself a moment of satisfaction as I watched Mistress Elizabeth, Wicked Bitch of the West, burn.

Shouts from inside the house startled me out of my dark pleasure. I ran across the garden, clutching the original pictures. Branches caught at my red t-shirt as I pushed between some thick bushes surrounding Lizzy's property. At least my jeans protected me from scratches. The busy street was visible through the hedge. I needed to make things right for Rurik.

My mind raced with excitement, I finally had the

evidence to prove his innocence. Who should I go to first? Colby, to stop any further attacks, or Rurik, to try and win him back?

CHAPTER EIGHTEEN

I ran through the busy streets disoriented as to where I was. Cars passed me and one honked when I stumbled too close to the road. The Buda Castle stood on the hill to my left, which meant the river would be east of me. I continued running, afraid one of Lizzy's minions would follow. Smells of spiced food drifted from the many restaurants between the storefronts. The late evening traffic clogged the boulevards as I got further from her estates.

My breath came in painful heaves with each step. I didn't know how many blocks I ran but it felt like I'd done a marathon. A bench invited me over to take a rest. I needed to stop and gather my thoughts.

No one caught me yet so I assumed Lizzy's people

too busy with the fire to wonder about me. They would need to regroup after the loss of their leader. I smiled in satisfaction at the memory. Happy her plans to murder me and destroy Rurik's clan had backfired.

The smell of smoke clung to the pictures still clutched in my hand, their edges singed in the initial blaze. I laid them on my lap and tried to flatten out the crinkles. They clearly showed someone else instead of Rurik. He looked similar but couldn't compare to Rurik's beauty.

Colby needed to see them. I hoped to convince him to decline the contract on Rurik's existence and switch it to double-crossing-rat-bastard Tane, if not Dragos himself. Colby wasn't a greedy man, justice would compensate for the monetary loss. There were no human laws that governed the paranormal world, so he elected himself to do it. Once he knew Rurik is innocent of the crime, he won't kill him. I knew how Colby worked.

Rurik needed to see the pictures too. Not so much for the images but that I got them for him. I wanted him to forgive me and trust me. He had to believe in me again. How would he react when I told him where I got the pictures and why Lizzy had them? I grimaced. And that I killed her?

He never expressed any affection for her.

A bus pulled in front of me. The door opened and the driver stared at me. I shook my head, even if I knew where to go I didn't have a cent on me. My wallet sat on Rurik's bedroom floor. This situation would have been my biggest nightmare a few days ago but after tonight, it was a cake walk.

Initially, I wanted to go to Rurik but my insides still felt tender and sore from our last conversation. If I knew for sure this could make things right between us I wouldn't hesitate to go to him first but I didn't know. It made more sense to find Colby and call off any further attacks. The least I could do was make sure Rurik stayed alive regardless of what became of us.

One of the wonderful things about Budapest was the abundance of pay phones. I scanned the area while I rested on the bench. Across the street and down half a block I spotted a pink phone stand.

It'd been years since I'd had to panhandle but the technique was simple. Locate a john and ask. Begging put food on my plate when things got rough after my grandma died and the landlord kicked me out of our rent-controlled apartment. I could always find some guy who wanted to play my hero. It was a gift. I had a good sense of character—I think this helped me be good bait. A big percentage of men would try to take advantage of the situation but it didn't take long for me to spot the right kind of gentlemen.

With my sweetest smile pasted on my face, I approached him. "Excuse me, sir. Do you speak English?"

He looked a little over fifty with some gray at his temples. It didn't touch the rest of his short black hair. The warm weather made it cozy enough for him to wear a short sleeve button down shirt with his black slacks.

He raised one thick eyebrow and shook his head.

Of course not. Only I, Colby's gang, and the vampires seemed to speak English. I pulled out my empty pockets and pretended to talk on the phone then rubbed my fingers together in the universal sign for moula.

He reached for his back pocket while laughing and offered me some change. The coins filled my hands, he gave me enough to make a few calls.

I placed them in my pockets and shook his hand. "Kosomo."

He nodded and as he passed behind me grabbed my ass.

I don't know what got me angrier, the squeak I made or my lack of judgment.

He winked and continued on his way. At least I had some cash. What's a little ass pinch in exchange for a life saving telephone call?

The phone was a short jog away. I dialed Colby's number. It rang, and rang, and rang. Finally a computerized voice answered to inform me to leave a message. Dang. "It's Connie. Don't kill Rurik, I have something to show you." The phone clicked as I hung up.

He always answered his phone. A shiver ran through me from head to toe. My grandma told me shivers like that meant someone just walked over my grave.

What could he be doing? Visions of Colby attacking Rurik's peaceful people wreaked havoc on my shot nerves.

I couldn't contact Rurik, I never had his number. Even the location of his home was vague. My heart raced again. I didn't know what to do. So much miscommunication and deceit would destroy the bud of change which bloomed in my soul. I didn't want to lose my hope. It brought me happiness, something I'd forgotten existed.

Only one other person in Budapest carried a cell phone whose number I knew. The thought of how angry he would be made me cringe. He would help, I could depend on him. Once he finished yelling.

I dialed his number and he answered after the first ring.

"What?"

"Red?"

CHAPTER NINETEEN

"Connie," Red growled over the phone. "You didn't board the plane. I told Colby we should have checked you out of that hotel ourselves."

Pieces of loose cement piled at the foot the phone stand. I toed one around. "I couldn't leave." Red wouldn't understand my falling for a vampire. Not just any vampire at that, but the one we set out to hunt and execute. My first hurdle would be to convince him of Rurik's innocence.

"Yeah, apparently Colby knows you too well."

"What do you mean?" I forgot my cement toy and stared hard at the phone as if I could see Red's pockmarked face through it.

"When you gonna learn? Colby's always a step

ahead. He planted a tracker on you in case you did somethin' like this. So we can watch over you and keep you safe."

"When? How?" I gasped. "That cold bastard didn't come to my hotel room to check on me. He came to plant that damn tracker." *Keep me safe, my ass.* He wanted to follow me to Rurik's lair. Use me like bait without me knowing and I led him straight to Marie's house. Pressure built inside my head from the molten anger bubbling.

"Nothin' would have made us happier if you just got on that plane and gone home like you were supposed to."

"Red." The fury in my voice could have melted the phone. "You have a blind spot when it comes to Colby." Pedestrians passing by gave me more space as my voice grew louder. "He doesn't want to keep me safe, you granny-humping butt sucker! He wants Rurik. Why would you let him trick me like that?"

"'Cause I care. You're runnin' around with a killer, baby. He's done somethin' to your mind."

"I sure needed your help a few minutes ago when the queen of the crazies wanted to suck me dry." I leaned my head against the phone suddenly tired. A few hours sleep and one meal wasn't enough if I kept this pace. "Please, tell me you haven't mobilized on Rurik's home." They used me. Rurik trusted me and took me home to protect me then I repay him by having Colby knock at his front door.

"Queen of the what? You tellin' me you're not in

the house?"

"No, damn it, aren't you tracking me? I've got important information for Colby and can't reach him."

"Tracker's planted on your suitcase, not you. He's not answerin' his phone?" I could picture Red scratching his chin.

"Red, tell me what's going on."

"We're only watchin' Rurik's place."

I closed my eyes in relief.

"Colby got a lead on one of the *Nosferatu*. He's checkin' it out."

I groaned, my relief short lived. Which one? He shouldn't go anywhere near them. "I need help, Red. Can you come get me?"

He sighed. "You're about to complicate things, aren't you?"

"Yeah, pick me up something to eat on the way. I'm starving."

"Where are you?"

Excellent question, I still didn't know.

"You've got no clue, do you?"

"No."

"Pass the phone to someone around you."

I scanned the area. "They're all Hungarian."

"How surprisin' considerin' what country your standin' in."

"You speak Hungarian?"

"I exercise the muscle between my ears as well. You should try it out sometime. Now get a person who's not drunk on the damn phone."

I got a middle-aged woman to speak to Red. It gave me time to examine the thing poking me from the back of my mind. Why didn't Colby answer his phone? I hoped he stayed out of trouble.

Red flipped through the pictures. He sat in the driver's seat of his parked non-nondescript white van and used the steering wheel as a desk. I ate *langos*, a foccacia-like bread, with tuna topping and plum dumplings as fast as I could without choking. I averaged one meal per day since my encounter with Rurik at the club. A few pounds lost wouldn't hurt but I could think of better ways to diet than running for my life and starving.

Red's brows furrowed as he bought one close to his face and used a pen light to see better since the street lights barely reached inside the cab. "Are you sure this ain't him?"

"Oh course, give me that." I grabbed the photo from his hand to take another look. "This isn't him. His chin is too round and shoulders too narrow. Look past the hair and suit, that's not his face." I tossed in on the sun-faded dash.

"I've never seen him up close. Not like you have." He grinned at me, wagging his eyebrows up and down.

"I sure hope not, I don't like to share." A horrid image of Red with Rurik in bed turned my stomach full of *langos* and plums. If this made me puke in his van then Red deserved it.

"I'm sure you don't."

An urge to punch the smug grin off his face almost overwhelmed me. I hated that he made me blush. Not like my wimpy strike would hurt his solid rock head. "I want to show these to Colby and stop any further action against Rurik."

"Baby, listen to me." He touched my shoulder and leaned in to face me, concern evident in his eyes. "Did it occur to you *these* pictures could be the fakes?"

"No." I searched my soul for any doubt but found none. "I believe he's innocent. What more evidence do you need?"

He sighed and scratched his chin.

"Red, why would Lizzy have them if they were fake?"

"My thoughts exactly, why did she give them to you if she wanted to frame Rurik for your murder? I'm just askin' you to look at this in an objective manner."

"She didn't give them to me. I took them from her. She used them gloat at my ignorance. Rurik had the opportunity to kill me a few times. Instead he's helped me. I trust him."

He stared at me a moment longer. "Okay then."

I hugged him as relief made me limp. The anxiety and stress of the last few days seemed more bearable now that Red would help me.

"Yeah but you gotta convince the boss. Once I can reach him." He handed me the thin stack of pictures. "Why do you smell like smoke?"

"I barbecued my first vampire." There should have

been fireworks and confetti but all I got was his glare.

"Tell me the rest."

"At Dragos' party I met a vampire named Elizabeth. She had a thing for Rurik so she snatched me from his place and tried to kill me. Her plan was to frame Rurik for my death so you guys would storm his home and kill his people. She'd save Rurik and keep him for herself."

"We guys? As in the troops? She knew about us?"

I nodded.

He hit the steering wheel. "Shit, how?"

It seemed like everyone knew about us but Rurik. So much for being a covert operations team, our time in Budapest was up. Tane knew about us, hell he hired us, and Dragos ordered him to do it. Once they found out about Lizzy, we were dead.

A chill ran through me. Dragos, Lizzy, and Tane were a storm of headaches. "We're in trouble," I whispered. "They're going to come after us."

Red dialed a number on his cell phone then hit the steering wheel again. "Still no answer. Colby was checkin' out somethin' on the *Nosferatu*. He said you told him not to trust his contact so he started a deeper investigation on him. It led to the one named Tane."

A small weight lifted from my shoulders. Finally, he found out who really hired us. My relief was short lived as I realized that I might have inadvertently sent Colby to his death. The weight fell back onto me and it felt heavier.

"You don't seem surprised." Red twisted in his seat

to face me.

"I'm not. What do we do now?" In the grand scheme of things the pictures were a small victory. Colby was missing and we would have *Nosferatu* hunting us soon. "We should warn the others to get out of town." I proved Rurik's innocence, my obligations to him were finished.

My heart ached with loss. If we could have had some time, without chaos and schemes, our relationship would have been nice. I still wanted that.

"You knew his contact to be a *Nosferatu* and didn't tell us?"

"Red." I poured a plea for mercy in his name. Tane's blackmail tied my hands behind my back. Or not. It sounded like the vampires would come after us anyway, especially with Colby missing. Tane just lost his leverage with me. Red and I stared at each other. "I couldn't at the time. Tane's been blackmailing me with the team's lives. He's the one who hired us and he wanted me to inform him of our actions."

"That's the secret you've been keepin'?"

I nodded and glanced out of the van's windshield.

"Hired by a bloodsucker. I'll call and warn the team but we don't leave people behind. We wait and search for Colby first." He started the van. "We also need to speak to Rurik." The van revved as he stuck it in drive and pressed the gas. We were out of the parking lot before what he said registered.

"Why?"

"He's more than just a hunk, Connie. He's

Overlord of Budapest and has a lot of resources. Ever hear the sayin', 'The enemy of my enemy is my friend.'? Sounds like we have a common enemy. Those *Nosferatu* know about us and I don't think they plan on being our friends. Maybe you can convince him to back us up."

"Uh, Red. That may not be the best idea." I held on to the van's dashboard as he took a corner then snatched at the seatbelt and buckled myself in. "He's upset with me, Evel Knievel."

He glanced at me. "Whatcha do?"

"He found the pictures Colby gave me in my suitcase. Then put two and two together to figure out I'd been used as bait. That we were hired to kill him." The words tumbled out as I spoke. It came out so fast I wondered if he understood.

I could see he rolled his eyes by the reflection in the windshield. He understood. "How much does he know about our operations?" His voice rumbled with irritation. Red used to be a drill Sergeant in the army and had great control over his vocal cords.

"I never really got the chance to explain anything."

"What about the rest?" He stopped for a traffic light, almost kissing fenders with the car ahead of us.

"There's more?"

"That you love him."

"I barely know him."

He chuckled. "You're a piece of work, ya know. You've lied for him, proved his innocence, then killed his mistress."

"She wasn't his mistress!"

"You're in love." He sped up with the green light.

The last thing I wanted to talk about with Red was my feelings.

Traffic thinned and buildings got further apart, we'd left the city. Rurik's neighborhood drew closer and my anxiety level rocketed. "This is a terrible idea." Red didn't hear my whisper over the roar of the van's engine.

"Sounds like you two need counselin'."

"You offering?" I cracked a small smile his way.

He barked a laugh. "If I had a death wish I'd go shark hunting in a chum bathing suit."

I laughed and it felt good. My redheaded grizzly bear had a wonderful knack for that. Colby may be the brains of the outfit but Red was the glue that kept it together.

We pulled into the long driveway and parked behind the rust bucket. My laughter died.

CHAPTER TWENTY

Marie wrapped herself around me when she opened the door. She mumbled incoherent Hungarian things then drew us into one of the sitting rooms, all the while calling out for Rurik.

"What happened to you? We were so worried. Who was that man who carried you off? Rurik has sent everyone out to find you and it's left us defense—"

"Enough, Marie." Rurik's quiet voice silenced her. He drank me in with his eyes from across the room as he stood in the doorway. The light reflected off his black untidy hair. Even after the fight at the party he'd maintained an impeccable appearance. In a few strides he'd crossed the room, almost too quick to see, and lifted me to his lips. He consumed me with his kiss.

My spirit soared to be in his arms again. I dropped the pictures and ran my fingers through his silken hair to pull him closer. All my reservations about him shattered. Who was I trying to fool? I loved him.

He pressed his tongue into my mouth to taste me in lazy sweeps. A deep moan vibrated in his chest.

"I guess you two don't need a counselor."

Rurik jerked away from our kiss. His moan turned into a growl as he twisted to set me down behind him, barring me from Red. With preternatural speed he snagged Red off the floor by his shirtfront. "Was this the slayer who stole you from me?" Red hung a foot from the floor and dangled from Rurik's grip as if he weighed like a child. He'd paled so his freckles stood out.

"Put me down." The order snapped with the expert confidence being a drill Sergeant gave you. "I didn't come here to fight."

"No, you came to stake me."

"A few hours ago I would have gladly done it but Connie's changed my mind."

Rurik twisted to glare at me. "How can you bring this here?" He shook Red with his last question. "You said you believed me."

"I do and I can prove but not if you hurt Red. Put him down."

His body tensed as he fought with indecision. I asked him to trust me after all I did so far betrayed him. Our decision to come here was a mistake. Red should have listened to me.

"Show him the pictures already, Connie, before this gets messy." Red grasped at the arm that held him for balance.

I touched my tormented lover's shoulder. "He's a friend and wants to help. Please."

He stared at me. Questions formed in his eyes and for the first time I saw doubt. It made me want to cry but he released Red. After all my secrets and a possible murder attempt he still wanted to believe in me. I hoped to earn it one day.

I retrieved one of the fallen pictures scattered around us and showed him. "The photos in my suitcase are altered. These are the originals."

He didn't even look at it. "I know the pictures were fake. I wish you didn't need proof."

His comment hurt me even more by stabbing me in the heart. Things between us were not forgiven after all. A relationship built on lies never had a chance.

I pointed at Red as I rounded on Rurik. "How do you expect me to convince them to stop hunting you? I've had faith in you since the bathhouse."

His expression softened. "You're trying to protect me?"

I rolled my eyes and crossed my arms. Why did I bother? He had a pretty face and a sexy body? Or was it for his tenacity to cling to an old rusted car because he loved it. That he built a happy clan that didn't prey on human kind but embraced it. Maybe the way he teased me and made me laugh.

"Ah hell. Stop bein' an idiot. Connie's been breakin'

all the rules tryin' to help you. She cares about you and you care about her. We've got proof you're innocent and are willing to make a truce. A fresh start for everyone." Red's cell phone buzzed. He pulled it from his pocket. "What?" He walked away to concentrate on whoever spoke.

I examined my worn running shoes. "I'm sorry." Nothing I said would express how much. I met his stare. "I really am."

The safety of his arms as he wrapped me in a hug felt divine after the turmoil of the last twenty-four hours. I closed my eyes and melted to his hard body.

He sighed. "A new start."

"We all made up now?" Red stood with his feet apart, cell phone crushed in one fist. "Great. Can you help us out? Looks like we've got ourselves caught up in a *Nosferatu* power struggle. I don't think any of us will survive this unless we make an alliance. Dragos is trying to kill you and it won't be long before he comes after us." He shook his head. "I can't believe I just said that. They were a myth until two days ago."

Rurik eyed Red, his arms slipped from my shoulders. "They need to remain myth. Do you understand? For your own safety."

Red nodded. "Don't spill the beans."

"They would discredit you then destroy you. Not just Dragos, but any of his kind. They guard their secrets well and have millennia of experience doing it."

I could see Red swallow.

"You wanted to offer me an alliance?" Rurik crossed

his arms over his chest and faced Red. "What could I gain from this?"

"Any intel we obtain and extra hands to fight. We'll also do our best to keep you in power."

"I want the original and forged pictures."

Red bent down and gathered some of the photos then stuffed them in Rurik's hand. "Done, what else?"

Rurik turned his head toward me.

"She's not for sale."

"Red!"

"I'm not makin' you stay if you don't wanna."

"I didn't imply for you to give her to me, only not to stop her if she chooses to stay."

Tired of fooling myself, I reached up on tiptoe and planted a soft kiss on his cheek as my answer.

Rurik scowled at Red, daring him to object but Red nodded to us.

"One more thing, I don't want any hunting of my clan. If you gain proof of their misdeeds, give it to me. I keep my own house."

"I can't speak for Colby but I'll do my best to convince him." He stuffed his cell phone in his pocket. "I'll gather the troops and bring them here. We've misplaced our boss. He was following a *Nosferatu* lead. Can you help us locate him?"

"I will make some inquires. We can defend ourselves better together but I will fight only against Dragos and his men. No others."

CHAPTER TWENTY-ONE

Marie escorted Red out of the house. Before the front door closed Rurik snatched me off my feet and embraced me. His kiss made all my aches and pains disappear.

Dizzy and short of breath, I held his shoulders when he set me down on my feet. The man could make a statue's knees wobble if he tried.

"You smell like smoke." He leaned his forehead against mine and closed his eyes. "Rabbit." The way he said my name, like he cherished it, melted any of my reservations that remained of his affection. "I'd never ... I would have..." He sighed. "I should never have chased you out."

I touched his pain-filled face. "You had good reason

to be angry. I kept a lot of secrets." This admission felt good. It helped me heal, allowed my wounds to scar over. Our relationship might have a chance at becoming something real. I'd been hollow and alone for so long and had nothing to lose until now. Maybe this would help me find what I wanted, a place to belong.

Yet, I still had secrets.

Tane still wanted the drug. It warred with my desire to be honest with Rurik, all for a stupid vial of mouthwash looking liquid. Maybe I could use it to get him to help us defend against Dragos.

He opened his eyes to gaze with worry into mine. "What happened to you? Who was brave enough to take you from my doorstep? This won't go unpunished, I promise."

I stepped out of the circle of his arms. Afraid once he heard of what I'd done to Lizzy he'd crush me. "Lizzy implemented it."

His eyes flared. "The audacity, she's overstepped her rights. She's a guest in my city." He paced as his voice rose. "Why do I tolerate that woman? She's always meddling-"

I stepped in front of him.

"Rabbit?"

"I smell like smoke because I set her on fire." I cringed expecting an explosion.

His feet stayed planted to the floor, his eyes stunned. "You did what?"

I explained her plans for murder and extortion. It poured from me like a river. "The original pictures came from her as well. She helped Dragos kill these people and frame you." I kicked at one of the pictures on the floor. "So I threw an oil lamp at her when she attacked me and she went up like a Roman candle. Furthermore," I poked him in the chest, "Tane's an ass, he's not your friend, and I'm sure he's trying to kill you too." I had to catch my breath.

As I ranted a huge grin developed on his face. "None of that surprises me, except you managed to escape unscathed."

"Why would that surprise you?" I stepped closer and stuck my face in his. "You expect Lizzy to be a murderous traitor and Tane to betray you but you're shocked that I can defend myself?" I poked his chest again. "I may be a girl but I can fight when cornered."

"It has to do with you being human." He ran his hands up and down my arms. "I appreciate you being a woman." He leered at me. "You're so hot, especially now." By the intensity of his stare, I didn't think he meant my body temperature. He leaned in until his lips found mine and assailed me with a wild hunger. It blew his last kiss out of the water, but no amount of sexy male flesh would cool my temper.

The frustration of being ordered and pushed around by egotistical, crazed vampires the past few days culminated. I struggled in Rurik's grasp but he wouldn't let me loose.

His hands held me to him in an iron grip.

So I bit him.

He cried out and shoved me away. A spot of blood

formed on his lip before he wiped it. When he saw it on the back of his hand, his eyes ignited with passion. He stepped forward and caught me in his arm then threw me over his shoulder with one hand.

I kicked out and pounded on his back. This caveman attitude turned me on, damn it. A thin line existed between passion and fury and mine just got real blurry. It's not what I wanted.

When we reached his room he dropped me on the bed.

I used the momentum of the bounce to roll and climb to my knees. Rurik stood by the edge of the bed, hair messed, cold blue eyes inflamed, and his bottom lip starting to swell. He'd never looked more delicious. I slid my fingers in his waistband and unbuttoned his jeans.

"What are you doing?" His voice held a hint of teasing as he stared at my hands in playful bewilderment.

"Shut up and get undressed." I lifted his shirt over his head and didn't need to order him twice. With centuries of practice Rurik stripped in seconds. His body was ready for me.

He bent forward to claim me but I leaned away. "Did I tell you to do that?"

The wicked grin he gave me made his lip bleed again. "No, Ma'am." But he crawled onto the bed anyway. "You're overdressed, Rabbit." He grabbed my ankle in an attempt to tug my jeans off.

The rough handling pissed me off. I'd remove my clothes when I was good and ready. In a twisted way, his attitude made me wet yet furious at myself for responding to it. I kicked at his hand but missed.

This only made him smile wider. The button on my pants snapped with a flick of his fingers then slipped off as if made of silk when he yanked. He gathered the edges of my panties in his large hands and slipped them from my hips.

"I chased you from this room because I feared I'd hurt you. It's been a long time since I lost control of myself." His fingers traced the collar of my t-shirt. "No more secrets from you, no more lies." With a single motion he tore it to the hem exposing my bra.

I struggled to crawl away. Not from fear, I wanted more control of the situation and didn't trust myself to not succumb to him, but he held me in place at the hips.

He leaned down to give me a more intimate kiss between my legs. The silken touch of his tongue made me writhe in his clutches as he licked me slow, as if savoring me like an ice cream cone. My anger should have faded but it didn't. I wanted to be free and I wanted control. He took those away from me, everyone had.

"Let me go."

His inflamed, dark stare caught my breath. "No," Rurik stated in a voice that held a tone I'd never heard him use. A thin line of a growl trickled from his throat as he bent to suckle.

The lightning shock of pleasure shot straight to my brain and overloaded my intelligence. Only a wanton beast remained pinned to the bed, a slave to his ministrations. I let him have my body.

He pressed his mouth deeper in me and drew harder until my cries stopped. I lay panting as he knelt next to me and reached for my bra. His cock pressed against his abdomen, hard and thick, ready with need.

I'd had enough of being prey. He wasn't the only one who knew his way around a bed. Power came with sex and I could wield it. Before things went any further I rolled over and licked his hard shaft from base to tip.

The sound of a sharp intake of breath told me of his surprise and pleasure.

No more taking orders from Colby, no more scolding from Red, and definitely no more pushing around by vampires. Rurik might be angry with me, but I was furious at the world. In a matter of days, my life had been turned inside out, my soul scrubbed raw, and my body battered.

I swallowed his cock whole and showed him no mercy. He was mine and I claimed him. My nails dug into the tender flesh of his ass and he cried out. From pain or ecstasy, I didn't care. I paced a hard, fast rhythm and didn't allow him a moment's reprieve. When I could taste his climax approaching I pulled away.

"Rabbit." The groan of my pet name was filled with yearning.

I kneeled to face him.

The chilling hunger in his stare fired my own lust. His skin felt smooth and firm under my hands as I touched his neck, his shoulders, then his chest.

He pulled me close.

"No." I whispered my command. "Lay on your back."

The expression on his face, as if contemplating his options, made me remember who and what I tried to boss. He gave me a small smirk and stretched across the bed with his arms behind his head. Despite his experience in politics, the Overlord tried in vain to intimidate me with that little smirk. All six feet of sexy, male flesh waited for my pleasure.

The emotional wave of anger drove me. He may be the Seducer of Budapest but I planned to break him of that role. I told the truth when I said I didn't share well with others. Rurik was mine now.

The remains of my t-shirt fell from my shoulders. Smudges of soot from the fire spotted my hands and now even I could smell the smoke trapped in my curls.

I held his gaze as I crawled on the bed up his legs and paused at his inner thighs to nibble at his tender tasty bits. Once again he tried to reach for me but I stopped my explorations until his hand returned behind his head accompanied by a frustrated growl. I smiled.

He allowed this charade of dominance. I wasn't a fool. It must be tiresome to have to lead all the time.

I slipped him inside after mounting his hips and rocked with a slow deliberate pace. His encouraging sweet moans fed my desire. I unclasped my bra, the last piece of cloth between us and let it fall from my shoulders. His eyes followed my hands as I caressed my body. It ignited not only him but me as well.

He matched my rhythm even though I could tell he wanted more.

As I licked around his nipple the little nub hardened. It elicited more encouraging noises from him.

"Bite." The word almost got lost in the midst of his other sounds. It only made sense that a vampire would like biting.

So I bit down, hard.

His back arched as his hands clenched the pillow.

I clung to him as his hips rose from the bed to beat in time with my growing needs. The pressure of an orgasm built but I could see in his face he still wanted more. I stretched out along his body and offered him what he wanted.

My neck.

A cry, seeming more creature than man, escaped him as he rolled us, pulled my head back and sank his fangs into me. No mind fog to distract me this time, so the sharp pain mingled with the climax. His cool lips pressed against my flesh as some of my warmth spilled into him. He continued to thrust as he fed until he brought both of us to completion.

Strong and all encompassing, Rurik's arms were the perfect resting place. I could have stayed there forever. He traced the bite mark I'd left around his aureole and chuckled.

"Nice."

"You're welcome."

He kissed the top of my head. "It's very promising. We've much to explore."

A loud crash from the downstairs interrupted my response. It sounded like the front door being battered down. I tumbled from his arms as Rurik opened the bedroom door before I even knew he'd moved.

I followed at my slower mortal speed.

He turned to me. "I love you." His lips pressed to mine in a quick impassioned kiss. "Forgive me."

"What—" A sharp pain across my jaw caught me by surprise then everything went black.

CHAPTER TWENTY-TWO

A coffin held me captive, bent in a fetal position and shoved inside its confines. The muscle in my back knotted strong enough to wake me up. Darkness blinded and confused me. My head bumped against the lid as I flashed back to waking at Lizzy's place. I could almost hear her shuffle her tarot cards.

My heart raced and my head felt split in two. Short of breath and a little shaky I pushed the top open and crawled out. I sat on the floor in Rurik's bedroom beside his now partially empty trunk, not a freaking coffin. His stuff lay scattered in the middle of the room, as if thrown there, but blended in well with all the other junk he left lying around.

Worse than anything else, my jaw ached. He must

have cold cocked me and stuffed me in the trunk. Why? I hoped this wasn't a kinky game. His excuse had better be good because I might change my mind and stake him myself.

The bedroom door hung at an angle as if kicked in. Maybe this wasn't a game after all. What happened while I lay unconscious? The room didn't have a window so I couldn't tell the time of day.

I scrambled into my pants and shirt that lay abandoned on the floor then peeked around the door. The house sat in silence and early afternoon sunlight streamed through a hallway window. I needed to control the urge to call out for Rurik. Nothing would have made me happier than for someone to stroll up the hall or the sound of Marie clanking pans in the kitchen.

I tiptoed down the curved staircase, my heart in my throat, and saw the front door stood open with the frame splintered. Dust filled the air with a musty smell. Stillness made it eerie. I waited for something to jump out and scare the crap out of me.

A breeze from the open door stirred little piles of dust gathered here and there. Where did it all come from? I knelt and pinched a bit between my fingers. It felt greasy.

This was an attack. Rurik must have heard something then K.O.'d me and hid me in the trunk. Damn, where could Red be? He should have been here to help.

There were no bodies. My heart dropped from my

throat to the pit of my stomach. What happened to Rurik? I glanced at the greasy dust I squished in my hand and gagged. Not dust, ashes. Specifically vampire ash. I brushed the stuff off my hand and retreated from it. How many vampires made this much ash? One, five? Was Rurik mixed in?

Tears burned behind my eyes. Could he be gone? His last words to me were of love. I continued to retreat, not wanting to step on any piles, and tripped over someone's foot.

I landed next to Marie. Face to face with her dead stare. My breath caught in my chest. Something had torn out her throat yet barely a drop of blood pooled from her wound. This kind of thing happened to evil people, not sweet motherly women. I crab walked from her body, trying to run from reality. I didn't want to see this. A horror movie come to life. My back hit the wall. The impact startled me enough to scream. The ear rupturing noise echoed through the empty house. I couldn't stop, not with Marie's lifeless eyes staring at me.

I'd seen a dead person before. The image of my late husband, Laurent, in his hospital bed was still vivid in my memory but this violent death shattered me. My whole body went numb, I couldn't feel anything below my neck. Kind Marie deserved better than this. She'd been sympathetic when Rurik frightened me from his room and genuinely happy upon my return.

That should have been me. Rurik, my lover, protected me, but were those his ashes on my feet? My screams grew hoarse until it was only a whisper. It was hard to concentrate. His last words to me, *forgive me, I love you*, whirled around my head. I tried to breathe and find a way out of this nightmare.

He was gone.

My happily ever after ... over before it started. He was supposed to live forever. I shouldn't have to go through this again.

I curled up, my eyes never leaving the crime that had occurred. As I lay there, I had a feeling that more time passed than I realized. Fine ash particles drifted through the bright sunlight, floating as if they tried to reach heaven.

Was there an afterlife for vampires? Were Rurik and Laurent together watching me? I shivered though I wasn't cold. The light faded from yellow to orange and the ash gave up its flight.

Sometime later, the roar of an engine woke me up. I didn't think I was asleep, just lost in an unthinking stupor, holding onto the numbness to prevent me from accepting the truth.

Someone shouted my name. I recognized the voice but I was dazed and it took me a while to come to the conclusion that I should answer.

"Connie," Red's tired face blocked my view of Marie. "Have you been hurt?"

I knew the words meant something but I could only stare. Nothing mattered anymore.

"I'm right here, baby." In a smooth, supple motion he scooped me in his arms and pressed my face to his chest to block my vision. The fresh cool air outside felt nice on my heated, wet face. My tears surprised me, I hadn't known I'd been crying until then. "They came last night," I croaked, my throat dry and raw.

Red settled me onto the front lawn. "We're here now. We'll take care of you." His voice sounded gruff. And then he was talking to someone else. "Secure the area and look for other survivors."

His men streamed into and around the house like a parade. "Connie?" He lifted my chin with a calloused finger and stared into my eyes. "You've a black cloud followin' you, kid. What the hell happened?"

The concern in his voice and the pity in his eyes made my grief real. "Rurik's ... d-dead." I tried out the words, confused by the way they sounded. Sobs burned inside my chest trying to escape.

"Why didn't you call me?"

"I just woke up." I managed to whisper before the first sob came out as a low moan. "Rurik knocked me out," I sobbed, "and hid me."

Red looked over my shoulder, not meeting my eyes. He knew I didn't want false reassurances. My new life fell apart earlier today. I wished I never came to Budapest. Things were fine before, I was dead inside but at least I didn't have this choking ache wrapped around my heart. It made falling into an active volcano like a swim in a pool. What had I done to deserve this? I was a plague to all the men I fell in love with.

Red hugged me and said what I needed to hear. "I'm so sorry." He stroked my hair while I cried.

I poured my sorrow onto his shoulder. The last time I did this I swore never again, yet I let my heartstrings get tangled once more. How stupid am I?

He touched my jaw and I winced at the contact. "You've a nasty bruise and some swellin'." With his fingertips he pressed along the bone. "No sharp pain?"

"It doesn't hurt," I lied and tried to swallow my tears. The words were honest enough for what he asked.

"I don't think it's broken." He touched my cheeks and drew my gaze. "Did you see anythin'? Why do you think Rurik's dead?

"There are ashes all over the place." Awareness began to seep through me, it trickled like ice in my veins. "Who do you think they belong to? He was the only vampire here last night and whoever did this killed Marie."

Dragos did this. I was sure and I wanted him dead.

One of the men returned. "No other survivors or bodies. Point of entry was through the front door. Not much damage and no notes."

Red nodded. "Clean the place of any trace of Connie the best you can." Then he shooed him away with a gesture.

I wiped my nose on his shirt.

He pulled back. "Hey, whatya doin'?"

"Where were you?" I asked with an openhanded smack to his shoulder. "You should have been here to help." Yet even with my angry words I reached out to him for more comfort. I'd suffered heartbreak before. It sucked.

"Connie, please stop cryin'. Your tears are makin' my knees weak." His voice sounded rough with emotion. "I've been out tryin' to find Colby. I checked everywhere and pulled in all my favors but still no word. He's in trouble."

"You don't think he's dead?"

"You kiddin'? Colby's larger than life. When it's time for him to go there'll be more than a silent disappearance."

"Like an explosion or something?" My tears began to dry. "What are the guys doing inside the house?"

"Can't have the Budapest authorities linkin' you to this crime scene. They're removin' any evidence of your bein' here. We'll have to work an alibi just in case."

Someone walked out to the van carrying my suitcase.

Red helped me to my feet. "We need to get out of town before they come for us. There's a few hours of daylight left. The airport's not far from here." He started toward the van.

"Red." I stepped toward him when he turned to me. What this cost him was etched across his face. It tore him up to leave Colby behind.

With his thumb, he cleared the tears from under my eyes. "We'll just get ourselves killed searchin'. I haven't any leads left, I don't even know where to look anymore." Red turned and walked to the vehicle with me in tow.

I crawled into the back with the men and lay on a pile of gear in the corner. No one met my eyes, they looked everywhere but me.

Brad, our shy computer tech, took off his jacket and draped it over my shoulders. I whispered my empty thanks.

"Well, in this situation we need to make a tactical retreat, boys. After we regroup, we'll come back for Colby." Red's voice drifted from the driver's area. The men around me sat with heads hung down and backs bent. Some still bore injuries from the fight at the party only a few nights ago. It felt like years.

I drifted in and out of alertness. I heard the murmurs of the team, felt the shift of the van as it turned a corner, and someone offered me a water bottle, which I drank greedily. I didn't want to be here anymore. I pulled the jacket over my head.

We sat in silence for a moment. A corner of a box poked me in the back so I shifted my hips. Something solid pressed against my leg from my pocket. I pulled out the vial of clear blue liquid.

The drug.

It sparkled in the fading sunlight and must have been sitting in my pants on the bedroom floor since the night I stole it from Rurik. I sat bolt upright and startled the guy next to me.

"You alright?" He looked at me askance.

"Where's my suitcase?"

He pointed toward the back door.

I shoved my way through male flesh and squeezed it open to their protests.

"What are you doin'?"

My purse sat inside. I took out my wallet and slid out a wrinkled card, careful not to tear it. "You said Colby followed a lead about Tane when he disappeared?" I shoved my way back to the front and showed Red the card with just a phone number on it. The one Tane gave me. "Give me your phone. This is our next lead."

I couldn't do anything about losing Rurik but I could help find Colby. Then we'd find who was responsible for this murder and destroy each person involved. It made me feel a smidge better and I needed to take what I could right now.

Red gave me his cell phone as he drove. "Who are you callin'?"

I dialed the number and ignored the question since I didn't feel like discussing my link to Tane.

A sleepy voice answered. "Hello?"

"This is Con-Rabbit. I'd like to leave a message for Tane." Red's eyebrows shot up to his hairline.

"Rabbit, nice to hear from you. This is Eric, Tane's companion." I remembered him from the jazz club on the A38. They were lovers. "We were wondering if you'd ever call. Guess Tane won this bet."

"Tell him I have what he wants."

"I'll come get it."

"I don't think so. I want to speak with him in person."

His low laughter carried over the phone. It made the hair on my arms stand. "You're either a ballsy girl or a silly one. No one ever *wants* to see him."

I sighed. "Fine, I *need* to see him."

"How good are you at following directions?"

"Pretty good."

CHAPTER TWENTY-THREE

My denial and numbness evaded me as I sat in the rowboat on the Danube River. It was a crippling thing, this sensation that my heart had been ripped out of my chest and torn to shreds. I knew it was still there but couldn't feel it beat. This pain would get better but not tonight, not for a long time. I curled over to press my face to one of the oars and tried to breathe with no lungs. I wanted a drink.

Bad. *Captain Morgan* and I had a date after this.

I needed to pull it together. To stuff my self-pity and sorrow in a deep dark hole. If things got better, if I survived the night, I could pull it out when I was alone and examine it. My strength would carry me through, I would prevail in some manner.

The pain became manageable.

Colby might be out on the river, in Tane's yacht. He needed me. I sat up, took a deep breath and started the boat moving again.

Rowing out to a yacht on the Danube River sounded a lot easier on the phone. No matter how I tried I couldn't coordinate the oars, so a ten minute ride turned into a thirty minute workout.

Red almost spontaneously combusted when I told him my story of Tane's blackmail. He understood my lies but it still hurt him. Our friendship had a dent now. He only agreed to this plan because it was a lead to Colby. Once more I wore the tracking chip. They worried it would get wet since we met on the water. If Red had his way I would have had to swallow it wrapped in a baggy like a drug mule. I vetoed that idea.

Once I pulled up to the hull of the ship I didn't see any kind of ladder to climb. You'd think a luxury liner would have a staircase.

"Hey, anyone there? I can use a hand." I looked at the rail along the deck for signs of life.

"The ladder is at the stern, Rabbit." Tane's soft voice carried well over the night.

I rowed a few strokes toward the front of the boat.

"That's the bow. Turn around and go to back."

Steam poured from my ears. Did I look like a sailor? I tried to change direction by swinging the oars in opposite directions but only managed to scrape the yacht's paint.

"Watch the ship." The curt command shot from

above. "You're late."

I settled the oars in the water. Even with the gentle lights that hung from the rigging I couldn't see Tane. "I'm lucky to have made it this far."

A rope flew over the edge of the yacht to land in my dingy. "Tie it to the boat, I'll reel you in."

I wrapped it around the bench and held the end as Tane guided it to the stern with ease.

As I pulled up he jumped in, rocking the row boat enough to make me hang on to the sides. He unwound the rope from the bench while he muttered under his breath then tied a complicated knot to moor it. After he climbed back out he turned and offered his hand. "Welcome aboard, Rabbit."

I accepted it and stepped onto the back platform beside him.

This time he didn't hide his origins under a hat. The moonlight gleamed off his smooth, bald head with his pointed ears folded along its side. His tattoo flowed down into the neckline of his pale-blue, button-down shirt and still remained obscure. He brushed some water beads from his dark gray slacks before directing me to the ladder.

It surprised me to see he was barefoot.

"Pay attention to your steps. I don't want to have to fish you out of the river."

I stared daggers at him before climbing up the ladder. He didn't seem to mind throwing me in it the other night.

His chuckle mocked me.

The deck spoke of wealth. White leather couches attached to the rails invited me to snuggle and the dark hard wood floor felt smooth under my feet. A glass pitcher of clear liquid and a full martini glass sat on a table by one of the couches.

Tane brushed past me and sat next to the table. He picked up the glass and sipped. "Would you like one? Eric makes a good dry martini."

I remained by the ladder. It made me feel safer, even though I couldn't do much if Tane decided to hurt me. "I don't drink anymore." I licked my lips, after this afternoon the pitcher looked tempting. "No olives?"

"We can only take liquids. You should know that." He sipped again. "Do you have the drug? The one he used on you?"

I pulled the vial out of my pocket. It weighed heavier than before like all my responsibilities sat in it.

He signaled me to bring it closer.

I never had the chance to ask Rurik why he owned it. What good could come from breaking down psychic abilities? I couldn't help wonder what crimes Tane would commit with it. But I didn't have any other leverage.

The energy to hold myself together drained my strength. I needed to get this over with. "I want Colby." It wasn't courage that had me making demands of a Nosferatu. A certain sense of freedom came with grief. I didn't have any fear of death, it would just send me to those I loved and missed. How can you be brave if you weren't afraid?

"Why would you think I have him?"

"He disappeared yesterday while investigating Eric. Only you could take him like that. You said if I got you the drug no harm would come to my people. Here it is. Now, give him back."

He leaned back into the couch and finished his drink. "The moment you stepped on this ship the drug was mine. You have nothing to bargain with."

I popped the cap to the vial and poured a little onto the floor. "If I destroy it then neither of us will have what we want."

Tane's hand gripped my wrist and restrained me from emptying it. His empty glass sat on the table. It still amazed me how fast a vampire could move. He took the bottle from my grasp. "Why do you have to make things so difficult? I don't see why Rurik obsesses about you."

The sound of his name stabbed me. "Rurik's dead." I could barely hear my own whisper.

"Really? How?" Tane stood so close if he took a deep breath he'd touch me.

"Dragos attacked his home last night."

"You saw him dead?"

"No, but his ashes were everywhere."

"The ashes. How interesting."

"We made a deal."

He turned his back to me and returned to his seat. "And?" The vial looked small in his hand as he lifted it to examine the contents.

"Is your word worth nothing?"

"My word? Now there's an old concept. I also remember the part of the deal which you're not to tell anyone I hired Colby."

"I didn't"

"Liar. You told him not to trust his source, may as well have told him. You sent him straight here and I'm going to keep him." He grinned at me, his fangs glinted in the dim light. "Unless you want to make another agreement. One that you will keep."

Red was right. This plan sucked. What other choice did we have? I didn't know what to do. Making another deal with Tane, my personal demon, seemed suicidal.

"What do you want?"

"I need you to agree to do it before I tell you what it is."

"Absolutely not."

"Very well, but listen to what I have to offer first." He leaned forward with his elbows on his knees. "I will give you Colby." His black soulless stare pierced me from across the deck. "And I will give you back your Rurik."

"What? How?" My heart raced at the thought. Could Tane be so powerful to resurrect the dead?

"Rurik lives. Those weren't his ashes."

The world spun. He lived. I could have cried if I had any tears left. My legs gave out and nausea boiled in my gut. I found myself sitting on the deck with Tane holding my head between my knees.

"If you vomit on my boat all deals are off."

I swallowed.

Tane released his hold on my head so I could sit. He settled himself onto the deck next to me. "Those ashes belonged to two of my men. Rurik killed them before we subdued him. They turned to ash with the sunrise." A ring on his little finger caught my attention. He lifted his hand for me to see. It was the Budapest Overlord's ring. "My reward from Dragos for Rurik. The city's mine now."

"He thought you were his friend. No matter how hard I tried to convince him he wouldn't believe me."

Tane's eyes widened. "I am his friend. If I wasn't would I bother giving you the chance to rescue him? I could have just offered you Colby but I'm generous enough to offer both."

"For a price." With a friend like Tane, I had to wonder how Rurik ever survived.

"Of course." He chuckled. "You mistake me for a modern vampire. A post-Christian one, maybe? I may enjoy some of Rurik's philosophies but at heart I'm still Dragos' kindred." An amused grin spread across his face as he leaned back and looked at the stars. "Do you truly love him as a man or does it border closer to worship?"

"He's not a god. I love him as a person." More than I probably should after only a few days.

"But he's not." He glanced at me. "We used to be. Once again you find yourself in a position of choice. You could stay here on the boat and ride out the on-coming storm or you can cast yourself out on the mercy of the waves."

"Or I can build my own damn ship and conquer the storm. I won't give up on Rurik. We're in love."

"Yes, oddly you are. You're not his type, he usually likes happy women. You're so raw and sore inside. You broadcast your pain to every vampire around you. 'I ache and grieve. Kill me.' To most you're a gourmet meal."

I was speechless. Embarrassed. Mortified. His words described what I'd felt when I arrived in Budapest but Rurik changed all that.

"You didn't know?"

"No."

"Beautiful." He chuckled. "He's so beautiful."

"Who?"

"Colby, of course, the way his mind works. The way he hunts us so efficiently, using someone that broadcasts like you as bait. Marvelous. You never wondered why most vampires were drawn to you?"

"No." I thought I was just easy pickings. How naïve. I ground my teeth in frustration. None of this mattered. It might have yesterday. Tane was the king of deceit, he told me this to hurt me, to make me angry at Colby. Yet, he's expressed his admiration of Colby many times. Did he have a crush? I shivered. Maybe he wanted me to hate Colby enough to leave him behind?

I wouldn't leave my worst enemy with Tane.

Even his confession of Rurik's captivity made me suspicious. I kept this news foreign to my heart to protect what was left. Hope made me more afraid than dealing with my demon. I wouldn't survive if Tane lied and I'd allowed myself to embrace the giggle of joy fluttering in my chest. I'd take any chance though to be reunited with my vampire lover, no matter how slim.

"Doesn't matter why Colby hired me, it's the past. Rurik's my future, I'll take the deal. What do you want in return?"

"What I've always wanted." He turned to face me, the earlier amusement replaced by a somber expression. "Dragos dead."

Chapter Twenty-Four

A sharp bark of laughter detonated from me. "You want me to kill Dragos? Maybe you've had one too many martinis. Have you looked at me? I can barely row a boat."

"Yes, your lack of physical prowess has crossed my mind." Tane stood and gestured me to sit with him on one of the white leather couches. "Fortunately, this doesn't require skill or I would have done it myself. My plan needs bait, someone who meets Dragos' tastes."

"Someone who broadcasts like me, you mean."

"It's why Rurik chose you at the club. Dragos expressed an interest in you when he'd seen you at the hot springs. We needed someone he wanted to feed on."

One shock after another, Tane didn't hold back on his info punches. "You were both working together to kill him then?"

"We've been allies in this for decades. Killing such a powerful Nosferatu takes careful planning. I've walked a fine line to remain close to our Magistrate for a long time and it's grown thinner since the party."

"But Rurik drugged me before he even asked me to the party, never even gave me a chance to refuse to accompany him. Why? How would that become an assassination attempt?"

"The drug in your system interrupts psychic abilities, both human and vampire. It decreases response time and thought processes, then the victim is easy pickings. The key is to get him to ingest it."

"So you want Dragos to feed from me. Why not spike his drink?"

"He doesn't indulge, not with drinks anyway." The way he trailed his eyes down my body explained what Dragos might want from me.

"Rurik made a deal with me at the party. If I allowed Dragos to feed he'd protect me from him drawing too much. Can you offer the same?"

Tane scratched his chin. "I don't see how. The party was a unique opportunity. There was a lot of public feeding. Who knew Colby's team would be so resourceful and almost kill Rurik instead. I could have staked myself. We were so close and I screwed up by hiring competent slayers." His fist hit the table and rattled the pitcher, it echoed over the water. "Then he falls in love with you, the imbecile. This time there can be no mistakes. You'll have to take the chance he won't bleed you out on his first bite. If you fail, not only do you die, but Rurik too."

He retrieved the drug vial from the table.

"You want me to drug myself and let Dragos feed from me." I'd felt terror before, especially these last few days, but not this bone-deep knowledge that I wouldn't live through this. "Then what?"

"You will need to free Rurik first. Then once Dragos is incapacitated, he has to kill him. It's the only way I can envision either of you making it out of there alive."

"That's a horrible plan. I wouldn't know where to find him or how to free him. Do I look like James Bond?"

Tane held out a key with the vial. "I will give you instructions on what to do and where to go."

I stared at what he held. Risk my life for Rurik's? He did it for me when he knocked me out and hid me in his trunk. I took both items from Tane. "Fine. Now, where's Colby?"

A crooked grin matched the amusement in his expression. "Below deck, watching Eric for me." He stood and strode barefoot across the deck, to a door leading into the heart of the yacht, before I could ask why. As he opened it he bowed. "Ladies first."

"I don't think so." Tane gained nothing by hurting me but I didn't need to take any unnecessary gambles. I followed him across a room that held a sitting area and books then down a spiral staircase to a large bedroom.

Eric laid on his stomach in the center of a king sized water bed unmoving. Tane paused to touch his short salt and pepper hair.

I came around the corner of the stairs to view the rest of the room.

Colby drew my attention straight away. He was chained upright to the far wall and watched Tane with dead eyes until they glanced at me. A light of hope sprung to life in them. "Connie?"

Tane twisted to face me. "Connie." My name rolled off his tongue as if to savor it.

"You didn't think my real name was Rabbit, did you?" I crossed the room to Colby, passing both Tane and the unresponsive Eric.

"I never gave it a thought."

Colby looked feverish as I drew closer. Sweat beaded on his forehead and trickled down the sides. His pale skin felt hot and clammy. I gave him a quick once over but couldn't see any injuries.

The quiet noise of weight being shifted on the bed caught my attention. Tane sat next to Eric, he stroked a broad hand down his pet's back. "I've decided to use you as a bargaining chip instead of keeping you since Eric still lives, Colby. You're very lucky he's strong enough to endure my trials. I think you would not have survived long with me."

A shiver ran through Colby's shoulder where my hand rested.

I examined Eric closer. He appeared paler than Colby. Sets of bite marks in different stages of healing decorated his skin all over his exposed body. A fresh set, still oozing, proclaimed themselves above the others. They rested on his neck, right by his jugular.

Another shiver shook Colby. "Tane thought we should play a game of chance."

"It wouldn't be fair for me to keep you both. The conflict would have been too much for me to bear. Eric's been a good companion, he deserved the opportunity to fight for his position." Tane continued to pet the silent Eric before meeting my stare. "If Eric proved strong enough to live through a deep and long feed then he could remain with me. If not, then Colby would replace him."

Colby growled before he shouted. "I never wanted to be your pet." The volume hurt my ears.

"That's inconsequential." The slight touch of disappointment in his voice surprised me. His desire to get rid of Dragos outweighed his yearning for Colby.

It was my turn to shiver.

"I'm letting you go. If you wish to return, my invitation will stand."

Colby spit on the floor.

"Tane," I pointed to the manacles. I wanted to get out before Colby gave Tane a reason to change his mind. We were just a few steps from freedom and he was going to blow it. I'd never seen this side of Colby. The uncontrolled, passionate man chained to wall must hide deep inside the cold, calculating one who sends me broadcasting my pain to vampire dens. I had to get him out of here before *I* changed my mind.

Tane opened a drawer in the bedside table and retrieved a set of keys. He tossed them to me.

I cupped Colby's face in my hand to draw his attention. "When I release you, behave. I need you. Focus." Our eyes met and an understanding passed.

He nodded. Once released from his bindings Colby staggered from the wall and almost fell but Tane, using his immortal powers of speed, caught him. He reacted as if touched by a hot iron and squirmed out of Tane's hands. I didn't want to think about what hardships Colby experienced on this yacht. He didn't have any injuries but not all wounds were physical.

Colby caught both of us by surprise when he threw a punch.

Tane took it in the chin and stumbled back. His knee caught on the corner of the bed and it tripped him. The fall turned into a roll. When he rose in a cat-like twist a serrated knife appeared in his hand from God knows where.

"Colby stop." I tried to grab his arm but he swatted me behind him like a gnat. "He's letting us go," I pleaded.

"He lies. This is just another fantasy he's created. You're not even real."

"I'm not? Tane, what is he talking about?"

"We shared a few dreams. I am very proficient at entering minds."

Before I could try to convince Colby of my existence, he launched himself at Tane and grappled for the knife. His momentum drove them over the bed and Eric to fall onto the other side out of my view.

"Stop! Stop! Stop!." I sounded like a deranged cheerleader. Most men would already be dead, but Colby had fought vampires for years and was strong with crazed rage. I ran to other side of the bed.

Tane lay under Colby. They both faced the ceiling and the sharp blade pressed against Colby's throat yet he still struggled. Tane appeared to not want to hurt him, just defend himself.

Colby jabbed his elbow into Tane's side causing the grip on the knife to waiver. He rolled off toward the knife arm and pulled the blade from Tane's hand.

Like an idiot, I jumped between them, a piece of tissue paper between two bulls.

The knife flashed and sliced across my upper arm. I cried out and pressed the wound with my hand. Blood seeped through my fingers.

Colby stared at the knife with my blood on it then back at me. "Connie?"

"Dumbass, look what you did. If I need stitches I'm going to get Red to give you an atomic wedgie." It burned like a son of a bitch. Stupid ass men thinking they could solve their issues with knives.

Tane tore at the white cotton bed sheets. He examined the wound. "It's just a graze. Stitches are unnecessary." With the strips of cloth he made a quick tight bandage around my arm. He sucked my blood off his fingers and shrugged at my horrified expression. "You have a mild flavor."

The blood oozed through the bandage. I covered it

with my hand. "You don't get seconds."

Colby had stuck the knife in his waistband. He stared at Tane. "This isn't a dream?"

"Nothing *I* say will convince you."

I stepped to Colby and pressed myself against his bare chest. The physical contact did the trick as he hugged me tight for moment before my boss' persona returned and he pushed me away.

I tried to aim him to the staircase.

"Why would he let me go?"

I glared back at Tane. "Is this permanent?"

"No, once he sleeps and eats he should return to normal. Not all our fantasies were bad. You enjoyed some of them, Colby."

"Stop taunting him." I pushed Colby harder. "Go up the stairs, I've got a row boat. Red's waiting for us."

At the mention of Red's name he straightened up. "You didn't answer my question, Tane."

"Connie is willing to trade a service for your life. I think it's profitable enough of a deal."

"No, I won't allow her to do anything for you. I'll stay."

I paused in my pushing efforts, not believing my ears. "Are you nuts?"

He gazed into my eyes. "I won't have you making deals with this bastard."

"Well, well, all my dreams have come true. I guess our deal is off then Rabbit. You'll have to figure out how to save Rurik on your own." Tane stood and sauntered toward Colby.

I felt him stiffen next to me.

"Enough. Colby, listen to me. I have to do this." I pointed at Tane with my uninjured arm. "Stop playing games. You want this more than I do."

A small smile played on Tane's lips.

Colby's arm snaked around my waist and lifted me in a fireman's lift then carried me up the stairs.

"What are you doing? I can walk."

He carried me to the back of the yacht where the rowboat waited and stepped into it before setting me onto a bench.

I looked over his shoulder to the deck but Tane didn't follow us.

"Take the boat back to Red. I can't believe he let you do this. I'll be all right, I can take care of myself."

"Sure you can." I tried to smile. "But they need you. Dragos is taking over the city. He knows about us, he's the one who told Tane to hire our team. They'll be dead soon, if not already, without you."

His eyebrows shot up.

"Dragos has Rurik prisoner. I love him. Tane is willing to help me with a rescue if I poison Dragos." I left out the details on how. "You're a bonus. Even if you stay, I'll still do this. Go help Red."

"How do you plan to poison a Nosferatu Prime?"

"Easy, do what I do best. Be bait." Before I climbed out of the boat I stopped and whispered in his ear. "Follow my chip."

His sharp stare told me he understood. They would track my signal and help out.

I climbed the ladder to the deck and watched Colby row away with much more skill than I had.

Tane stepped up next to me, a long range rifle in his hands.

"What's that for?"

"Just in case he left with you, I can't have loose ends." He turned to me. "Let's go save your boyfriend."

CHAPTER TWENTY-FIVE

"You're coming with me?" I faced Tane not trusting a thing he said or did.

"Someone has to get you inside the compound."

"When you say compound, I envision high fences and guards."

"You've an accurate imagination." He rested the rifle against his shoulder and watched Colby row.

I tried to comb my fingers through my tangled curls and cleared my throat. "You'll leave him be?"

Tane glanced at me, a touch of sorrow in his eyes. "He'll come back." Then he returned inside the boat.

For Colby's sake, I hope he didn't. I followed Tane to the living room.

He poured himself another martini. "We need to

discuss my plan." A wide armchair dominated the far side of the room and he sank onto it. "Once the drug affects you, your mind will not have any defenses what-so-ever to invasion and manipulation. Dragos will have control over you and be able read all your thoughts."

"He did that during our dance at the party. I'm not looking forward to re-experience it." I remained by the door and chewed my lower lip. The false reassurance of an exit comforted me.

"He'll know of our plan to drug and kill him."

This thought never occurred to me. No one worried about that at the party. Then again, I didn't know their plans, only suspected Rurik of drugging me to control my actions. "That's not good, Genius."

"Don't worry, Rabbit." He took a sip of his drink and grinned at me. "I have it covered."

"Why doesn't that make me feel better? And how come you didn't mention this before?" I crossed my arms. This boded ill for me.

He stared at me, his expression blank, from across the room while he finished his drink. "You would never have agreed. I have to alter your memories, build blocks to prevent Dragos from seeing them. This means I have to enter your mind."

Eww.

My face must have reflected the thought since he grimaced and said, "I'm not anticipating this anymore than you are. Being surrounded by pink ponies and rainbows does not appeal to me."

"You're not rummaging through my brain. That's

not part of the deal."

"It's necessary. None of us will survive Dragos' wrath if he learns the truth. I will get ten times worse whatever tortures he concocts for you. It's the only way you'll be able to retrieve Rurik alive since Dragos will be able to read your intentions."

I sighed and felt deflated. Rurik. He'd sacrificed himself for me and now I must do the same. "Will there be any permanent damage?" I tapped my temple with my finger.

"Altering memories is very difficult. It makes up what you are. I can only do a temporary change and the closer to reality, the better it will fit."

I sat in the closest seat by the entrance. Tane would need to change all my memories of tonight. "Can you tell me in detail what you plan to switch?"

He shrugged. "I can wipe it away after. I will tell Dragos that I exchanged Colby for you."

"My team would never do that."

"He'll believe it. Trading a useless girl for their leader will make perfect sense to him. He doesn't have a taste for men like I do. Colby holds no appeal to him but you, on the other hand, do."

"Yeah, he likes women with poor common sense," I mumbled to myself.

Eric climbed the stairs and joined us. He looked like road kill. His eyes shone with fever from the dark pits encircling them. "Is Colby dead?" A pair of black plaid PJ bottoms threatened to fall from his narrow hips and a red blanket hung over his shoulders. The color made him paler.

"No, I traded Rabbit for him." Tane lied.

Eric glanced at me as if surprised to find me in the room. "Why?"

I would have given him the one finger salute but I felt more pity for him than anger.

Tane's eyes narrowed as he stared at his pet who visibly shrank from him.

"We're taking Rabbit to Dragos as a gift. Start the boat and sail us there."

Eric nodded and exited to the deck.

"Are you sure he should be driving? He might pass out."

Tane gave me the same stare he'd directed at Eric. It froze my soul. "Let's get this done. It won't be long before we're at the compound." He gestured for me to approach.

I didn't hesitate. If I did I might have changed my mind.

He scooted over in the armchair and made room for me. Barely. Our legs touched when I squeezed in.

"How am I supposed to follow your directions to save Rurik if you're going to wipe it away?"

"Smart girl, I'm going to leave compulsions for you. Certain visual cues will stimulate you to act. They'll guide you. I've thought this through. Trust me."

Said the spider to the fly.

"I hate this plan." I ran my fingers through my curls in a Colby-stressed-out fashion.

"Do you have any other suggestions?"

"Storm the castle and rescue the dude in distress." I rubbed my eyes. When did I sleep last? A truly deep, eight hours of uninterrupted, blissful rest. Must have been the day before I found Rurik at the club. That vampire wasn't good for my health and well being.

Tane didn't even give my suggestion a response. "It won't hurt if you relax your mental shields." His touch on my mind slid over my barriers. A gentle pressure asking to come in.

"Easier said than done. Give me a second." Colby taught how to build them, not how to take them down. It never occurred to either of us that I would want to. I closed my eyes and tried to picture a door opening.

The roar of the yacht's engine startled me. My mental door disintegrated quicker than it materialized.

"Try again." Tane angled his body so he could face me.

I started the process over. These shields became a part of a person over time. Images held in place consciously, at first, but after some time you forgot they existed. Until some vampire asked you to take them down.

"Concentrate," he whispered.

I scrunched my eyes and poured all my effort into the door's existence.

"Hmm, it looks like you're trying to lay an egg instead."

I sighed and opened my eyes. "Your comments are not helping."

Chin in hand, he sat observing me, not amused. "It

takes only a few minutes to sail to Dragos' temporary compound."

"Where are you both from?"

He shook his head. "None of that should concern you. Try again."

"At the A38 you gave me the impression that you could break through my mental shields."

"It would hurt."

He cared if he hurt me? I took a deep breath and blew it out slow. The door came easier this time. Something knocked from the other side. It wanted to come in but it frightened me. Instinct took over and I shrank from the door. I heard a faint growl of frustration. The door bulged inward. It hurt. I ran forward to brace it, to prevent it from shattering but the pain became too much.

I heard a scream then realized it belonged to me.

A hole appeared where the door should have been and darkness flowed in.

Strong arms held me in a firm hug. My face rested on a shoulder and long fingers ran through my hair. I loved it when someone played with my hair. It relaxed me and made me feel loved.

Laurent.

No, I wiped the sleepy cobwebs from my brain cells. Rurik. I pulled him closer and snuggled deeper in his arms.

A deep chuckle vibrated in his chest. "I doubt you'd survive if Eric caught you in my arms, Rabbit."

Tane's voice skewered me. A thousand questions

assaulted my thoughts. I jerked out of his arms and stumbled out of a wide armchair. The room rocked and swayed with a steady motion.

Where the hell was I? The last I remembered I'd been in Red's van.

Tane remained curled up in the chair with a small satisfied smile.

"How'd I get here?" The view from a window showed the river. We were on a boat.

"Your people brought you to me as a trade for Colby."

I recalled Colby's disappearance and my suspicions that Tane had him. Did I tell Red? "They wouldn't do such a thing." I sounded more confident than I felt. They needed Colby, he ran everything. I was just bait. "I don't want to believe you." It came out wrong but honest.

"Doesn't matter."

The ship shuddered and stopped. I made a futile attempt for the door but Tane caught me in his steel hard arms.

"Save your energy. Dragos likes his prey to be feisty."

"No." I wanted the pain of Rurik's death to go away but not like this. Dragos would make my end long and painful, if he ever let me die.

Tane kept a tight grasp on my arm and guided me to the deck. Eric tied their ship to the dock. He looked awful, like he'd been used as a vampire all-you-can-eat buffet.

We were moored to a small private island. A large stone mansion, or better yet a castle, stood on the gently sloped hill.

Dragging me onto the pier, Tane stopped by Eric. "Stay here and rest. I won't be long." We continued to a guarded gate where we were greeted.

"Master Tane, we weren't expecting you. The Master is in the city at present." The pale faces of these vampires watched me with interest.

"I brought him a midnight snack." He pulled me in front of him as they laughed. "Send him a message that I've caught him a rabbit."

They opened the gate and let us through.

"I'll lock her in his study."

CHAPTER TWENTY-SIX

Tane dragged me through the front doors into a large open foyer. The place oozed of history with old paintings and tapestries covering the walls. A huge chandelier hung above us, not illuminated by modern bulbs but by candles. Crystals decorated the piece and they sparkled with the soft light. He didn't hesitate to admire anything, just continued to pull me up a wide marble staircase, and made a right down a hallway. A set of double wooden doors stood open and we entered the dark wood paneled room where he escorted me to a delicate Victorian chair.

A large black granite fireplace stained with age and use sat across from me. It was full of kindling but no fire.

"I'll make you a drink." Tane's offer rang strange.

Yet, I found myself saying, "Thank you." My thirst grew as I watched him pour orange juice in a glass at the bar. He stirred in a small vial of blue liquid into the drink. It reminded me of the one I found in Rurik's trunk but how would Tane have gotten it?

Ever since we walked into the house a veil of calm enveloped me. *Everything would be fine as long as I followed my instincts,* a little voice told me. This mantra repeated itself. My personal demon squatted in front of me to hand over the drink. "This will quench your thirst."

How did he know I was parched? I sipped it, the taste pleasant.

"Finish it, Rabbit." He watched as I emptied the glass. When did he become kind? "The windows in these rooms are huge almost the size of doors. They must let in a good quantity of sunlight during the day."

I twisted in my seat to see them. They were thin and tall. Only a foot of wall under and over them. "Maybe you should stay and find out, Tane."

"We were being so civil to each other until now." He ruffled my curls with his hand as he rose. "But I would have been disappointed if you remained polite." Before exiting the room he glanced at me and stated, "Windows." Then he closed the doors and the lock tumbled into place.

That word stuck in my mind. What about them? So they were big, whoopee shit. I set the empty glass down and crossed the room to one. Why didn't Tane tie me up? Did he think I wouldn't try to escape? Maybe that's what he wanted me to do. He said something about Dragos liking his prey to be feisty. A midnight hunt for the runaway rabbit? I could be reading too much into things. If I stayed I was dead, if I ran it would take a miracle for me to escape but at least I had a chance.

In my hand the window knob turned and the panel swung inward. A stone ledge ran the length of the house. Like an idiot, I looked at the ground. I changed my mind, this idea sucked. I'd try to pick the lock on the door first.

The boat dock was visible from here. Tane's boat floated by it while another smaller one pulled up behind.

I almost closed the window completely when I remembered who was on his way home from the city anticipating a rabbit dinner when he returned. Dragos.

The window rattled in my haste to open it again. I took my first tentative step onto the ledge. This ranked as the second stupidest things I'd ever done. Letting Johnny Turner convince me to give him my virginity in the seventh grade still took first place.

A breeze blew around my legs as I hugged the building. Even with the cool spring weather, sweat trickled down my back and made my palms slick. Inch by terrifying inch I groped away from Dragos' study. My plan only went as far as to escape the room. The overcast night sky hid the moon so the darkness surrounding me seemed endless. We only climbed one set of stairs to get to the study, which meant I should be on the second floor. The ground looked far, then I remembered the house sat on a hill and the land must slope away.

A decorative stone protrusion blocked my path. Every ten feet one marked the ledge. Their width gave me pause. Five inches sounded small until you hung from the side of a building like Spiderman. Except when I fell I wouldn't swing away safe. I'd go splat.

I wiped my sweaty hands on my jeans before reaching around the obstacle to search for a handhold. An outcrop of what felt like mortar met my fingertips after searching forever. I grabbed it and hugged the pillar with my knees.

My heart drummed against my chest as my palms got moist again. I glanced down. Even though I could barely see the ground the muscles in my legs registered danger and froze.

I clung to my perch like a love-struck loon, closed my eyes and tried not to be sick. A lightheaded swirl took me all of a sudden. Heights made me nervous but they never made me dizzy. I leaned my head against the structure, I couldn't stay here all night yet my limbs refused to listen.

The cold stone on my face cooled some of the hot flush of my fear and the sound of my panting filled the night.

Left foot already around the obstacle, only the right one needed to get to the other side, I concentrated on shuffling with my eyes closed and body glued to the wall. Muffled male voices floated from the dock, followed by laughter.

My fear of Tane's master slapped me on the ass. It made me deal with my spinning head and rebellious limbs quick.

I swung my right leg around the pillar and shuffled along the ledge. At the corner of the building I ran into a thorny rose bush. The sharp pricks on my skin, like fangs, startled me and I choked on a scream. By the scent of the soft flowers, which grew on it, and upon a closer inspection of the plant in the dark, I concluded it to be a rose vine intertwined on a trellis that grew to the roof. In other words, a makeshift ladder.

Hand and foot holds were easy to find, I tested my weight on both trellis and ancient vine by bouncing. Nothing snapped or groaned. I leaned back and watched the upper sections by the roof and it appeared to stay attached to the building.

The window above me had thick iron bars over them. It struck me as odd for the third floor, unless they were trying to keep something in the room instead of out.

A strong curiosity washed over me, almost a compulsion, to look inside. Determined, I climbed the trellis to the next level instead of to the ground.

Thorns hooked to my clothes and skin, slowing me. I tried my best not to make a racket. At times I didn't know if I stepped on the trellis or the vine.

I transferred to the third floor ledge and ignored the little voice screaming about the heights.

What I saw through the barred window should

have rocked my world but something inside me said I already expected this.

Rurik.

I grabbed onto a bar and touched the window as if I could reach him.

They had him chained to a black free-standing stone pillar with thick, heavy metal bindings. He wore only a pair of briefs so his multiple wounds were exposed for my view. My stomach churned at the pool of blood under his feet. It trickled from the multiple large cuts at key arterial areas. He hung limp like a corpse.

A strange man came into the room. With a sharp knife he sliced at my lover and refreshed the cuts.

Rurik cried out. He strained against the chains and snapped his teeth at the man, who yelped in surprise, slipped in the blood, and fell to the floor.

The metal from the window's bar cut into my palm as I squeezed it tight. I guess to keep a vampire weak you would need to drain him of his source of power, blood, but he healed so damn fast his captors needed to keep re-opening the wounds.

I had to rescue him. I didn't know how but I had to.

Two sills over a window stood ajar. I shimmied over to it and listened for movement inside the room but heard nothing. The window sill sat only a foot from the floor and I stepped into the building. My earlier lightheadedness returned with a vengeance, I grabbed onto something cold and metallic to steady myself. As my vision cleared I saw that I held an arm. With a small gasp I released it and jumped back. Suits of armor stood at attention along the wall.

I entered a medieval armory. The only weapons I recognized were the swords, all the other toys of mayhem remained nameless, except a nice Connie-sized hammer dangling from a belt. A weapon could be handy, so I pushed my sleeves to my elbows before taking hold of it. Wrapped around my wrist was a delicate silver bracelet holding a key. Where did I get that? My memories weren't adding up, Swiss cheese had fewer holes. The chain bent and curved in an intricate pattern. Very pretty and antique, maybe Rurik gave it to me?

I slipped the hammer out of the belt loop. It weighed more than I hoped but with a two handed grip I could dent heads. A simple and insane plan formed.

The hallway appeared empty. I knocked on the door to the room where Rurik remained captive and prepared the hammer, like a baseball bat, over my shoulder. My arms shook with the restrained effort. I shifted my weight to my back leg. Grandma taught me to play baseball. Her voice flashed in my mind, "Keep your eye on the target, put your back into it, and follow through!"

The door opened and I swung the hammer with all my strength. It was a home run.

The man who had cut Rurik sprawled back onto the floor after my hammer connected with his chest. He never had a chance to make a noise.

I prepared for retaliation but he didn't move. Was

he playing possum? His feet blocked the doorway. I would have to step over them to get in. I kicked his shoe and scooted back. Damn, I'd been expecting more of a fight from a vampire.

A weak groan came from inside the room. It drove me to jump over the man's legs. As I landed I spun with the hammer in hand to face the body on the floor, afraid of a surprise attack.

No wonder my plan worked. He was human. A bite mark on his neck declared it. His chest rose and fell in a shallow, irregular rhythm. Guilt, satisfaction, shame, and joy jumbled inside of me. I'd never hurt a fellow human being before.

"Connie?"

The whisper of my name reminded me of my objective. I turned at the sound of his voice.

Rurik stared at me with wide astonished eyes. His skin, the palest of whites, made the sharp angles of his face more apparent. Dark strands hair framed his face as he stared at me from dark wells. The predator in his soul closer to the surface than I'd ever witnessed.

"My Rabbit, what are you doing here?"

I rushed to hug him. To convince myself this was real. He felt frigid. "I thought you were dead."

"Get out. He's here-"

I kissed him. Foolish, carefree, and happy to have my Rurik back. Once more my head spun and I found myself hanging on to him instead of hugging him.

"Sorry, I'm a little dizzy."

"Look at me, baby"

I gazed into his ice blue eyes and poured all my love and affection for him into it.

"Something's wrong with you. Are you drunk?"

Rurik's soft caress brushed my thoughts. It triggered a reflex to strengthen my mental shields but nothing happened. I stepped back and concentrated on my defenses. As much as I tried, they were gone.

"What have you done?" The panic in Rurik's voice frightened me more than my stroll on the ledge. "Connie." He snapped. "Check the guard for keys. You have to free me." His arms jerked the chains with renewed vigor.

A set of keys, why did those words bring on a sense of deja vu?

"Quick, Connie. Move." Rurik strained from the stone pillar. "Dragos is trying to find you. I'm shielding you but I can't keep it up for long. They've bled me and I'm too weak. How the fuck did you get my drug in your system?"

Drug? That would explain the dizzy spells. I lifted my left hand and showed Rurik the key on my new pretty bracelet. "Did you give this to me? I like it."

His eyes widened. They shone with tears. "No, sweetheart. It must be from someone who's trying to help us. Can you use it to unlock the manacles?"

"Sure." The world became disjointed as if I watched myself from afar. I removed the bracelet and inserted the key into the lock.

Rabbit... A whisper trailed through the air or in my thoughts. I wasn't sure anymore. *Why are you doing that, Rabbit? It displeases me.* Dragos' presence in my head shut everything out.

"No." Rurik shook his head. "Listen to *me*, Connie. Unlock it, twist the key."

Come to me. Leave Rurik there to greet the dawn.

I pivoted to see the curtainless windows that faced the east. The black stains on the pillar must have come from earlier victims of this type of punishment. Rurik would burn and join their ashes.

Come. One simple elegant command. Why did I ever doubt Dragos? His power, strength, and intelligence spanned millennia. Only the unwise would oppose him.

I left the room. Rurik screamed my name over and over but Connie no longer existed, only Rabbit.

Dragos' Rabbit.

CHAPTER TWENTY-SEVEN

As I arrived to the same dark, wooden paneled study where Tane had locked me in, Dragos reclined on a plain wood chair. With one sandaled foot resting on his knee and his arm thrown over the chair back, he stared at a large broad sword that rested over the fireplace mantle.

I stepped through the threshold as quiet as a mouse, not wanting to disturb him, and took this opportunity to admire his male beauty. Muscular and strong, his chest and arms strained against the gray t-shirt he wore. The electric lights were off and he must have lit some candles, while I'd been gone, so the flickering glow caste shadows on the walls. His black leather pants clung to his long legs and ended in a pair of brown, worn sandals.

Why did I ever fear him or think him monstrous? His tattooed baldhead and pointed ears made him more exotic, not repulsive.

"Why would you run from me?" He echoed my thoughts. Soft and compelling, his voice had the timber of someone who never yelled. I wanted to hear more. "It would have displeased me if you'd left and taken Rurik with you."

All the trouble I went through to escape and release Rurik appeared silly now. I should have stayed here and waited. What sort of horrible person was I to make him unhappy? I knelt to cower on my hands and knees, ashamed of my selfishness. "I'm so sorry , Master."

"Since you're still young and foolish, Rabbit, I forgive you. I'll teach you to be a proper pet. Look at me."

Still bent low to the ground I gazed up at his magnificence. He'd uncrossed his legs and now leaned forward with his elbows on his knees.

"You and your merry band of slayers have entertained Tane to no end during our visit to Budapest. He's offered you as a token for leaving me out." He gestured to his lap. "Approach me."

My legs shook so much I couldn't stand. Not from fear but from anticipation of his touch. So I crawled.

His presence filled the room. Energy and malevolence pulsed from him in imperceptible waves.

When I reached his legs I couldn't resist rubbing my face against them like a cat in heat.

"Much better." He ran his fingers through my curls then pinched the material of my long-sleeved t-shirt between two fingers. "I hate these modern fashions on women. Take it off."

I started to remove my shirt but his touch on my arm stopped me. "Stand, I want to watch."

Something bothered me about his request. It made me uncomfortable but I couldn't understand why. I stood and undid my jeans then slid them down my legs in a slow manner. My earlier hesitation lifted and my purpose to make Dragos happy returned. The shirt, socks and shoes joined my jeans in quick succession.

I stood in my matching white lace bra and thong, happy I'd thought to wear these today instead of my sports stuff.

The cold heat of his scrutiny burned as his stare traced up my legs, over the generous curves of my hips, and stopped at the mounds of my breasts. "Turn."

I did a slow three-sixty. If Tane wouldn't have hurried me so much I might have thought to wear some make-up or done my hair. Instead, I came here as a windblown, nut case.

"I think I'd like you better with heels but this will do for now." He tapped his lap once more with his hand.

The gesture triggered a reflexive annoyance but it vanished almost as soon as it materialized. I scurried to him and perched on his trunk-like thighs. The skintight leather of his pants felt smooth and slick under my behind. I could feel every hard muscle in his legs. This god-like creature wanted me and it thrilled me that he did. I'd make him a very, very happy Master.

His fingers traced a line down my spine sending shivers straight to my scalp, raising the hairs on my body. "Like a god?" He whispered close to my ear. "You have it wrong, Rabbit. I *am* a god."

I started with the confirmation of his words. He really could read my thoughts. My repressed self bubbled up from where Dragos hid her. I grasped at my non-existent mental shield and panicked as a wave of calm poured over me before I could fight back. It allowed me to breathe easier and relax into his arms.

"You like to fight." His tone sounded approving. "And you don't believe me. Let me show you our godhood."

Visions of an ancient stone temple towering over a dense jungle intruded my thoughts like a video clip. Dragos stood on a dais at the top of the stairs, which climbed the side of the building, as people were dragged to him one at a time. *Sacrifices.* His soft voice echoed in my head. The moonlight glinted off his pale skin and baldhead, a giant surrounded by his worshippers.

Precious life and blood, taken for granted, spilled for a monster that cared nothing for them. Who probably terrorized this simple culture into extinction.

One after another the faces of victims played for me until I recognized a handsome and arrogant expression. The love in his eyes for his god shone bright. Tane, before Dragos made him a Nosferatu vampire.

As a human, he appeared so angelic.

My personal trip in history faded to present day, where Dragos attempted to convert me to his religion.

I'm not sure when I moved but now I straddled him, pressed up against his massive chest with my arms wrapped around his thick corded neck. The scent of the Danube River still clung to him.

His fingers played up and down my spine while he kissed a line from my shoulder to my ear. "Rurik's changed you. I don't like it."

I pushed myself away to meet his gaze. "What do you mean?" Rurik should have minded his own business and left me alone. I needed to fix things for Dragos so he'd like me again.

"He's made you happy. I can barely hear your grief. Even my visions of death don't stir it." He gripped a handful of my hair and yanked it so far back I had to arch my torso to prevent him snapping me in two.

I groaned at the strain on my back. My hands tried to find purchase but only found his arms to grasp. I wanted to give him what he wanted but didn't know how. It made me ache with incompetence.

"We'll have to fix this. I want to taste the salty grief that almost drowned you when we met." His fangs dragged and scraped the tender skin of my neck. "Let's explore this together and dig it back up. It was so fresh, it couldn't have healed in this short span of time." Pressure built in my head as Dragos sank himself into my memories. "I think this is the source of your grief."

Dragos and Budapest disappeared, replaced by a heart monitor on a hospital nightstand. The soft blips

BAIT

sounded familiar and the smell, of something dying, filled the room. I turned, already expecting what would be there.

Laurent, my deceased husband, lay in a hospital bed. Blankets pulled up to his waist, his exposed arms so thin and skeletal. The cancer had eaten away all of his strength.

A mass of wild blond curls rested next to his lap on the other side of the bed. He twirled one around his finger then let it fall away only to start over again, a bitter sweet smile on his face.

The head of hair stirred and lifted from the bed. I watched myself rub the sleep from my eyes.

"I didn't mean to wake you." Laurent touched my face.

"Nonsense, I'd have been upset if you let me sleep too long. Are you hurting? Do you need the nurse?"

"I'm all right, Connie. You really should get more sleep."

"I get plenty of sleep." The lie sat in the room like an elephant. At the time I believed myself. But as I looked at the dark circles under my eyes and my own weight loss I knew I'd only fooled myself. Laurent could see my suffering no matter how hard I tried to conceal it.

That hurt. A lot.

I reached for an open book that sat on the bedside table. "Do you want me to continue reading to you?" *The Princess Bride* scrawled across the cover in bold letters. He'd given it to me on our first date. I'd been more in a Romeo and Juliet kind of mood that day but we both loved this story.

He nodded. "As you wish, but lay next to me." He tried to scoot over but the pain made him grimace.

"Let me help." My younger self raced around the bed to help him shift over then I crawled in next to him.

He placed his head above my heart and snuggled in tight. His left hand caressed my breast until the nipple budded.

"How can I read with you fooling around?"

"I may be dying but I'm not dead." His chuckle tore my heart apart just like it did then. He glanced at my face and sucked in a breath. "Oh baby, don't cry." He pulled me down and kissed the tears that rolled over my cheeks.

"That's not funny." I sounded choked up on tears.

I'd buried this day deep, deep in my subconscious. I didn't want to be here, I couldn't survive this again. I wasn't strong enough yet to face this moment.

The last time we'd made love.

I tried to get out, but the room had no door. The pleasant noises from the bed drove me mad with guilt. I couldn't watch my younger self with my dead husband. This was why memories faded. How could I have continued living without him? I pressed my hands to my ears and curled up in a corner but I could still hear his climax.

The sound changed, it became shriller. I recognized it. Time had shifted to a few days later. The heart monitor no longer blipped. I uncurled myself and approached his bed.

Dead. Just as I remembered it.

The horrid ear piercing cries came from the younger me on the other side of the bed. A nurse tried to console her but I was beyond that. Grief held me prisoner, then and now. Neither of us had any family, only each other.

I was alone.

I don't know who howled louder at this point, me or the vision of me. Whatever healed since his death, ripped open. I knelt by the side of his bed, grasped his cold hand, and cried as if I'd never been through this before.

Alone, again.

A ripple of laughter cut through my grief. "Much better, Rabbit. This isn't the source though but I see it now." Dragos' voice pulled me from Laurent's bedside.

Instead, I knelt on the grass in a cemetery. I recognized the place even though I hadn't been there in ages. A cold dread seeped into me. Quiet weeping to my left drew my attention. A teenage Connie Bence sat on the fresh dirt covering a grave, all alone. My grandmother, my grandma, the only family I grew up with and knew of. I wanted to tell my younger self that everything would be all right. In a few years we'd meet a great guy who'd set us straight. Who'd show us there really were good people in the world. That they weren't a myth.

Helpless, I watched the younger me draw away from the world. Left in New York City, known for eating its young and destroying their innocence, to fend for myself.

This grief didn't stab me like the other but Dragos was right, it all started here.

I wanted to crawl into a hole and die. What happiness I knew became a forgotten memory.

A sudden sharp pain in my neck snatched me from my inner turmoil. Dragos ended the torture, satisfied at last with my state of mind. My blood salty enough with grief for him to feed.

He drank deep, his arms holding me fast and tight as he pulled my life's essence from my body.

I didn't struggle, I wanted it to end. It felt right to give him what he wanted.

Moans of pleasure emanated from Dragos. He bit down harder to increase the flow.

The pain caused me to cry out. It helped clear some of the fog clouding my reason. Why would I want Dragos to drink from me? He would kill me with his thirst. Laurent and my grandmother would never want me to give up.

The face of my new love returned, a fresh start, and a chance for a happily ever after. I'd left Rurik chained to a stone pillar, weak from being bled, to face the dawn. Then I crawled and undressed for Dragos? Worse, I let him touch me.

When did I lose my mind?

This triggered a cascade of memory blocks, the ones Tane built to hide our intentions. They crashed one after another. Colby's rescue, Tane's plan, and my involvement in both rushed back to me. I drank the drug and Dragos now drank me but I had failed to release my hero.

Shit.

Chapter Twenty-Eight

I wedged my hand between the two of us and pushed Dragos' chest. Even at full strength I wouldn't have been able to break free of his hold but I wiggled in his grasp and shoved his face. Another lightheaded spell came over me. It interrupted my weak struggles and felt different than the other ones. This time a wave of nausea accompanied it with a bone deep weariness.

He'd drawn too much blood.

Short of breath, I tried to attract his attention, to make him stop. "You're killing me. You won't be able to feed from me again."

His sucking eased as he pulled away from my neck. "Good point, my little Rabbit." He cocked his head and licked the wound then paused as if to listen to something.

My heart fluttered like a fledgling batting its wings. Pressure built on my chest as if someone sat on it. It became more difficult to breath.

"It may already be too late." He traced a finger under my chin to stabilize the wobble in my neck. "I could cross you over as a replacement for Elizabeth, an eye for eye kind of deal."

"No."

"Not that I blame you for killing her. She didn't have the right to destroy what's mine and you *do* belong to me, Rabbit. Rurik presented you as a gift, remember?" Our eyes met. "I should reward you for disposing Elizabeth for me. She was such a possessive pest." A glaze veiled his eyes.

At first I thought him caught up in a memory of Lizzy but his mouth hung open a bit as if stoned. He released me. Unprepared for this unexpected action I slumped against his chest like a rag doll. A cold sweat covered my body.

I was dying.

Dragos gasped and shook his head. "What the hell was that?" He stood and I tumbled to the floor. "What did you do to me?" His hands clutched his head as he stepped over me toward the fireplace mantle and gripped it.

I had enough strength to roll onto my side and watch him.

An explosion of wooden splinters caused me to flinch. The study doors slanted inward and dust floated in the air. Dragos crouched in a defensive position as Rurik strode through the gap bearing a saber in each hand. His wounds appeared healed, which meant he must have fed. Clad only in a pair of briefs with dried blood coating his skin like tribal paint, he swung one blade in Dragos' direction.

Dragos stepped into the attack, blocking it with his right arm while the left punched Rurik in the face. The cut in the Nosferatu's forearm knitted back together. "Who set you free?"

Rurik caught his footing and shook his head. He appraised the bigger vampire then advanced with more care. "I set myself free." He raised an arm and rattled the manacle that still clung to it.

Pride filled my heart. Even weak from being bled, he managed to break the chains and come to my rescue despite my abandonment of him to watch the dawn. I couldn't have loved him more.

In one smooth motion Dragos reached above the mantle for the huge double handed broad sword and sliced it through the air with one hand. He glanced my way.

Before he reached me Rurik blocked his path. "Connie belongs to me." The air rang with the tintinnabulation of singing blades as he attempted to pound and batter Dragos into the ground. Rurik drove him away from me.

I tried to raise myself on an elbow but nausea raged in my gut and the room tilted at an odd angle. My head hit the floor with a thud. The hardwood felt solid and the empty echo it made caused me to giggle. The devil-spawned bastard did this to me. My blood loss affected not just my body but my mind too.

Rurik's saber slipped past Dragos' defense and slashed for his throat.

I silently cheered. If this was to be my last moment then I wanted the satisfaction of watching him kick Dragos' ass.

Dragos dodged and laughed as if having wonderful time. "Good strategy."

Their weapons didn't make sense to me until then. Being stabbed hurts but won't kill a vampire, wooden stakes would have been a better choice, but Rurik kept aiming for the neck. Decapitation worked as well as a stake.

When Dragos slashed backhanded in a return blow, Rurik thrust his blade vertically and caught it with both of his before it cut him in half. "Why did you have to come to Budapest? You destroy everything you touch. What have I or my people done to deserve such a punishment?"

"You exist." Dragos blinked as if coming out of a daze. "You try to change our ways. Make our race docile. We're predators, not herders." He lunged with his last statement and missed Rurik's torso but pierced the wall where he had stood. With a puff of wall plaster Dragos yanked the weapon free.

They circled each other. "The laws want us to stay hidden and not kill humans. I didn't make those rules, you and your kindred did. Lurking in the shadows, always taking what you want and never giving back. Eternally alone."

His last word struck a chord in me. I knew what he described and how it felt. Neither of us wanted to be alone anymore. We needed to belong.

"My way makes life more bearable." Rurik feigned an attack.

Knocking a scimitar from Rurik's hand Dragos then kicked him in the chest and laughed. Even drugged he remained formidable. We would never have had a chance with him at full capacity.

Rurik staggered backwards toward the study's shattered doors.

A rumble below us shook the house. I recognized it. Red's van. It sounded like he drove it through the front door. Gunfire followed shouts as I heard the call to clear for UV light grenades.

I wanted to shout for help but I couldn't draw enough breath. The Calvary had arrived and I just needed to hang on.

A trickle of blood oozed out of Rurik's nose from the earlier punch he'd received. He wiped it with the back of his hand. "Sounds like the slayers have found you."

"They can't oppose my soldiers."

Colby stormed into the room with two of his men. "We don't want them, just you." With a UV grenade in hand he took aim.

"Stop. No!" I reached out to Colby finally finding my voice. "You'll kill Rurik too." My plea made him

BAIT

falter which left Dragos an opportunity.

Would my actions haunt me? Yes. Did I regret it? No, I'd have done it again.

One slice of Dragos' board sword cut the first of the mercenaries in half. An arc of blood splattered the other two human men.

Colby grabbed Dragos' wrist to prevent him from running it through his other man, who only stared at the carnage. His weight and strength only slowed the ancient vampire as the stained blade extended from the man's back after Dragos stabbed him. The victim stared at his injury as if in wonder before collapsing.

The howl of fury Colby released vibrated in the room. He pounded on Dragos' back with fists and feet, all reason lost in his actions.

I covered my face with my hands unable to witness what would happen to my mentor. Dragos had moved so quick, Rurik never could have helped them. Three humans and a vampire versus one drugged up Nosferatu who seemed to be winning, what a botched up assassination attempt.

Why did I think this would work? Dragos survived millennia because he possessed the strength and the power to.

A loud thump close to me caused me to peek. Colby lay by my feet unmoving. The sounds of battle ensued in the background as Rurik engaged Dragos again. I tried to move. This time I stayed flat as I rolled onto my stomach, my head still spun but I didn't pass out. I slithered to Colby.

By the time I crossed the few feet to him, my chest ached with heaviness and my breath came in gasps. I needed to lie down next to his body. His chest expanded and hope spurred in me. A nice huge lump grew on his forehead.

I watched the vampires fight across from us. Rurik had regained his lost sword and now held two. He spun around Dragos and landed a blow on his back.

Dragos gave an inhuman growl from the pain as Rurik withdrew the weapon. He raised one of his sabers over the Master's head, like a headsman, to chop at his neck.

In a move which required centuries of skill and grace Dragos pivoted and ran his broad sword into the center of Rurik's chest half way to the hilt.

This couldn't kill him, yet I screamed, despite my knowledge. No one wishes to see their loved one hurt and I knew this only precluded what would happen next. If we were going to die I selfishly wanted to go first. I'd watched too many people I loved die.

With his eyes wide, he gave me a fleeting look over Dragos' shoulder and offered me a wink, then stepped forward to drive the blade further through himself.

Dragos still held the hilt, which gave Rurik access to what he wanted. With a barbaric cry, he forced himself closer to the Master and crossed his sabers over Dragos' throat.

CHAPTER TWENTY-NINE

By sheer luck or the devil's grace Dragos escaped Rurik's assault by arching his back. A thin line of blood, from lacerated skin, arose where the razor sharp edges grazed him.

In his escape he'd released his hold on the broad sword. Eyebrows raised he touched his throat and laughed. "Nice move. You almost got me." Then he gripped the weapon protruding through Rurik's chest and twisted it.

His pain-filled cry shattered me. Tears spilled from my eyes. The move didn't work like he wanted it to, now he suffered. I prayed for a miracle but would God help a vampire? If someone from the team came they'd only add to the body count and there were too many corpses in this room already. I lay my head on Colby's chest too weak to help and needing any comfort I could get.

Rurik dropped his weapons in an attempt to grab and pull out the slick blade. His hands slipped with each try, cutting at his palms.

Dragos strolled around him, a crooked grin on his face. Vindication poured from him. He kicked at the back of my love's knees so he fell forward onto them with a grunt.

Blood streamed from his wound down his abdomen. It reminded me of the bathhouse where I saw him naked for the first time and watched the water run down his torso in the same manner. Our eyes met and locked. Deep sorrow pooled in his ice blue irises. They asked to be forgiven and offered an apology. Neither of which I wanted.

"Looks like I've missed all the fun." Tane leaned on the cracked door frame, arms crossed over his chest, still impeccably dressed in his white dress shirt and gray slacks. Pale Eric was in tow, subdued in jeans and t-shirt. "What's going on, brother? I thought you wanted Rurik to watch the dawn, not hack him up to pieces."

Tangled in conflicting emotions my heart soared with hope and plummeted with dread at the sight of Tane. What was my personal demon doing here? He'd given me the impression he wanted to sit on the fence and watch the outcome of this farce he created.

Dragos' grin widened into a smile. "An interesting

gift you left me. She's poisoned." He gestured to his head. "It affects my mental abilities and slows my movements."

"Really?" Tane stepped into the room and examined his friend who glared at him from his knees. "How ingenious of Rurik to come up with such a plan."

Rurik struggled, his movements strong with new ambition to remove the object from his chest. The size made it awkward as it continued to slip through his grasp. It moved a slow inch and caused him to moan with a new wave of agony.

Both Nosferatu circled him like sharks, in slow deliberate steps as if wondering in shared silences what manner to end his existence.

He narrowed his eyes as he glared with defiance at one then the other.

When Dragos came around to face him he shoved the sword back in the inches Rurik fought to bring out. The motion made Rurik fall to his side. His face contorted in a quiet scream.

Tane watched but glanced at me with a small secretive smile. I sucked in a sharp breath of surprise. My demon was up to something but I couldn't tell if it would benefit or harm me. Either way, I was tired of the mind games.

He strolled across the room and knelt by Colby who lay motionless between us. Tane touched the lump on his forehead. "He should be fine, maybe with a mild concussion." He directed this soft comment to me then spoke to Dragos. "You should have restrained yourself and not drained her so. It will be difficult to trace the drug once she's dead."

"I tire of listening to you preach these beliefs of taking only what we need, Tane." He kicked Rurik in the head. "This one's had too much influence on you. Kill her and be done with it. We have a bigger rodent to play with."

Tane rolled up his sleeve to expose his wrist.

"What are you doing?" His Master approached from behind and glanced over Tane's shoulder. Dragos' eyes flared when he saw what Tane planned and pulled him away from me to fling him toward the broken door.

With an agile dignity Tane unfolded from the floor after being manhandled by his Master. He brushed the wrinkles from his pants. "I was going to heal her."

"She'd be bound to you."

Tane rounded on Dragos. "A dead human is of no use to us."

The still body under me stirred to startle my weak fluttering heart. Colby lifted his head and assessed his surroundings. He pressed his fingers over my lips as I opened my mouth. They traced down my chin to touch the swollen bite mark on my neck. He frowned.

"So what?" Both Nosferatu argued and ignored us mere mortals but Rurik watched intently.

My pulse trembled at the concern on both of their faces. It made me want to cry. I felt awful but now I knew I looked it too. They knew I was dying.

"We can use her to control Rurik. I won't need to

stay in control of this city and can continue to travel with you."

"I want him dead not controlled."

With a warrior's training Colby rolled to his knees and picked me up in his arms. He rose and pivoted but Eric blocked our way.

"She won't make it to the hospital, Colby." Rurik's pain-filled voice croaked across the room. "I can hear her heart weaken with every beat. Bring her to me. I can help."

For the first time since I'd started working for him, I saw Colby hesitate. I knew my situation was dire. He didn't need to fight to hide his worry from me.

I touched his cheek then saw Eric over his shoulder. He held murder in his eyes. Something must have shown on my face since Colby twisted us to the side as Eric pointed a gun in our direction.

"Stop." Tane continued to face-off with Dragos as he spoke his quiet command.

Eric stepped back as if struck by the word.

"Go secure the house."

The plaything didn't relinquish his aim at Colby.

"Don't try my tolerance tonight, Eric." Tane turned his stare on him.

He slipped the safety back on his weapon and ran from the room.

I'm not sure what Colby would have done if he didn't have his arms full with me. From the tension radiating around him I'd say Eric just got away with his life still intact.

Tane sauntered around Rurik, his friend, and paused to kick him in the small of his back.

Dragos nodded his approval.

"Enough." I couldn't view anymore abuse to my lover. "If you're going to kill us get it over with."

"I don't think we should." Tane drew nearer and brushed a curl from my eyes. "You've all proven to be useful. *I'm* not a wasteful master." He glanced at Dragos over his shoulder. "Or a lax one. Place her on the divan, Colby. Then you can tend to your men."

"I'm not your lackey. Connie is a member of my team. I won't leave her behind."

"See what I mean." Dragos chuckled. "They're too much trouble."

Tane rolled his eyes. "Then lay her down and watch as I help if that suits you better."

"Connie." Rurik kicked and struggled then reached for me.

In turn, Tane looked at each of us then gestured to the couch. "She's getting worse. It won't be long before she's dead."

"Let me do this, Tane. I beg of you." Rurik sat up, he grimaced with the motion as the sword cut deeper.

As Colby sat on the divan he hugged me closer. "I don't know what to do for you, Connie." He whispered in my ear. Neither did I. The pressure on my chest grew. It became more difficult to draw breath. The edges of warmth blanketed me, starting from my toes it moved up my body. Exhaustion prevailed over my soul.

"She's either bound to me or she passes to other

side. Decide before it's too late."

Colby hugged me. "Connie?" The anxiety mixed into my name called me back to my situation.

"Tane, please don't do this." Rurik pleaded.

Tane ignored him. He rolled up one sleeve to expose his wrist and brought it to my lips. With a pointed fingernail he punctured his skin at the pulse site. "You'll need to drink some of this, Rabbit, if you want to live."

I pressed my lips together and shook my head.

"You're being difficult again. Soon you'll be beyond even my help. Drink."

I felt my eyes bulge in their sockets. "I don't want to be a vampire." My voice so soft I could barely hear it.

He sighed with impatience. "There's more to that than a little lick of blood. This will strengthen you and heal your blood loss."

"But I'll be bound to you."

"Yes, you'll be getting your life spark from me."

"I don't want—" He dripped a couple of drops into my mouth while I spoke. I tried to spit them out. Being eternally tied to Tane was worse than hell. I'd take my chances.

"I've had enough of these theatrics. End it." Dragos laughed. "She doesn't even want to be saved."

Tane shoved the wound to my mouth and coaxed more blood into it. Metallic, salty flavor assaulted my tongue. I fought not to swallow it and tried to make eye contact with my lover.

Rurik stood behind Dragos. The broad sword

braced in two hands he dragged it out of his chest. Sweat beaded on his forehead as the muscles on his neck corded with exertion. It glided out. Rurik took the hilt in his hands and brought the huge sharp blade over his shoulder. *"Master."* As Dragos twisted at the sound of his title, Rurik beheaded him. The body fell at his feet and the head flew next to the door. It rolled until stopped by one of the bodies blocking the doorway.

Tane rubbed his thumb down my throat which caused me to swallow reflexively.

"Bastard." Rurik shoved him from me and lifted my head to his chest wound. "Drink from me as well, baby. It might prevent the binding if you drink from both of us."

Tane staggered away from us. "You don't know that."

I drank from Rurik's heart wound. It tasted different from Tane's, smoother with less metallic flavor.

"This ends any ties between us, Tane."

"On the contrary, this shackles you to me."

Night surrounded me and swallowed me whole. I floated away and waited for the light. The one you hear about on daytime talk shows but it didn't show up. Someone came toward me and I extended my hand to him. "Rurik, my sweet-souled vampire, won't you come and wash away my pain?"

He smiled. "Even unconscious you steal my heart. Follow me home, Rabbit. Back to consciousness, I won't lose you now I've finally found you."

My eyes fluttered open to find myself in his arms,

where I belonged. "You did it. You killed Dragos and saved me." I whispered.

"It's about bloody time, too." Tane stood over Dragos' body. "You were supposed to spare me this, Rurik." His voice cracked with emotion. "He may have become mad but I still loved him." Recent events still unprocessed I watched in shock as he pulled the serrated knife from his rolled up sleeve. He knelt by Dragos' body and tore his t-shirt open. With a confident grip on the dagger he made an incision below the breast bone. He reached inside, under the rib cage, and ripped out the heart. It still pumped, slow and steady, his organ as black as his soul.

I retched. My empty stomach heaved again as the smell reached me.

Tane regarded me. "Well done, Rabbit."

I wiped the spit from my mouth. "Asshole."

A scuffing at the door caught my attention. Eric waited until Tane acknowledged him with a nod. "The house is secure with his men's assistance." He pointed to Colby.

"Good, toss me the head." The fireplace ignited with flames high enough to lick at the mantle.

I jumped at the sight and Rurik tightened his hold on me.

Eric tossed the head to Tane who waited by the fire with the heart. He dropped both in. The flames died down to just the small intense blue ones as if afraid to touch the flesh.

Tane growled and closed his eyes. "Don't be so

stubborn, Dragos. You've lost, your reign is over." He spoke as if Dragos could hear. The flames returned with new vigor and a dark smoke leaked into the room.

Good riddance. We won, the thought sank in and I twisted to smile at Rurik. Somehow we prevailed against the dark god of old. Even though our relationship was only days old, we'd both been willing to risk our lives for each other, those acts spoke volumes. He never needed to tell me how much he loved me, he'd shown me.

We all watched fire. For what, I'm not sure. Maybe for Dragos' ghost to appear or his decapitated body to rise. Neither happened.

Instead, Red stomped into the room. "What the fuck is goin' on around here?" He glanced at my blood stained lips. "Colby, you lettin' her drink from that thing?" He loomed over everyone, a bandage on one arm and a machete in the other.

Rurik backed away from the two experienced slayers with me clasped in his arms.

Both of them followed.

"I want to stay with him. Red you promised me." I pointedly looked in Tane's direction. "You should go. Get the team out."

"You're part of that team." Colby didn't budge.

"Not anymore." I slid my hand up Rurik's healed chest. "I've been compromised."

Colby's eyes swam with sorrow. He understood. It was the biggest risk to being bait, to get caught. "Damn."

CHAPTER THIRTY

I don't mind the sun sometimes and watched the last of its rays dance on the horizon before the night tucked them in for bed. The sky darkened but the city's golden lights held back my gloom. I loved Budapest.

A wall of overstuffed pillows surrounded me and I snuggled deeper into the blankets. I could sleep for a week. Some of the bedding accompanied Rurik to the bathroom with the dawn. Coffins made sense now that I tucked him into a tub twice since we've met. A bedroom with no windows would be nice but not common.

The bathroom door opened and the subject of my thoughts strutted across the room naked. Lean and graceful muscles moved below his pale skin. His black thick hair curled around his ears. The wounds were all healed, not even a scar. I could watch him all day.

He slid under the warm covers and wrapped me in his arms. "I can get use to this."

"Sleeping in tubs?"

He gave a low, deep chuckle. "No, having a warm naked body to curl next to when I wake." He nuzzled my earlobe and it shot sparks of desire straight to my core. "Did you sleep well?"

"Yes."

His voice caressed something needy and hurt inside of me. "I'm glad I fed before the dawn. I don't think I could have resisted you."

"No feedings for awhile." I cleared my throat and shifted in his arms. Dragos tainted that for me. The physical pains of my bite would fade with time but the emotional scars he reopened frightened me. It took so much energy to heal them the first time.

Rurik brushed his lips on my cheeks. "You're not alone anymore. I'm here for you. No feeding, no mental touches until you're ready."

The concern in his voice soothed the raw tender bits of my soul. He really would wait and support me. Never leave me alone. I touched his chin and drew him close. "I love you."

Those magical words brought beautiful warmth to his wintry eyes. "I love you too, my Rabbit."

"Just *your* Rabbit. No one else can call me that. Not even that bastard Tane. If an eternity passes it will still be too soon for me to see him again." I wanted to spend the night like this, just the two of us, no emergencies, fights, or Nosferatu.

"You rescued me from the darkness, after I lost consciousness. Where were we?"

"Close to your end, I think. I've never been before, I followed you there." He touched his lips to mine and gave me slow, gentle kisses taking his time to savor each touch. "After only five nights, I found myself willing to battle death himself for you." He raised himself on his elbow, concern pulled at the corners of his eyes. "You are staying with me?"

Budapest's sexiest creature wore his insecurities on his sleeve. The idea of teasing him tempted me but after all the lies I'd told we needed a fresh honest start. "Yes, as long as we can be together. I want you to know from this day forward you are my number one confidante. No more deceiving, I swear." I placed my hand over my heart next to the healed love bite Rurik had given me.

He touched the little circular scars. "I know but what do you mean by as long as we can? What would stop us?"

I sighed. Rurik may be older but he missed seeing the big picture of us staying together. "I'm going to grow old." The things I loved about him included his inability to get sick or age. He would never leave me alone but one day I would leave him and it made me sad.

"No, you won't."

His statement slapped me across the face. I sat up in bed and the world spun with the sudden movement.

"Rabbit." Rurik grabbed my shoulders and pushed me against the pillows. "You're still too weak to be jumping around. It's why I wanted to wait to discuss this."

Blood rushed back to my head when I lay down and the world righted itself. "Why am I not better?"

"On the contrary, you are much, much better. Any shortness of breath or chest pain?"

I shook my head. No nausea or bone deep exhaustion either.

"Drinking my blood doesn't work like magic. It takes time. For now, it will keep you alive until your body produces the volume of cells you need." He rushed to the bathroom then returned with a glass of water. "Drink. You need to stay hydrated."

"Yes, nurse." I chugged it down as best I could, being prone. Fantasies of Rurik giving me a bed-bath tickled my fancies. I placed the empty glass on the nightstand.

"You will need to take some of my blood from time to time to refresh the bonds between us. It's what will keep you alive."

He scooped me into his arms as he lay next to me. "It'll be all right. It had to be done. Between Dragos feasting on you and the amount of drug you ingested, you didn't have a chance, baby. No matter what, death would have claimed you. I couldn't bear it." He whispered those last words in my hair.

"You wanted to do it." I remembered him begging Tane.

"Of course." He set me on his lap. "It's not all bad."
A mischievous smile played at the corners of his lips.
"You won't age or get sick."

My breath caught in my throat again. "Really?"

He nodded. "As long as we're bound."

"Do vampires bind humans to them often?"

"No, it can become a strain physically and
emotionally. The younger the vampire, the more the
human will need to feed." He caressed my sides to my
hips and back as he pressed himself to me. "I have great
stamina and can ... sustain you for a long time." His
voice grew husky.

"I'm sure you can." I rolled over to face him. "What
happens now? Should I move to Budapest?"

Rurik held up his hands. No Overlord ring sat
upon any of his fingers. "Not unless you insist. My
people began leaving this city as soon as Dragos arrived.
There's nothing holding me here."

"I'm sorry."

"For what? Loving me? Giving me joy and laughter?"
His soft, full lips found mine. He kissed with more
passion as his hands wandered over my body. "Hmm,
you're not forgiven." He crawled on top of me, bearing
his weight on his arms. "We're not only bound in blood
but with something stronger. Love. Forever."

THE END

About the Author

Annie Nicholas hibernates in the rural, green mountains of Vermont where she dreams of different worlds, heroes, and heroines. When spring arrives the stories pour from her, in hopes to share them with the masses one day.

Mother, daughter, wife are some of the hats she happily wears while trudging after her cubs through the hills and dales. The four seasons an inspiration and muse.

And now turn the page for a preview of

THE OMEGAS

Now available from Lyrical Press
www.lyricalpress.com/the_omegas

"I found the solution to our problem!" Eric strode into Sugar's living room holding an envelope. He handed it to her and joined the rest of his werewolf pack lounging on her mismatched furniture.

Sugar examined the front, then the back of it. "Pal Robi Incorporated. What's this?"

"It's our salvation." Eric shifted in his seat to lean forward. "Read it to everyone."

She slid her fingernail in a corner, tearing it open. The letter was printed on good quality paper with a huge golden company emblem stamped at the top. An errant blond curl slid in front of her eyes, she shoved it back behind her ear.

To the Omega pack:

I have reviewed the details of your plight. Pal Robi Incorporated deals mostly in security issues, but I find your problem worthy of my personal attention. Enclosed you will find a non-negotiable contract. Please review it closely, and have your signature notarized. The return fax number is listed on the contract so proceedings can begin. Mail the original to my office. Thank you for your business.

Sincerely,

Daedalus Pal Robi

As Sugar scanned the contract a cold surge of intuition clenched her stomach. Shocked confusion exploded inside her mind, robbing her of any coherent thought. "You hired a vampire?" Her shout shattered the silence around them.

The pack responded to her outburst with low growls directed at Eric.

On days like this she wondered what she'd gotten herself tangled in. She wasn't pack, just a plain vanilla human. The Omegas were her neighbors. They were also her best friends.

Every full moon they became werewolves, each of them outcasts from their old packs. Driven by loneliness, Eric had solicited Sugar to help him search for others like himself. Werewolves with no attitude. Geeks of the underworld. Pansies of the paranormal.

Their friendship spanned years, since high school, when he'd rescued her from a home of drug abuse. Eric had treated her like a little sister, advising her on life in general. When he survived his werewolf attack, both their worlds shattered and their roles reversed.

Eric found four others to join him: Sam, Tyler, Katrina and Robert. No alphas ruled in this pack. They needed each other, so they became a family. All five lived in the apartment next to her.

Eyes wide, Eric held his hands out in front of him. "Mr. Pal Robi is offering to teach us how to fight."

Sugar tilted her head as she surveyed her friend. "Yeah, for a substantial fee. How can you guys afford this?" He always thought with his heart.

Eric looked at his pack, pleading. "Before you make any judgments, let's have Sugar read the contract

ANNIE NICHOLAS

out loud."

She held it in front of her.

This is an agreement between Pal Robi Incorporated and Eric, Sam, Katrina, Tyler, and Robert, from here forward to be known as the Omegas.

Scope:

1. *Pal Robi Inc. will provide to the Omegas, training in defense, hand-to-hand combat and small weapons use.*

2. *Training will take place for the duration of the period beginning with the trainer's arrival until the challenge date.*

3. *Combat training is inherently dangerous. Pal Robi Inc. is not responsible for injury or death sustained during such training.*

4. *Trainer will not intentionally hurt and-or kill any Omega during the period of this agreement.*

Responsibilities of the Omegas:

1. *Omegas will provide trainer from Pal Robi with appropriate lodgings.*

2. *Omegas will provide daylight security of said trainer.*

3. *Omegas will submit to the direction of the trainer without question for the duration of the training.*

Fees:

1. *Omegas agree to pay Pal Robi Inc. $8,000 in cash prior to the beginning of training.*

2. *In addition, Omegas will provide the trainer with fresh, consumable blood upon request.*

Penalties:

1. *Failure to provide payment renders this agreement null and void.*

2. *Failure to abide by the terms specified represents a breach of contract which renders the agreement null and void.*

3. *Breach of contract will result in an immediate investigation. Vengeance will be swift and unmerciful.*

Sugar placed the contract on her lap while waiting for their reactions.

Robert held up his hand to speak, like a kid in a classroom.

She sighed. How could this pack of puppies fight a pack of wolves? "Robert, speak up. You don't need to ask permission to talk anymore, remember?"

He grinned sheepishly. "What do they mean 'vengeance will be swift and unmerciful?'"

They turned to Eric, but it was Tyler who answered. "It means if anything happens to the vamp, we can kiss our asses goodbye."

Eric stood to face his pack mates, staring at each one in turn. "How can we not hire him? The Ayumu pack officially challenged us. One of us has to fight and beat one of their alphas in a month. There's no other way."

"We be absorbed again," Katrina whispered in her exotic oriental accent, as she hugged her knees tight against her chest. Being a submissive female in a pack equated to being anyone's meat. Sugar tried to help Katrina open up and come to terms with those old wounds, but they kept her captive, stuck in this phase for life.

Tyler shuffled closer to Katrina, petting her long, black, silken tresses. She shrank from him, fear etched on her delicate features.

He looked at Sugar and shrugged. It made her furious to watch Katrina cringe. Nothing would make her happier than to get some kind of revenge on the pack mates that did this to her dainty friend. How did preying on weaker members equate to strength? She just couldn't understand werewolves.

"Couldn't you run away?" The weight of Sugar's words hung in the air.

Eric crossed his arms. "There will always be another Ayumu pack wherever we go. We're finally happy. We have jobs, friends, and a home. It's all worth fighting for, right guys?"

Sugar looked around her disorganized living room at her stray werewolf friends. They nodded to each other, sealing their fates.

There went her quiet life.

A vampire would be moving in next door.

—

Two nights later Sugar heard struggling outside her apartment door. The book in her hand didn't grab her attention like the racket in the hall did. Standing, she left the book behind and tiptoed to the door. She cracked it open to peek outside. Eric, Tyler and Robert were carrying a large, black, shiny coffin past her apartment.

Sugar sighed and rubbed her chin. She'd like to hide in here for a month, not wanting to meet the trainer. It was silly to worry about this stranger, but he meant change.

Vampires had announced their existence years ago, becoming legal citizens. This one apparently ran his own business, which would help her friends. It wasn't like he'd be something from the horror movies that had kept her awake with nightmares when she was a kid. She squared her shoulders. Time she faced her own demons and met this new neighbor.

She padded down the carpeted hall barefoot, to where the boys were trying to wedge the coffin through their doorway.

The thin Weres battled with the box, and she smiled at the sight. "I think you need to turn it sideways and slide it at an angle." The coffin shone like glass. Temptation got the best of her, and she ran a finger along the surface. It felt cool. "Is he in there?"

"No, he's not." A rich, masculine voice drifted over her shoulder.

Sugar spun around, sucked in a hard breath, and stepped back against the coffin. Magazines ran pictures of mainstream vampires. TV even showed a few interviews with them, but nothing prepared her for this particular one.

The deep blue color of his eyes reminded her of the sea. Well-defined cheekbones led to a strong jaw and a slight teasing smile on his full, sensual lips.

A stirring began deep inside her. He wasn't beautiful, more sexy and hot.

Breathless, Sugar experienced an impulsive urge to ask him to rub the smooth, pale skin of his bald head all over her body. A hunger awoke, one she thought lay dormant. It unfurled inside of her and wanted to be fed.

"You're not wolf." He loomed over her. A black tattoo on his well-developed chest peeked out from underneath his partially unbuttoned white dress shirt.

Eric tapped her chin with his finger, silently instructing her to close her mouth. "Sugar is our neighbor." He gestured to the rakish vampire. "This is Mr. Pal Robi."

Heat crept up her cheeks. She stuck out her hand. "Nice to meet you."

His hand engulfed hers while he shook it tenderly. "Is that your real name?" He didn't release his hold.

She dropped her chin. A thrill ran through her. "My parents have a poor sense of humor. I have a twin named Spice."

Amusement creased the skin around his eyes. "Sugar and spice, and everything nice."

The poem annoyed her more every time someone quoted it. "Yes, I've heard the rest. I'm not a little girl anymore." She withdrew her hand from his. Maybe the phenomenal packaging was only skin deep.

A carnal light sparked in his eyes. "Definitely not a little girl. You may call me Daedalus." His gaze traced her face and slipped lower, caressing the curves of her breasts, then down along her hips.

Sugar gasped as this alarming man studied her. She could almost hear the Omegas leering at her response to Daedalus. "I'll get out of your way."

He didn't move as she pressed herself against the wall to squeeze by him. The tips of her breasts brushed his well-muscled arm. They pebbled, pushing through her blouse. Naughty images of him running those large palms over her nipples played in her mind.

Her panties got damp as a flash of desire burned through her. She realized he'd wanted her to brush against him. He was such a cad, and it made her want him even more.

Daedalus watched her heart-shaped ass wiggle back down the hall. She was ravishing. He would never mix business with pleasure, but she didn't belong to the pack. Just a neighbor and a bonus.

She reminded him of the 1950's pin-up poster

ANNIE NICHOLAS

girls, pretty and full of luscious curves. He still kept those posters in storage.

Sugar. His thoughts sprang to the hard caramelized shell on crème brulee. He would like to ignite her sweetness into a passionate inferno.

Daedalus had felt her response to him as she brushed his arm. The flush of color in her face pleased him. He wanted her to turn and look his way one more time before she entered her home.

The Omegas began wrestling with his coffin again. "Can we call you Daedalus?" one of them piped up.

Sugar glanced back at him.

"No." He gave her a shameless wink.

And now turn the page for a preview of

RED DAWN

Now available from Eirelander Publishing
www.eirelander-publishing.com/reddawn.htm

The butterflies in Sadie's stomach turned to lead and slammed into her gut. Glitch, her data processing POD, descended from the ceiling and floated in front of her. Various glyphs appeared then disappeared on its silver surface, much like a mirrored bubble.

The space station caught it hacking into their computer system.

"Frik." The POD stored the majority of her data and ran her more complex programs when she needed it to, like trying to break into the Cyngi database through the firewall.

"You never get snagged." A wave of nausea crashed over her.

She shouldn't have skipped breakfast. If the Red Dawn was docked at any other space station, she'd just get a slap on the wrist for the intrusion. It didn't hurt that she was protected by her status as a Liaison. She could get away with small injunctions most other places.

Working with government officials as a translator and a cultural expert had its perks. With so many different aliens involved in the Central Worlds government, the Liaison's office was developed to smooth over any confusion between races and to avoid misunderstandings that could lead to conflict. Every dignitary received a Liaison, so when an ambassador for the Cyngi had requested an audience with the political Assembly at Center Station—the main hub of trade and politics—she jumped at the opportunity.

Since the Cyngi guarded their privacy with intense

fervor, she didn't know how they would react to her and Glitch's transgression. The proof was in the file they sent to acquaint her on their own customs and behaviors. Minimal information. A few language files she could use to barely get by, a child's version of their history, basic cultural faux pas.

She had to admit she got more from her own research through rare vid files provided by the Liaison office. The media streams showed her things, like the desire to touch. They leaned against one another or held hands, didn't matter what sex or age. So she expected her new assignment, Xau, to need physical contact; but she'd need to have a little talk with her about restraining those urges around other races. That's if she didn't get fired for hacking their computer. It worried her a bit and butterflies fluttered around her insides.

A bang echoed from the cargo bay below her as the crew unloaded the ship of goods for the space station that orbited the Cyngi home world on the outer reaches of the galaxy. If they took legal action for her unauthorized information hunt, it would be a long time before the Liaison office rallied to her defense.

"Liaison, the ambassador is at the airlock requesting permission to board the ship." The captain's voice interrupted her dread. He and his family crewed the freighter. They were Denobola, a bipedal, panther-like race.

"Oh my cotton joy, she's early." Sadie dropped the wet towel from her head into the laundry reciprocal.

"I can stall if you need more time, Liaison."

"I'd appreciate that, but don't let her get upset. If she does, just let her in." She yanked open the drawer under the cot and grabbed a clean red jumper.

Most of the freighter comprised of cargo and little living space so their room consisted of two fold-up bunks, a bathroom, and a wall-bench. No passenger liners came to this remote part of the galaxy so both she and the ambassador needed to make do with the sparse dull surroundings.

"The Cyngi do not upset easily. He'll wait." The captain cut the connection.

She stopped dressing, only a leg in the one-piece suit. "He?"

More symbols flashed in rapid succession over Glitch's surface. She didn't need to read them. It had a link to her internal processor and communicated directly with her brain. She suspected it did symbol gyrations to express its emotions, which she knew it contained. They shared this odd habit. She did a similar thing by talking out loud to get her message across.

"I refuse to review the file again Glitch. It's flawed. According to the information provided, the ambassador is supposed to be female." She pulled her jumper on, over the thin underwear and camisole she already wore, and zipped it up.

Not the most flattering outfit, but the Cyngi wore minimal clothes.

Why would he care about fashion? Why did they switch ambassadors? Why didn't someone send her a message about them doing this?

She ran her fingers through her tight black curls to knock loose any beads of water and forced a deep, slow breath.

"By the Dark Void, I wish they'd sent me more info on their race. I'm working blind." She slipped on her heavy boots.

The room's door disappeared into the wall when she activated it. Outside, the bare narrow hallway led to an elevator. Pipes and tubes ran along the ceiling; and she passed a steep metallic emergency stairwell, which she'd hate to have to climb.

Glitch floated above her head. "Let's go meet our new employer. Maybe he can keep us out of prison." She made the statement as light and humorous as possible for Glitch's sake but wiped her sweaty palms on her jump suit. No point in both of them worrying.

A bell announced the lift's arrival on her floor. Once the doors slid open, a set of pale green eyes met hers. She restrained the gut reaction to jump back. Thousands of years of instincts bred into human DNA cried out predator. Ten years as a Liaison taught her to repress those impulses.

Kaille, one of the captain's wives, stared at her eye-to-eye. "Are you ready, Liaison?"

Shaped like a human but with the features and nature of a panther, Kaille's slim, lithe body moved with a beast-of-prey's grace as she stepped out of the elevator. Large, soft lower paws glided over the floor without making a noise when she circled her. The golden fur of her pelt shone as if groomed for hours, and a small black nose glistened on the tip of her short, narrow muzzle. Vertically slit green eyes peered with intelligence while they assessed her from head to toe.

"Sadie has given you permission to address her by name." Cine, another of the captain's wives, followed Kaille out of the elevator.

Her fur shimmered too, but her coat was a paler shade of gold, which complimented her dark blue eyes.

"You shouldn't meet the ambassador dressed like that."

Both sister-wives wore purple and navy blue silk sarongs, which clung to their hips. She'd never seen them in anything but work attire.

No Denobola wore shirts; both sexes displayed their fine-furred muscular chest. Though the females were narrower of shoulder, they were beautiful.

"The Cyngi wear little clothes, so I doubt he'll care or notice what I'm wearing."

"That's not so," The tips of Kaille's ears flattened a bit with anxiety. "They appreciate beauty and will be flattered at the effort. We mean no offense to your knowledge or your position, but we have dealt with the Cyngi for many decades. Please accept our advice."

"No offense taken. They did not send me much data on their culture or customs. Any suggestions would be appreciated."

"At least apply some of your war paint. It gives you more color and draws attention to your pretty copper eyes." Cine almost skipped while she led them back into Sadie's room.

Her 'war paint' was the make-up she'd packed and the most expensive items she owned since they came all the way from Earth. A little piece of home. The wives were intrigued when she'd worn some on her arrival to their ship.

Sadie applied some of her 'war paint' as the sister-wives observed from the wall-bench. They ignored Glitch, who hovered by them. Some green eye shadow and a heavy swipe of black mascara helped accentuate the almond shape of her eyes. She turned around for their inspection and smiled, careful not to expose her teeth. The time she'd made that mistake, she was a new recruit and it almost cost her life since they interpreted it as a threat.

Kaille crossed the small space and took the application brush from her hand. "You should add some gold on your face." She made a few more strokes, then physically turned Sadie to look in the mirror. "See? It highlights your dark skin tones."

For a female who could never wear the 'war-paints', the suggestion was sound. It did look better.

Finding the right color for dark brown skin could be a challenge. She wasn't a pretty chocolate shade; she was a spent-your-life-on-the-Serengeti-plains deep brown, almost a black with blue highlight in the right illumination.

Kaille applied a few more swipes along her cheekbones, which helped to soften their sharp prominence.

"She's ready, Maol." Sadie watched as Cine shut

off the intercom then turn to her. "We'll go greet the ambassador now." The delicate Denobola female activated the door and stepped into the corridor followed by the taller Kaille.

Sadie followed them through the dull gray hallways of the ship. The lack of color bothered her. Never one to need luxury, it surprised her how the monotony dragged at her soul. She gave herself a mental shake. When was the last time she'd seen the sky? "Do you know who this ambassador is?" The need to ask grated at her. "My files state it's supposed to be Xau, a female Cyngi, but the captain said it's a male waiting to board."

"No, they all look the same to us." Kaille flicked her ears and pressed the button to call the elevator.

The Denobola were the only race allowed into this system. The treaty they held granted them sole shipping rights for the Cyngi. Yet even they never went on the space station, let alone the planet.

They took the lift down to the airlock. She thought this meeting must be important for the crew, maybe as trade relations, for them to deem it necessary to inspect her.

In thinking, she recalled a similar freighter where she'd played among the cargo bins and fallen in love with space travel. Her father worked as a miner in the Sol System asteroid belt. One summer he convinced her mother to try and live on the space station Earth maintained in the area. They traveled there via a freighter. The maze of corridors and cargo bins were a perfect playground for an eleven-year-old girl with an active imagination. To bad her mother cracked under the isolation and limited living space. Within two months, they were back on a ship. She saw her father every two months for a few weeks afterward, and every time he visited she begged him to take her with him.

The opportunity to become a Liaison fulfilled her every dream. Nothing could make her happier. She got to travel the universe, learn new languages, and meet aliens of all sorts. The Cyngi topped her list since they were the most mysterious. They stayed aloof from aliens and never left their system.

Until now.

They had requested her to be their Liaison and accompany their ambassador to Central Station.

The lift stopped and she exited to find Captain Maol's family, including the children, gathered around the ship's main entrance. At the front stood the captain, his two adult sons, and his dominant wife, Len, who still wore her pilot's jumpsuit.

Sadie made a small half bow in their direction, a sign of respect for the bridge crew. This wasn't always required except at official meetings. The captain activated the airlock cycle, so the ambassador could enter from the space station dock.

While they waited, Glitch sent her images of the security programs it had encountered while trying to get her more intel on the Cyngi. It wanted to show her the complexity of the system. The data streamed via her internal computer CHIP implanted in her brain.

This integration made her capable of being a

ANNIE NICHOLAS

Liaison. Languages and cultures could be downloaded to her within seconds. As an unaltered human, it would have been impossible for her to study them all.

Amazing software, and that's only the firewall. The urge to explore it, to meld with its artistry, almost overwhelmed her. She wiped her mouth and checked for drool.

This race was light years ahead of Central World programming. She'd never seen anything like it. You could have been fried. For a race living on a back world planet, they're pretty advanced. I don't think you escaped, I think they let you go. This probably means we may not be in as much trouble as I thought.

The thick metal door hissed as it opened with a loud clank before the Cyngi dignitary stepped in. He bowed to the Denobola in the same manner she had.

She bowed back with the ship family.

"Nual, it's a surprise to see you. We expected Xau." Captain Maol spoke galactic patwa with a heavy accent. "Welcome aboard the Red Dawn."

"Most happy to be welcomed. Today, Xau found out she is with child, and since we have no knowledge of how space travel would affect the baby's development, she chose to remain home." He turned his solemn blue eyes her way and stepped forward to offer his hand. "I am Nual."

She stared at his hand. Nothing in her files on the Cyngi said they had a hand greeting. Should she grab his forearm like a Zair warrior, kiss it like a Kenish maid, or entwine her fingers in his like a Morian noble?

326

He withdrew a little. "Is it not customary among humans to shake hands when introducing themselves?"

She blinked and felt akin to a human ass. "Yes, it is. I apologize for the misunderstanding." His hand engulfed hers as they shook. "I am Sadie Beckit, your Liaison."

His skin was a brighter shade of blue than she'd expected, similar to Earth's sky on a clear summer day. A small hat of feathers of the same color sat on his bald head. Each overlapped the other in a tight configuration, so it looked as if a cap surrounded the top of his head.

Nual exchanged names with the ship family. He loomed over them, easily six feet tall.

Maol gestured to the beige canvas bag slung across Nual's bare chest. "Do you have any other luggage to store?

"Only the case that came through the bay doors earlier today. Is it secured?"

"The box has its own storage bin as requested."

From this angle, Sadie could see Nual had small, dark blue freckles, which flowed both down the back of his neck from the feathered cap and around his well-defined abdomen. They trailed lower to disappear under the short, white linen cloth wrapped tight around his hips.

He glanced at her while she stared. Some races approved blatant admiration, others didn't. She didn't know how to deal with her instant attraction. There could be so many possibilities but the files they sent her

ANNIE NICHOLAS

were on the females of his race, not the Adonis-shaped males.

Glitch floated over her head and approached Nual's face. It never went to strangers. The self-preservation programs loaded into these precious machines erred on the side of caution since they were too valuable to be stolen or damaged. Symbols flashed across its reflective surface in slow succession. Her POD spelled its name using computer glyphs.

"Nice to meet you, Glitch." The ambassador gave a slight bow as if to an equal.

With an audible click, her mouth snapped shut after hanging open at the exchange. No one ever treated her POD like a person. Most didn't even acknowledge its presence in the room. Glitch was a high-tech computer to non-POD users but she suspected a deeper sentience to it. When she'd discussed her suspicions with a systems developer, he'd told her that she only saw a reflection of herself in the gadget.

Not many could read glyphs. His intelligence increased her interest. Her chip processed his abilities as she took in his handsome appearance. The combination of these things made something low in her abdomen tighten. She could get a pretty face at any station stop if she wanted, but a sharp mind was difficult to find and sexy as hell.

She pulled her scattered wits together and tried to remember the office she represented. "If you will follow me, Ambassador, I'll show you to our quarters." The calm serene voice that flowed from her did not reflect the riptide of attraction she felt. It took years of practice to learn professional detachment while freaking out inside.

The captain escorted them to the lift and left Nual in her care after the door slid shut. They stood side-by-side while they waited for their level. She glanced his way and found him staring at her.

He gave a small smile. "You're much more exotic in person," he whispered.

CPSIA information can be obtained at www.ICGtesting.com
Printed in the USA
LVOW131549220412

278650LV00001B/16/P